"No police,"

Linn said, much too quickly, the fear back in her eyes again. She swallowed and looked away, hunching her shoulders slightly as though suddenly chilled.

Trey's eyes narrowed. There was a sudden awareness between them, a silence filled with a thousand unspoken things that both of them sensed, yet neither acknowledged. It seemed to grow, filling the night, and he shifted restlessly. The woman felt it, too. She seemed smaller suddenly, and very vulnerable. And when she finally looked back up at him, her eyes were filled with misery and fear.

That look, it held and caught him. It was the look of something trapped and afraid, something that had been pushed almost to the end.

"Please," she whispered, hugging the boy tightly against her. "I . . . I know you're angry. But I can't get involved. I just can't. . . ."

Dear Reader,

This month brings more excitement your way, starting with Emilie Richards's *The Way Back Home*, the sequel to last month's *Runaway*. Rosie Jensen has taken on another name and begun another life, hoping to be safe from her past. But trouble has a way of catching up to people, and only Grady Clayton—a man who has a lot to lose himself if the truth about Rosie is ever revealed—is strong enough both to love her and to keep her safe.

Paula Detmer Riggs returns us to New Mexico's Santa Ysabel pueblo in *A Lasting Promise*, a book that will bring tears amidst the smiles. Maura Seger is back after too long a time with *Painted Lady*, an intriguing mystery set amongst the beauties of Block Island. And Silhouette Desire favorite Naomi Horton makes her second appearance in the line with *In Safekeeping*.

In months to come look for Linda Howard, Barbara Faith, Emilie Richards (with *Fugitive*, a follow-up to her current duo) and more of your favorites to keep the fires burning here at Silhouette Intimate Moments.

Leslie J. Wainger
Senior Editor and Editorial Coordinator

In Safekeeping
NAOMI HORTON

Silhouette Intimate Moments

Published by Silhouette Books New York

America's Publisher of Contemporary Romance

SILHOUETTE BOOKS
300 East 42nd St., New York, N.Y. 10017

ISBN: 0-373-07343-7

First Silhouette Books printing July 1990

Printed in the U.S.A.

NAOMI HORTON

was born in northern Alberta, where the winters are long and the libraries far apart. "When I'd run out of books," she says, "I'd simply create my own—entire worlds filled with people, adventure and romance. I guess it's not surprising that I'm still at it!" An engineering technologist, she presently lives in Nanaimo, British Columbia, with her collection of assorted pets.

Chapter 1

There's a man following us."

Linn's heart did a distinct somersault. On her knees beside the tide pool that she and Nathan had been examining, she looked up and saw him staring at something behind her, his small face pinched with sudden fear. She dropped the shell she was holding and got to her feet swiftly, trying—for the boy's sake—not to appear too concerned.

"It's probably just someone out for an evening stroll, like us," she said offhandedly. "We can't always expect to have the whole beach to ourselves." But she scanned the wide sweep of sand behind them nervously. It ran on for miles, the hard-packed sand glistening where the retreating tide had washed it clean. The setting sun had turned it to scarlet and gold, but the colors were fading now and in a few more minutes the grayed dusk would be upon them.

There was no one there. Linn eased her breath out. "Well, whoever it was, he's gone now. He's probably staying in the campground or one of the motels."

But Nathan shook his head, still staring down the beach. "He went behind that big pile of logs."

Linn looked around again, trying to ignore a jab of raw terror. Odds were the man was simply a tourist, enjoying the sunset and a few minutes of solitude before retiring for the night. Odds were...

She wet her lips and stared hard at the weathered logs lying in jumbled piles along the foot of the steeply rising shoreline. Some of them were whole trees, torn off the rugged coast by winter storms, their tangled roots rising like frozen coils of rope. But most were strays that had slipped free of the big offshore log booms. They'd been tossed ashore by the relentless waves and wind and lay in huge drifts, jammed so tightly that they built an almost impenetrable wall running the entire length of the coast. They looked for all the world like a set of pickup sticks cast down by a giant's hand, and they created a rabbit warren that could hide anyone who wanted to stay hidden.

Sternly she hauled in her runaway imagination. The odds that he had followed them this far were all but impossible. She and Nathan had left Florida three weeks ago, and she'd laid a dizzying crisscross of false trails across eight states that was guaranteed to lose the most determined pursuer.

Something gave a sharp cry from the tall, silent pines hemming the beach. Some night bird probably, out for the hunt, but it made her start badly and she swore under her breath as she realized that her own nervousness had transmitted itself to Nathan.

Suddenly he looked very small and defenseless, his eyes shadowed with a weary kind of fear far at odds with his age. He stepped nearer to her, the delight and laughter that had lighted his face only minutes ago gone now. As always, it made Linn's heart ache. This nightmare was taking a horrifying toll on everyone it touched, but perhaps the worst was the effect it was having on Nathan. Boys of five were supposed to be filled with laughter and the reckless joy of just being alive, but Nathan had become withdrawn and silent over the past few weeks, his small face growing paler and more pinched as the days went by.

Linn caught the sudden bite of anger and swallowed it, knowing from experience that giving in to either the anger or the relentless dread behind it would accomplish nothing.

She smiled at Nathan and touched him on the shoulder. "I'm about ready for a cup of cocoa," she said lightly. "Do you want to head back now?"

He nodded vigorously, reaching for her hand. Two months ago, like any rambunctious five-year-old, he wouldn't have been caught dead reaching for the security of an adult's hand. But all that had changed.

His sea-damp fingers fastened anxiously around hers. "Let's walk by the edge of the water." He tugged her toward the lower beach where long combers were spilling across the sand. Away from the jumbled piles of logs and whatever he'd seen there to frighten him.

But there was no one waiting for them. The shadows where Nathan had thought he'd seen the man were empty, and they walked on undisturbed. Nathan seemed to relax after a few minutes, and after a while Linn managed to shake off her own unease. They were safe. Santos couldn't have tracked them this far. As long as she didn't get careless, there was nothing to worry about. Nothing at all.

She was raven-haired and blue-eyed, and from the first time he saw her, Steele knew she was the kind of trouble that no man needed. It came like that sometimes, gift-wrapped in satin and sin and long, smoldering glances that kept you coming back for more. The kind of trouble that left good men dead.

Raven-haired and blue-eyed...

Trey gave a snort. It wasn't difficult to tell where *that* had come from. He raised his eyes from the computer screen and looked out at the beach. It filled his entire view from the expanse of glass that made up the west wall of his study, blood-red now in the setting sun. The restless Pacific swept onto the shelving sand a few hundred yards out, but he gave the long, foamstreaked combers only a cursory glance, more interested in the empty beach stretching southward, curved and clean. And empty.

Damn it, where was she?

He glanced at the clock on the bookcase. It was nearly nine, well past the time she and the boy were usually back.

Suddenly restless for no reason he could pin down, he got up and wandered across to the big windows, frowning slightly as he stared along the tide-damp beach. Where was she, anyway, his raven-haired, blue-eyed mystery lady?

If she *was* blue-eyed, Trey reminded himself. He'd never gotten close enough to her to find out. As elusive as sea mist, she ventured out only in the evening or early morning to stroll the deserted beach with the boy he presumed was her son. She'd rented the beach house beside his about a week ago, but he'd never caught more than the occasional tantalizing glimpse of her since. And although he'd asked around the village, no one knew anything about her.

The big German shepherd lying on the rug in front of the fireplace lifted his head and whined softly, ears pricked. He got to his feet and walked over to stand beside Trey, staring out at the beach as though he, too, sensed that something was amiss.

"It isn't any of our damned business," Trey reminded the big dog irritably. He reached down to rub the puckered scar running diagonally across his left thigh, kneading the aching muscles almost absently. He'd gotten *that* by not minding his own business, by being in the wrong place at the wrong time and taking a bullet meant for someone else.

He swore under his breath and walked back to the desk. The woman wasn't his problem. Getting this damned book written *was*. He sat down again and forced himself to re-read the last paragraph, frowning again.

Steele was in trouble. Not the usual kind, the kind that a bit of heavy armament and natural guile could get him out of. No, the trouble was closer to home than that. The truth was, after eight books, Steele was bored.

Correction, Trey reminded himself with a faint smile. Author T. C. Hollister was bored.

There *was* a difference, in spite of the efforts of various critics and media types to convince the reading public that Steele, cold-eyed hero of the Man of Action espionage novels, and T. C. Hollister, ex-marine, were one and the same.

Eyes narrowed, he reached for the cigarette sitting in the ashtray and drew deeply on it, realizing with annoyance that he'd smoked it half down without even tasting it. It was the second—and last—of the day, the one he looked forward to most because it *was* the last, and the fact he'd wasted a good part of it irritated the hell out of him. He drew on it again, slowly this time, forcing himself to concentrate on the acrid bite of the smoke as he contemplated the words staring back at him.

Not bad. Although where she was taking him, this raven-haired beauty, he had no idea. She'd appeared out of nowhere a few hours ago, taking Steele as much by surprise as she'd taken her creator. And as he'd typed the words, something had happened. Suddenly he'd found himself wanting to get the next sentence down and then the next, wanting to know what was going to happen. Wanting to know who she was, this blue-eyed woman who had captured Steele's imagination as she'd captured his. . . .

He glanced at the clock again. Where was she? She'd never been this late coming back before.

After looking down at the computer once more, he swore softly and stabbed a finger at the keyboard, clearing the screen. He turned the machine off and ground what was left of the cigarette into the ashtray. To hell with it. He'd finish it tomorrow.

Trey walked downstairs and into the kitchen and poured himself a cup of coffee, trying not to look at the pack of cigarettes lying on the counter. It had been a mistake, taking his precious last of the day early like that. He'd thought the familiar ritual might help jar loose some sudden bolt of creativity, but all it had done was underscore how little he'd accomplished today.

She was raven-haired and blue-eyed. . . .

In spite of himself he smiled. Maybe the alchemy of caffeine and nicotine *had* worked. He was on to something there. Something good. Maybe *Steele on Ice* was going to get written, after all.

He strolled onto the wide sun deck and took a sip of the coffee, squinting as he scanned the beach through rising steam. The shore was completely deserted, nothing moving but the long, white-frilled breakers rolling up the beach. A lone gull sailed overhead, its cry desolate, and Trey's frown deepened as he stared southward, eyes narrowed. It would be dark in another few minutes. She should have been back by now.

Finally he caught himself and turned away from the railing with a soft oath. Hell, it wasn't any of his business if she stayed out there all night! He didn't even know her. Not where she was from, not how long she was staying, not even her name. Just that she and the boy were alone. And that she was scared to death.

He'd recognized it the moment he'd seen it in her eyes that day he'd come up behind her on the beach, unseen and unheard. She'd turned around and had found him standing only a few feet away. He'd said something to reassure her— what, he couldn't even remember now—but she'd hurried off and now would only come out when no one else was on the beach.

But there had been no mistaking the terror on her face. He'd seen fear like that before and had hoped never to see it again: the wild, frightened look of something hunted.

And that was when it had started, this habit he'd gotten into of sitting out here on the deck each night with a coffee and his last cigarette of the day. Not that he was watching over her, exactly. But the truth was that he rested easier when he knew where she was.

Just habit, he told himself. Watching over people was his business, and he was damned good at it. As he was at anticipating trouble....

Murphy whined softly, and Trey glanced at him. The big dog was staring intently down the beach, every muscle of his body taut. "You feel it too, don't you, old fella?" he murmured, staring at the long, dusk-grayed stretch of sand. "Something's wrong. She should have been back by now...."

Murphy responded with a whimper, then turned and trotted toward the steps leading down to the beach. He looked over his shoulder at Trey and gave a quiet bark, as though wondering what was taking so long, and Trey whispered an oath under his breath. This was crazy, damn it! She'd made it pretty plain that she wanted to be left alone. If he went wandering out there and met her in the dark, he'd scare the daylights out of her. And for all he knew, she was carrying a gun. . . .

He rubbed his aching thigh, unable to stop a grim smile from lifting one corner of his mouth. That would be the ultimate irony, all right: T. C. Hollister, original man of action, getting shot by a mysterious raven-haired, blue-eyed beauty on a deserted beach in the middle of the night. Hell, it would probably double his book sales. If he lived to enjoy it.

The man stepped in front of them with no warning at all.

Nathan had been telling her about starfish, and Linn, concentrating on the boy's story and lulled by the rhythmic surge and ebb of the waves washing around their feet, had relaxed her watchfulness. Head down, hands tucked into the pockets of her windbreaker, she'd been strolling along with her mind on the mysteries of tide and sand and shell instead of possible danger, which was why she hadn't spotted him until he stepped from behind a huge, tide-tangled pile of weathered logs right into their path.

Linn stopped so abruptly that Nathan, who had dropped behind a step or two to look at some piece of tidal debris, very nearly ran into her. He saw the man and stopped as abruptly as Linn had, his eyes wide and frightened.

The man grinned at her. "Hi, gorgeous."

Linn swallowed. Common sense said she had nothing to fear. Common sense said he was just a local resident, looking for clams or doing a little illegal fishing. It couldn't be one of Santos's men. There was no way he could have tracked her this far. . . .

"I been waitin' for you." The man's grin widened with anticipation. It was as though he could sense her fear, fed off it. "You're late tonight."

Linn could taste the panic now, felt light-headed with it, but fought it desperately, knowing that she couldn't afford the luxury of falling apart. "I think you've made a mistake," she said coldly.

"No, I don't think so." His words sounded faintly slurred. "You're stayin' in one a' them ritzy beach houses up a ways." It was less a question than a statement, somehow all the more threatening for its certainty.

"What do you want?" She snapped the words out, her mind racing. He was big, damn it. And beefy, with wall-to-wall shoulders and arms like tree boles, biceps straining at his shirt sleeves. If he got his hands on her, she wouldn't have a chance. But she had to keep him away from Nathan. A weapon . . . if only there was a rock, even a piece of driftwood . . . anything . . .

"Jus' wanna talk." His grin widened sloppily. "I been watchin' ya. You don't come out much, do ya? 'Cept at night."

There was something about his voice that made Linn look at him sharply. He grinned back at her congenially, weaving ever so slightly in the soft sand, and suddenly she gave a gasp of strangled laughter. He was drunk!

He wasn't one of Santos's thugs at all, just a local barfly with a couple too many under his belt. Reckless with relief, she put her hand on Nathan's shoulder and started to walk around the man. "Perhaps some other time. It's gotten cold and it's past my son's bedtime, so—"

"Pas' my bedtime, too." Still grinning, he stepped in front of her. He glanced at Nathan. "You go on home, kid. Your mom an' me are goin' to have a party."

"You're drunk," Linn said icily. "Get out of my way."

"Not too drunk to show you a good time, honey," he assured her with an ugly laugh.

"You leave her alone!" Nathan's voice rose with indignation; he pulled away from Linn's hand and planted himself squarely between her and the man. "My daddy's a policeman, and he'll put you in jail if you—"

"But your old man ain't here, is he?" The man's grin widened and he aimed a lazy swat at Nathan. "Now you get before I—"

"Get away from him!" Linn grabbed the man's arm and wrenched it down. "Nathan, run!"

The man gave a grunt of surprise and Linn caught a glimpse of Nathan stumbling back out of reach just before the arm she was holding pulled her sharply off balance. She tripped in the soft sand and would have gone down if her assailant hadn't caught her. He grabbed both wrists and wrenched her upright, giving an unpleasant laugh. "Well, well, looks like I got me a real little spitfire." He laughed again, enveloping her in a bearlike embrace. "You jus' go ahead and fight all you want, honey. I like it rough."

He tried to kiss her, but Linn gave a yelp of disgust and wrenched her face away. He stank of diesel fuel and stale beer and the combination made Linn's stomach heave as she struggled futilely against his powerful grip. The fear was back now, a more basic, primitive kind; she realized with a sudden, sickening clarity that by walking the beach at night to avoid one danger she'd left herself wide open to another.

"You leave her alone!"

It was Nathan's voice, the anger in it overriding the fear, and Linn heard her assailant's breath sucked in on a gasp of pain. He swore and swung his left arm around and Linn caught a glimpse of Nathan stumbling backward to avoid the blow, a heavy piece of weathered pine clutched in both hands. His footing betrayed him and he fell sprawling, but as Linn's assailant made a lunge for the boy, she flung herself sideways with every ounce of strength she had.

Caught by surprise, the man made a wild grab for Linn. He caught the back of her jacket and wrenched her back so violently that she tripped in the deep sand and fell heavily.

"Run, Nathan!" she shouted. "Get out of here! Run!" The man snarled something and reached down for her, his face twisted with anger, and with more instinct than rational thought she grabbed a fistful of sand and flung it squarely into his eyes.

He threw up his hands with a roar and in that instant Linn was on her feet, screaming to Nathan to run, run, even as she herself was running. But not fast enough. Her assailant was on her with a bellow and as his hand clamped down on her shoulder, Linn tried to twist free. She stumbled heavily, her feet sinking into the deep, loose sand, and then she went sprawling facedown, landing against two posts, embedded firmly in the sand.

It was only when they moved that she realized they weren't posts at all, but legs. Sun-browned and well-muscled male legs, widespread for balance. They were bare, as were the feet in front of her, and it took Linn a befuddled moment or two to realize that they didn't belong to her attacker.

"Just what in the hell," a husky baritone above her asked very calmly, "is going on here?"

"Nothin' that's any of *your* business," Linn's assailant warned with drunken bravado. "Butt out before I—"

"By the look of it, buddy," the baritone went on conversationally, "I'd say the lady wasn't interested."

"She's interested, all right. She comes out here every night, looking for company. Figured I'd give her some of what she's bin lookin' for, that's all. But I ain't in no sharing mood, so get lost."

Linn heard a throaty growl above her, so animal-like it made the hair on her neck stir. She went motionless, terrified to move, not even daring to look up as another growl rumbled around her, the sound filled with deadly threat.

The legs beside her stirred. "I don't think so," the husky voice said, deceptively soft.

"This ain't got nothin' to do with you," she heard the other man say belligerently. "You an' the mutt don't scare me none." He took a step forward and Linn recoiled. "Come on, doll-face. The party's just started. We're goin' to—"

Linn wasn't too sure what happened next. There was a spitting snarl behind her, then something large and black shot out of the shadows just as the tanned legs moved. The stranger stepped across her in one smooth stride, bracing his right foot in the sand and pivoting on it. Linn blinked as his other foot rose in a clean, sweeping arc, lashing up and around so fast that the movement was just a blur.

The kick caught her attacker solidly in the solar plexus; he gave a grunt of surprised agony and staggered backward. The stranger, both feet on solid ground again, stepped forward lightly. His fist shot out and landed on the man's jaw with a satisfyingly meaty thud, and Linn watched in astonishment as her assailant went sprawling across the sand.

"Murphy, watch him!"

The black shadow that Linn was only starting to realize was a huge German shepherd pounced on the prone man with a snarl.

"Get him off me! Get him off me!" The man's voice lifted in a shriek of terror.

"Lie still or he'll tear your throat out," the newcomer snapped. "Guard, Murphy!"

The big dog stood fully astride the downed man, lips curled back, the wet, gleaming fangs hovering mere inches from the man's face. The fur across the dog's shoulders stood up like a brush and Linn could see him quivering with anticipation, poised like a cat over a mouse, every muscle as tight as coiled steel.

Her attacker was babbling something, his voice just a wordless squeal of fear that was all but lost under the dog's snarls. Linn swallowed and sat up very slowly, dazed, brushing a tangle of hair out of her eyes. "Nathan?" she whispered hoarsely.

Another dark shape detached itself from the deepening shadows and hurled itself at her with a low wail. Nathan's arms went around her neck in a stranglehold and he clung to her, shaking so badly that Linn could hear his teeth chattering.

She hugged him fiercely, holding back her own tears of fright through sheer force of will. "Are you all right, Nathan? He didn't hurt you, did he?"

Nathan shook his head, snuffling and sobbing against her neck. "I hit him, b-but he wouldn't l-let go!"

"I know, honey, I know." Linn buried her face in his damp, tangled hair and squeezed her eyes shut, too shaken to do more than simply rock him against her. "I know you were trying to help me, Nathan, but you should have run. We talked about what to do if something like this happened, remember?"

"B-but he wasn't trying to hurt *me*," the boy sobbed, his arms clasped so tightly around Linn's throat that she was having trouble breathing. "H-he was trying to hurt *you*, Aunt Linn. He was—"

"Nathan!" She spoke his name with quiet urgency, praying the stranger was too occupied with her attacker to

have caught the boy's slip. She felt Nathan flinch slightly
and hugged him even tighter. *He's just a child,* something
in her cried out. He was too young to understand the impli-
cations of even one tiny mistake, and yet—for his own
safety—he *had* to understand. The charade had to continue, no matter what the circumstances, no matter how
afraid he was.

"It's all right, Nathan," she murmured reassuringly.
"And I'm all right, too. He didn't hurt me."

He drew back slightly to look at her, his eyes blurred with
tears. "W-was he one of the bad men after my daddy?" he
whispered. "D-did they follow us here?"

The fear on his face made Linn's heart ache. "No,
honey," she said softly, knowing the stranger was listening
but suddenly not caring. "He was just some man who
wanted to scare us. He had too much to drink and was being
obnoxious, that's all. We'll never see him again, I promise."

Nathan drew in a deep, unsteady breath and wiped his
eyes with the back of his hand. His lower lip was still trembling but he held the tears back manfully. "Are we going to
put him in jail?"

"Damned right," a gruff baritone muttered behind her.
"The cops are going to *love* finally getting something solid
on this guy."

Linn swallowed, a sudden smothering panic washing over
her again. She fought it again, only half-successfully, and
glanced up as the stranger walked around and into view.

He looked, she found herself thinking inanely, like
someone who'd be more at home on a battlefield in ancient
Gaul than a modern-day beach. She had a sudden, crystalline image of him on the back of a war chariot, a plumed
helmet on his head and good Roman iron in his hand. She
could almost smell the horse sweat for an instant, could hear
the clash of weaponry. Then it all vanished and she was back
on the cool, tide-damp sand, Nathan tight in her arms and
the stranger standing there silently, looking down at her.

Except he wasn't a stranger.

She'd seen him before. On the sun deck of the big beach
house beside hers, as a matter of fact. And once on this very

beach. She'd turned around one evening and had found him standing not five feet from her, startling her so badly that she'd still been shaking an hour later. He'd said something to her—she couldn't remember what—but she'd grabbed Nathan's hand and had headed for the safety of her beach house at a near run. She'd seen him two or three times since then, but always at a safe distance, and to her relief he'd never attempted to approach her again.

But it was definitely the same man. He had the kind of face a woman wouldn't easily forget. His features were strong and straight and ruggedly male, with just enough sensuality in the mouth and around the eyes to send a little tingle through any female old enough—and woman enough—to recognize the promise it held.

His hair was long and thick and tousled, and it lay in wind-tossed waves around his ears and neck, almost but not quite hiding the glint of gold in his left ear. It gave him a rough, slightly dangerous look she wasn't sure she liked and she swallowed, holding Nathan a little tighter. He was taller than she would have liked, too, and lean and well-muscled enough to be real trouble if he wanted to be.

And he was fast, she already knew that. He moved like a street fighter, quick and sure on his feet, not making a single move that was wasted, and there was something about the way he was just standing there now, loose and relaxed yet quietly alert, that put her nerves on edge. It was as though he were waiting for her to make the first move, as though whatever happened next was going to depend on what she did—or didn't—do.

It was only then that she realized, even more uneasily, that he was all but naked. He was wearing nothing but a deep golden tan and a pair of very brief denim shorts that had in an earlier life been real jeans. Threadbare and tattered, they rode so low on his hips and hugged his contours so audaciously that it was impossible not to notice he was wearing nothing under them.

And for the first time since he'd appeared, Linn found herself suddenly wondering *why* he was there. What had brought him out to this far end of the beach? It was almost

as though he'd known she was going to be there. As
though...

Without warning, he dropped onto one knee just in front
of her and she flinched, her arms tightening around Nathan.

"Easy..." His voice was just a murmur of reassurance
and he made no move to touch her. "Are you all right?"

Wetting her lips, Linn nodded. She drew in a deep breath,
trying for Nathan's sake to sound calm and in control. "I—
I'm fine," she managed to whisper, her voice so rough it
didn't even sound like her. "Thank you. For c-coming when
you did, I mean. For helping."

"That's me. Trey Hollister, man of action."

She looked up at him uncertainly, hearing the edge of
bitterness to his voice, and Trey gritted his teeth against the
pain. It was like a physical presence, pressing on him, blur-
ring his vision. It felt as though he'd just torn part of his leg
away, and through the haze of agony it occurred to him that
he might have done just that. The wound in his thigh had
gone bone deep, the layers of muscle and tendon and liga-
ment and flesh were only just starting to draw together, and
that damned kick he'd used on Rolfson had sure as hell
ripped *something* loose.

"I don't suppose you'd mind telling me what the hell
you're doing out here this time of night?" He bit the words
out, teeth still gritted.

She flinched, saying nothing, and Trey swallowed the rest
of his tirade, not even sure why he was so angry. Maybe it
was the way she'd risked her own life; maybe it was the way
she'd risked the boy. And part of it was just the realization,
like a stone in his gut, that if he hadn't decided to come out
here after her, he'd have had to live with that on his conscience, too. And he had enough there already without some
damned woman deliberately putting herself in danger.

He kneaded his throbbing thigh with his hand, half
expecting to bring his palm away bloody. But although it felt
as though he'd ripped his leg open, he hadn't, of course. The
ridged scar merely stood out red and ugly against the tanned
skin around it.

She was still kneeling in the sand, her head so low that her face was hidden by a silken curtain of hair, and it was only when he saw the tear splash onto the back of her hand and glitter in the moonlight that he realized she was crying. He stared down at her, feeling his fierce anger dissipate. It all but disappeared after a moment or two, leaving nothing behind but a bone-deep weariness and an emptiness that seemed to go on forever.

For a split second he found himself tempted to slip his arms around her and cradle her against him, to just let her cry and get it all out—all the terror and anger and pain—but he managed to catch himself. First off, odds were that she'd figured he was planning to finish what Rolfson had started and would claw his eyes out, and second, nowhere was it written that Trey Hollister had an obligation to take on the mantle of savior. Whatever was scaring this woman half to death went beyond this moment and this beach, but that wasn't any of his business. He'd done what any man would have done under the circumstances, but his responsibilities ended right here.

Slowly he eased himself to his feet, teeth clenched against the pain in his leg. The boy in her arms gave him a quick, uncertain look and then, to Trey's surprise, broke into a tentative but very real smile. Trey smiled back, a private smile passed man to man over the woman's head that made the boy practically beam with pleasure. The fear in his eyes vanished and was replaced by such utter uncomplicated trust that Trey groaned inwardly.

Now what in the hell had he done! The kid's mother had taught him that fear for some damned good reason, and she wasn't going to appreciate having it tampered with.

He wheeled around with a muttered oath and limped through the loose sand to where Murphy was still standing guard over the woman's attacker. The dog hadn't moved so much as a hair in the intervening few minutes and was still rumbling threatening growls. Trey had to smile at his enthusiasm. Murphy always had taken his heroics seriously, but tonight he'd pulled out all the stops. Obviously as big a pushover for ladies in distress as his owner.

Trey didn't find the thought particularly cheering. "Okay, Murph, back off," he ordered gruffly. The big dog whined and looked up. The man made the mistake of moving slightly and Murphy gave a coughing snarl and snapped the air inches from the man's face, spraying him with saliva and hot, canine breath.

The man gave a squeal of fear and covered his face with his hands, and Trey chuckled and nudged Murphy aside. "Let him up," he said quietly. "You've done your part. It's my turn now."

Murphy whined again a couple of times but did move back a few steps. He circled slowly, bristling and growling, obviously hoping the man would make a break for it and try to run. And for a split second or two, Trey was almost hoping the same thing, wanting nothing more than some excuse to work off some of his remaining anger and adrenaline. He reached down and grabbed the man's shirt-front and pulled him to his feet, feeling disgust rise like bile in his throat. It took all his willpower to keep from planting his bruised, aching fist solidly in the man's face.

Breathing a little quickly he released him instead and flexed his fist. "You should have stayed home tonight, Rolfson. Because you just bought yourself some jail time."

The man gave a derisive snort, trying to keep one eye on the circling dog and glower at Trey at the same time. "And *you* just bought yourself some serious trouble, chump. You can't go around punching people for no reason. The lady 'n' me were just having ourselves a friendly visit, that's all." His scare had sobered him up considerably, but he still sounded badly shaken.

Trey smiled grimly. "Save it for the cops, *chump*. But I wouldn't count on it getting you anywhere. They've been trying to get something solid on you for months—I figure they'll give me a good citizen's award for getting you off the street."

"She was asking for it." Rolfson gave the woman an angry look. "No woman goes walkin' on the beach at night unless she's looking for some action."

Trey's right fist itched, but he drew in a deep, calming breath and kept his hand by his side, satisfying his urge for violence by giving the man a ferocious shove toward the piles of driftwood. "I told you to save it. Now get over there and stand real still or I'll let my dog have a go at you. Murphy! Guard!"

The big shepherd sprang forward with a snarl and stood in front of the man, legs widespread and braced, hackles raised. The man paled slightly and swallowed, licking his lips, seemingly transfixed by the dog's burning stare.

Trey turned to the woman. She hadn't moved, but the color had come back into her cheeks and the wild panic he'd first seen in her eyes was gone. In its place was an odd mixture of emotions: fear, suspicion, relief and, just perhaps, a hint of gratitude. Or maybe he'd just imagined the gratitude, he decided as he got closer. There didn't seem to be anything in the troubled gaze now but wariness and mistrust.

Which was fine by him, he reminded himself impatiently. He didn't want her thinking she owed him anything. Debts just made things complicated. "If you're ready, let's head back. Your place is closer. We can call the police from there and—"

"No." She said it quietly, but the one word, crystal clear, seemed very loud. "I won't . . . be pressing charges."

Trey stared down at her. "What the hell are you talking about? He tried to rape you, for—!"

Her chin lifted fractionally and she held his glare without faltering. "I appreciate your help, but it ends here. You can call your dog off and let him go."

"Like hell I'm letting him go," Trey said heatedly. "Damn it, lady, I don't know what your problem is, but you're not turning this guy loose to prey on some other unsuspecting woman! If you're afraid he'll get off and come after you and your son, don't be. The local cops have had their eye on him for over a year—they'll be only too glad to get him behind bars."

"No." She said it much too quickly, the fear back in her eyes again. She swallowed and looked away, hunching her shoulders slightly as though suddenly chilled. "No police."

Trey's eyes narrowed. There was a sudden awareness between them, a silence filled with a thousand unworded things that both were aware of, yet neither acknowledged. It seemed to grow, filling the night, and Trey shifted restlessly. The woman clearly felt it, too. Suddenly she seemed smaller and very vulnerable, and when she finally looked back up at him, her eyes were filled with misery and desperation.

It held and caught him, that look. It was the look of something trapped and afraid, something that's been pushed almost to the end. "Please," she whispered, hugging the boy more tightly against her. "I . . . I know you're angry. But I can't get involved. I just can't. . . ."

Chapter 2

Her voice trailed off, lost under the rhythmic wash of surf on sand, and she looked away again, her eyes sliding from his as though she knew exactly what he was thinking.

Hell. Trey drew in a deep, angry breath and exhaled it noisily, staring out across the darkening sea. Common sense said he should get out now, before whatever trouble she was in sucked him in, too. But he'd chucked common sense out the window the minute he'd decided to follow her tonight. In fact, it had probably gone out the window when she'd first turned up a week ago and he'd let himself get slowly entangled in the web of mystery around her.

His oath was short and pungent, and it made her blink. She flinched slightly as he strode by her, flushing at the unspoken anger and censure in his face.

Her attacker smirked as Trey approached. "Told you it wasn't none of your business. You're goin' to pay for this, buddy. Nobody's goin' to take a swing at me and not—" He gave a squeal of surprised fear as Trey's hand shot out and grabbed him by the shirtfront.

Trey lifted him off his feet and threw him back against the pile of weathered logs, hard, then moved in close and fast before his opponent could do more than struggle to catch his breath.

He put his splayed fingers lightly on the man's chest and leaned in close. "One more word, and you're dog meat. I'm going to let you go because that's the way the lady wants it, but that's not the way I want it. I'll be watching you, Rolfson. And I'll be waiting. One wrong move and I'm taking you out. Fast and clean, with no witnesses."

"Y-you can't do nothing," the man babbled with false bravado. "It's harassment. I'll go to the cops. I'll—"

"You do that. I'm sure they'll be real worried about what happens to you." Trey gave the man another violent shove. "I'm dead serious, Rolfson. Right now I'm the biggest problem you've got, understand? If I see you hanging around this beach or find out you've been bothering this woman or her kid, I'll kill you."

Once again he wrapped his fists around the man's shirtfront and hauled him to the end of the pile of logs, then gave him a ferocious push that sent him sprawling into the sand. Murphy pounced on him with a snarl, stopping only at a sharp command from Trey. The man clawed himself to all fours and started scrambling away. Finally he managed to get his feet under him and headed down the beach at a dead run without so much as a glance over his shoulder. Murphy was dancing with excitement, yelping in frustration as he watched the man speed away without being given the command to go after him.

"Lie down," Trey told him sharply, knowing exactly how the big dog felt.

Something moved behind him and Trey looked around, finding the boy—Nathan?—standing there wide-eyed with awe. He looked up at Trey. "Wow! Is your dog a police dog, mister?"

The small, dirty face gazing up at him was filled with such undisguised worship that Trey felt something inside him catch. He thought of another little boy looking up at him in that same way. That had been nearly eighteen years ago. The boy was a man now, close to twenty. Maybe even married with a son of his own....

Trey forced the thought away brutally, trying to ignore Nathan's gaze. That was exactly what he needed, some hero-worshiping kid underfoot every time he turned around. Not bothering to answer, he strode by the boy without looking at him.

But even as he tried to ignore it, Trey couldn't miss the way the boy's face crumpled with hurt, the way the small shoulders slumped under his denim windbreaker. He blinked hard, as though fighting sudden tears, and Trey swore again, silently this time, and dropped stiffly onto one knee with an inward sigh. "Come on over here," he said gently. The boy looked at him mistrustfully, and Trey impatiently motioned him to come nearer.

"Nathan..." The woman's voice was vibrant with warning.

"Look, lady, would you lighten up?" Trey gave her a mildly hostile look, not knowing if it was her suspicions he was annoyed with, or himself for giving a damn. "Murph here is worth his weight in marines when it counts, and when he's around I can guarantee that nothing's going to happen to the kid. Or to you. So do me a favor and just ease up a bit."

She flushed and looked away, her mouth tightening with what he figured was instinctive anger. But to Trey's relief, common sense won out over raw pride. "It's all right, Nathan," she said in a hoarse whisper, not looking at Trey. "Do as he says."

Nathan walked over slowly, clearly still uncertain after his initial rebuff. Trey smiled at the boy, knowing the woman was watching him, her eyes dark and private in the deepening dusk. "Murph, come here." Trey snapped his fingers and the big dog came bounding over, tail windmilling, tongue lolling. "Sit." Murphy did so instantly, giving Trey a goofy, good-natured look, as though wondering what kind of game they were playing now. "Murph, this is—" Trey looked at the boy. "What's your name, kid?"

"My name's Nathan Val—" He stopped abruptly. "Nathan Stee—" Again he stopped, giving the woman a stricken look.

"Stevens...son," she said, stumbling awkwardly over what was obviously a spur-of-the-moment alias. "Nathan Stevenson."

Her eyes dared him to argue. "Stevenson," he repeated, holding her gaze just long enough to tell her he knew damned well that she was lying. She held his gaze steadily, refusing to rise to the bait, and he nearly had to smile. "Okay. Stevenson it is. Nathan, this is Murphy." Hearing his name, Murphy beamed. "Well, Nat...does anyone call you Nat?"

The boy smiled. "My daddy sometimes calls me—" He bit it off, sliding his mother a quick, nervous glance. "Sometimes," he whispered, looking down. His fingers twisted in the hem of his windbreaker and he dug at the sand with one small, sneaker-clad foot. "Most people call me Nathan."

"How about me?" Trey asked gently. It was a judgment call, and he didn't even know why he was bothering, but the look of desolation on the boy's face tore at him. "Would you like me to call you Nathan or Nat?"

"Nat...would be okay," he whispered, looking up shyly. His words were casual enough, but he was still too young to be able to disguise his pleasure at the nickname.

Careful, Hollister, Trey warned himself, knowing the woman was watching him with a cool, speculative expression. He found himself thinking of lion cubs and their mothers, and the fate awaiting any man foolish enough to come between them. "Okay, Nat. Hold your hand out so he can get used to your scent. That's right." Trey nodded as the boy hesitantly extended his hand. Murphy, as though sensing the boy's nervousness, reached out very gently and nudged the waiting fingers with his nose, then, even more gently, ran a large, wet tongue across them.

The age-old gesture of acceptance made Nathan giggle with delight. "Can I pet him?"

"Sure. You're friends now. If you're ever in trouble and need help, just sing out and Murph will be right there."

"Wow." Nathan's eyes shone as he ran his hand down Murphy's broad head and between his ears. The dog wriggled with pleasure and eased himself a little closer, giving the boy's face an enthusiastic swipe with his tongue.

Nathan gave a sputter of laughter and wiped his face with his arm. Grinning, he looked up at Trey. "Thanks, Mr. Hollister."

"Trey, to friends." Trey held out his hand. Nathan took it and they shook solemnly. "Okay, kid, I think it's time I took you and your mother home."

"Is that man going to come back?"

"He won't be back," Trey assured him. "That was a pretty brave thing you did, trying to drive him off with that piece of driftwood. But your mother was right—it *was* dangerous. If anything like that happens again, you clear out, fast, and get help. Understand?"

"Yes, sir," Nathan said firmly, looking very much older than his four or five years. He scrubbed a handful of tousled hair off his forehead and for a moment Trey almost thought he was going to salute. Shoulders back, he looked Trey straight in the eye. "I think we should go home now."

Trey looked down at the boy curiously. "Your daddy wouldn't happen to be a soldier, would he?"

"No, sir," came the prompt and proud reply. "My daddy's a pol—"

"Nathan." The woman's quiet voice silenced the boy abruptly. Nathan gave Trey a nervous glance, as though aware he'd said too much, and turned to walk back to his mother.

My daddy's a policeman, Trey finished for him thoughtfully. Now that was interesting....

His gaze met the woman's almost by accident, and he could see the fear in her eyes, the mistrust. She was still kneeling on the sand and looked scared and cold and miserable, arms wrapped around herself as though trying to hold out the chill. The sea wind had whipped her hair into tangles and the small oval of her face seemed even paler than usual, the dark pools of her eyes haunted as she stared up at him, as though uncertain of what he was going to do next.

What in God's name was she mixed up in? he found himself wondering. She didn't strike him as the kind of woman who would frighten easily. She'd been shaken up over tonight's ordeal, for instance, but was far from hysterical, so whatever had put that kind of fear in her eyes must be pretty serious. The kind of seriousness that a man didn't want to get mixed up in if he didn't have to.

"I don't know about you," he said quietly, reaching down for her, "but Murphy and I have had enough excitement for one night. Let's go home."

He felt her flinch slightly as he took her by the upper arm and lifted her to her feet, but she didn't argue or even pull away. Probably too damned cold to make the effort, he decided as a spasm of shivers ran through her, making her stumble slightly. It was shock, mainly. If he didn't get her home soon, he was going to wind up carrying her.

"Let's get this jacket buttoned up." He reached for the front of her windbreaker, but she recoiled from his touch like a horse shying from the whip.

She clutched her gaping jacket and started walking away, so stiff with cold that she stumbled again. "I'm all right," she mumbled, hunching her shoulders. "Nathan and I c-can get back by ourselves."

"You're not all right," Trey told her bluntly, catching her by the shoulders and swinging her around to face him. She gave a squeak of shock but he ignored it and zipped up the jacket, then turned the collar up around her ears. "Quit being such a hard case, Stevenson. You don't get points for stubbornness."

She stared up at him, half frightened and half outraged, and Trey watched her struggle to make up her mind which to give in to first. But in the end, much to his satisfaction, she resisted both of them. Her shoulders sagged, she simply nodded and started walking, shivering so badly he could actually see the tremors as they ran through her.

I'd like to know your story, lady, he told her silently as he fell into step beside her. What's out there that's scaring you so badly?

The walk back to her beach house took hours.

In reality, Linn knew, it couldn't have been more than twenty minutes. It had taken Nathan and her nearly an hour to walk the same distance, exploring salt pools and drifts of tidal debris along the way, and it was only when she started to realize how far they'd gone that she also became aware how much danger she'd put herself and Nathan in.

Rolfson would have known how deserted the beach was at night. Hers was the nearest house, nearly a mile from where he'd attacked her. There was nothing out here but eagles and gulls and the endless keening of the wind. The forest rising into the mountains from the beach was so thick and wild that there were no campgrounds, no hiking trails. Nothing. No one would have heard her screams. No one would have come.

She shivered violently. The tears flooded her eyes so unexpectedly she couldn't even blink them back and she stumbled heavily against Hollister, blinded. He steadied her, then wrapped one large, warm hand gently around hers. "Almost there. How are you doing?"

"Okay," she lied bravely, dabbing at her nose with her sleeve. The shivers just wouldn't let up and all she wanted to do was sit down in the cold sand and burst into tears. But aside from the fact that it would frighten poor Nathan even more, she was also damned if she was going to fall apart in front of Hollister. Half of it was the stubborn Irish pride that had gotten her through worse situations than this, and half of it was—perhaps—a matter of survival.

The timing of Hollister's rescue still bothered her. He must have been right behind them to have gotten there that quickly, yet neither she nor Nathan had seen him.

Unless he'd been waiting for her, too.

She glanced at Hollister uneasily. His fingers were still meshed warmly with hers, but was he holding her hand simply to reassure her—or to keep her from escaping?

Her heart did a quick little flip-flop and she wet her lips, wondering how far she'd get if she wrenched her hand free, scooped up Nathan and started running.

Not far at all, she advised herself grimly. Not even on her best day, and without the burden of Nathan. She'd seen Hollister move.

She shivered again, more violently. God, the expression on his face when he'd had Rolfson pinned against those logs! He'd spoken about death as though it were something casual, his words less a threat than a promise, delivered in a flat, calm voice that had chilled her to the bone. And there had been something in his eyes, something cold and still and lethal, that made her shiver again just thinking about it.

She dared another sidelong glance at him. If he *was* working for Santos, she'd escaped one nightmare tonight just to fall into another one—this one far more deadly than attempted rape. They wanted Nathan, not her. To Santos she was just someone who was in the way, someone who had something he wanted.

And yet, if Hollister's plan was to kill her and kidnap Nathan, why go through this silly charade?

Unless he hadn't wanted a witness. Rolfson had been drunk, but not that drunk. If her body washed up on the beach in a few days, he'd have no trouble remembering Hollister's face. But that didn't make sense, either, because if Hollister was on Santos's payroll, he'd have no qualms about killing Rolfson, too. In fact, that probably would have been ideal, setting the whole thing up as a murder-suicide or something. It wouldn't have been difficult. Rolfson hadn't been much of an opponent; she'd have been even less so. A quick judo chop to the throat, and—

"You and the boy are staying with me tonight."

Hollister's voice made Linn blink, and she slowly realized that they were in front of her rented beach house.

It was set back in a stand of pines on the embankment overlooking the beach, low and weathered, looking so much a natural part of the rugged landscape that most people didn't even notice it. A sun deck jutted off the front, wide enough to hang over the bank, supported by huge pilings.

From the deck ran the wooden steps that were the only access from the beach, complete with the large No Trespassing sign nailed to a post at the bottom to discourage sightseers and tourists. There was another sign under it, smaller and obviously added as a whimsical touch. Until now Linn had always found the graphically drawn skull and crossbones amusing; tonight it just made her shiver.

The house was dark and silent. And oddly ominous. She swallowed and put her foot on the bottom step.

"I said—"

"I heard you," Linn replied. "I appreciate the offer, but we'll be staying here tonight."

"Not so fast." Hollister's hand caught her wrist and Linn's heart gave a leap of raw fear. "You're in no shape to be here by yourself tonight."

Linn twisted her arm free and stared up at him defiantly. "I'm perfectly all right."

Hollister's eyes narrowed. For an instant Linn thought he was going to try to force her to go with him and she braced herself. "Damn it, lady, you really are a pain in the—" He swallowed the rest, his eyes glinting dangerously in the near darkness. "Wait here, then. And don't come up until I tell you it's clear."

Linn had her mouth half open to argue, but it suddenly seemed like too much trouble. Numbed with cold and the residue of what she supposed was shock, she simply nodded and watched as he padded lightly up the dew-damp steps, silent as a cat.

He gave a sharp whistle after a moment or two and motioned her to join him, and Linn started climbing the stairs slowly. He was waiting by a big sliding door leading into the living room when she finally reached the top. He held his hand out and wiggled his fingers impatiently. "Give me the key."

Wearily Linn fumbled in the pocket of her windbreaker. Her fear had vanished under the leaden weight of exhaustion, and suddenly all she wanted was to get inside and into bed. "You don't have to do this," she mumbled through chattering teeth. "I'm okay now. Nobody could have—" She frowned and went through her pockets again, more slowly this time, aware that Trey was looking down at her impatiently.

She looked up at him, stricken. "I can't find it." He whispered a soft oath and Linn checked the pockets of her jeans. A feeling of hopeless despair washed over her and she had to bite her lower lip to hold it steady. This was too much! Sudden tears welled, threatening to overflow. "I—I had it. I know I had it!"

"It probably fell out of your pocket when you were struggling with Rolfson. Hang on a minute—I'll be right back." He vaulted the deck railing and vanished around the side of the house.

"Trey'll get it open," Nathan said confidently.

"But the front door's locked. There's no way he can get inside to—" The faint tinkle of breaking glass stopped her.

Nathan smiled up at her knowingly. "Told ya."

"But he can't just break in like a . . . a thief!" He was too good at this sort of thing: from martial arts to breaking and entering, there didn't seem to be anything he couldn't—or wouldn't—do.

The curtains on the inside of the glass were pulled aside and Trey looked out at her. He unlocked the catch and slid the heavy door open and Nathan scurried through, glad to be out of the cold, and Linn unhappily followed a moment later. "You broke a window," she said accusingly as she stepped by him.

"Give me a break," he said wearily as he pulled the door closed behind her and locked it. "What did you want me to do? Leave you and Nathan out there in the cold while I went back to look for your key? Hell, I could have just gone home and let you find your own way in. You could have walked back up to the end of the beach yourself and looked for the key. There's only about twenty square miles of loose sand out there to sift through."

It cut through the cold and misery, as it was probably supposed to. Linn felt her cheeks color. "I'm sorry. You're right," she whispered, so cold and tired that she was having trouble holding back the treacherous flood of tears again.

Damn it, what was the matter with her! She wasn't a cryer. Bursting into tears when all else failed was Kathy's way of coping, not hers. But right now it was taking every bit of willpower she had not to do just that. "But I'm all right now, so you d-don't have to s-stay." She could sense more than see him moving through the darkness, and flinched when he turned on one of the table lamps.

"Like hell you're all right," he growled, striding across the room toward her. "You're scared and you're cold and you're this far from losing it." He held his hand up, thumb and forefinger a scant inch apart. "Now I'm going to take a quick look through the rest of the house, and I don't want you or the kid moving out of this room until I get back. I'll leave Murphy with you in case I scare something loose. Then, once that's done, you're going to put the kid to bed, and you and I are going to have a long talk. Got all that?''

If she'd had the strength, Linn thought wearily, she'd have gotten a lot of satisfaction out of telling Trey Hollister to go to hell. As it was, it took almost more strength than she possessed just to nod. He had to be one of the most overbearing men she'd ever met. If she got out of this mess alive, she was going to take the time to tell him off properly.

If she got out of this mess alive...

She looked around the room miserably, only to discover that he'd vanished. As promised, the big shepherd was still there, sitting by the door with his ears pricked up and his chocolate eyes alert and watchful. Keeping watch or standing guard? If she walked across to that door, would he hold her at bay until his master got back? And had Trey gone to check for intruders, or just to ensure that the house was empty before—?

Stop it, Linn told herself angrily. Enough was enough. She couldn't go on like this, second-guessing herself and everyone around her, or she was going to drive herself crazy. Staying alive and keeping Nathan safe depended on keeping her wits about her, and she couldn't do that if she worked herself into such a knot of panic that she couldn't even think straight.

"Okay, the place is clean." Trey was suddenly there again, startling her slightly. "Everything's secure—both doors and all the windows, except the one in the kitchen I broke to get in. But I jammed the lock on it. Do you have a gun?''

"A *gun*?'' She stared at him blankly.

"I just figured that under the circumstances—'' He shrugged, leaving the rest unsaid. "Probably better that way. Guns have the bad habit of killing the wrong person, anyway.'' He turned and looked down at Nathan. "Okay, kid, time to hit the hay.''

"I usually get a cup of hot chocolate,'' Nathan said doubtfully. "With mushmallows.''

"I'll bring it in to you, honey," Linn said through chattering teeth. "But it is past your bedtime."

"Can Murphy stay with me?"

"Honey, I don't think—"

"Sure," Trey interrupted smoothly. "Just don't feed him any of those marsh—mushmallows. Even if he begs."

"Promise! Come on, Murphy!" Nathan was out of his windbreaker in a flash, and he and Murphy raced down the hallway to the bedrooms.

"One down, one to go." Trey turned toward her. He reached out and unzipped her jacket, then deftly pulled her arms out of it and tossed it onto the sofa. "I'm going to make Nathan's hot chocolate, and while I'm doing that, you're going to get under a boiling-hot shower and stay there until you thaw out."

Linn wrenched away from him. "Damn it, you c-can't just come in here and—"

"Either you get those clothes off and get into a hot shower on your own," he said in a dangerously calm voice, "or I'll take them off and *put* you in."

"Just because you rescued me from Rolfson tonight doesn't give you any right to—" Linn stopped dead, stumbling back as Trey started toward her. "Come near me and I swear I . . . I'll . . ."

"Call the police?" he asked dryly. "Lady, I'm just about done arguing with you. You've got to the count of three. *One.*"

"I'll…" Linn sputtered to a halt. Damn him! He'd called her bluff, and she was fresh out of options. And there was something about the set of his mouth and the way he was moving, slowly yet deliberately, toward her that made her think that he just might carry through his threat if she gave him enough provocation.

"Two."

"Hollister, I'm warning you!" Linn looked around for a weapon. She spotted the set of brass fireplace tools and snatched up the poker, brandishing it like a saber. "Come another step closer and I'll spit you like a cocktail olive!"

"That's it, by God," Trey rumbled, his patience evaporating. "Lady, I don't need this! I'm tired, I'm sore and I just want to go home and lose myself in a very large glass of bourbon—but I can't do that. And you know why? Because I'm stuck here, watching over some scared, stubborn woman who's too damn obstinate to admit she just might not be able to hold it together much longer." He took two long strides toward her, grabbing her wrist in one hand and the poker in the other, and had wrenched the weapon from her before she'd even had to time to to react.

"Enough is enough!" He tossed the poker away and it ricocheted off the stone hearth with a clatter. Her eyes had gone wide with terror and Trey inwardly sighed, the agony in his throbbing leg forgotten for a moment or two as he realized he'd frightened her half to death.

"You're close to frozen and you're in shock," he told her quietly. "By tomorrow morning all of this will just be a bad dream, but you've got to get through tonight." He released her wrist and she stumbled back, pale and wide-eyed, staring up at him through a haze of fear. "You're not in any condition to take care of yourself, let alone that boy in there. And I'm not leaving here until I know you've gotten things under control and that he's safe. Got that?"

He watched her struggle with it. She was smart enough to know he was right, but could she overcome her fear and suspicion of strangers long enough to trust him? "If I were going to hurt you or the boy," he told her softly, "I'd have done it by now."

She stared at him in silence, mouth tight with anger, eyes still mistrustful. Then she drew in a deep breath, releasing it through clenched teeth. "The cocoa," she said with chilled precision, "is in the cupboard above the stove. Make it with hot milk, not water, and he likes exactly five miniature marshmallows in it." Her chin went up a notch and eyes filled with defiance held his. "And I do *not* appreciate being bullied, Mr. Hollister, regardless of how well-intentioned. I am quite able to take care of myself and my son, and I don't need—"

"Like you were taking care of him down on the beach with Rolfson?" Trey held her stare just as defiantly, feeling the anger flare through him. At her, or at himself? Or was it just rage at an imperfect world where women lived in fear and little boys never saw their fathers again?

He thought she was going to say something, but at the last moment she bit back the words and drew herself up to her full five feet three inches. The effect was spoiled by the fact that she was shivering so badly she could scarcely stand, but she made the best of it as she turned on one heel and strode across the room.

"This backwoods he-man routine may endear you to the women around here," she said icily, "but it doesn't do a damned thing for me." She paused in the corridor to turn and glare at him. "I want you *out* of here before I get back, Mr. Hollister. Out of my house and out of my life. Do you understand me?"

Trey nearly laughed. She reminded him of a stray kitten he'd taken in once, so small it fitted in the palm of his hand but full of enough spit and hiss to hold Murphy at bay. "Two and a half..."

She wheeled away and marched down the corridor, back ramrod straight, and he had to wince as the bathroom door was slammed with enough force to rattle the windows.

He had a roaring fire going in the big fieldstone fireplace by the time Linn got out of the shower. His back was to her as he added another pine log to the flames, and as she stepped into the room and saw him, Linn's breath caught.

Her shock lasted only a split second. Just long enough for her heart to give an odd, quick little twist of recognition before her mind, always logical, always practical, reminded her that what she was seeing was quite impossible.

Jack was dead. He'd been dead for nearly four years now. And that tall, dark-haired man across the room from her right now, moving catlike and quickly and wearing that achingly familiar old plaid shirt, was a stranger.

Damn.

The old memories hadn't caught her unawares like that for a long, long while; she was surprised how sharp the pain of loss could still be. It wasn't Trey's fault. He'd obviously found that old shirt of Jack's on the back of the chair where she'd left it that morning and had slipped it on without even thinking. And why should he? He didn't know anything about her or the man she'd once loved, or the memories that faded old shirt held....

Chapter 3

Trey didn't know if Linn had said something, or if he had just sensed her standing behind him. But whatever the reason, he suddenly knew she was there; he straightened and turned around, mouth half-open to ask her if she wanted a drink.

The question turned to dust in his mouth as his eyes met hers. She was looking at him with an expression of such radiance and love that his heart literally missed a beat and he completely forgot what he'd been about to say.

Then, abruptly, the look was gone. A flicker of what might have been pain crossed her face and then she was looking at *him*, Trey Hollister, and not the man whom, for one magical heartbeat of time, she thought she'd seen.

She held his gaze for a moment longer, her expression curiously vulnerable, then lifted the towel she was carrying and started rubbing her hair dry. "I thought I told you to get out."

"And I told you to stop being such a hard case." Trey eased his breath out tightly, feeling a sudden, violent surge of jealousy for the man that look had been for. Where the hell was he? Trey found himself thinking. Why wasn't he here, taking care of his woman? And what was he? Husband? Lover?

He swore under his breath and turned back to the fire, shoving another log into the crackling flames. It was crazy, being jealous of a man he'd never met over a woman he hardly knew. But if a woman ever looked at *him* that way, he'd damned well be there when she needed him. If it had been *him*...

But it wasn't him. Trey swore again and roughly closed the fire screen. He straightened and turned away from the fire, trying to ignore a treacherous little feeling of wistfulness. No woman had ever looked at him like that. No woman but Diane, anyway, and even then it had only lasted three months.

It had taken her that long to realize the man she'd married was a marine first and a husband second, and by the time his orders had come through for Vietnam, the rift between them was already irreparable. She'd stayed another year, then she'd left, taking with her the only family he'd ever known. And the son he scarcely knew....

He shrugged the memories away impatiently. Linn was sitting on the wide stone hearth, vigorously rubbing her hair, and he poured her a generous shot of the scotch he'd found in one of the kitchen cabinets.

"Here." He touched her on the shoulder and she drew the towel from her hair and looked up warily. "Drink as much of this as you can get down. It'll help stop the shakes."

To his surprise, she smiled faintly as she reached up to take the glass. "You're very good at this, Mr. Hollister."

"Trey," he reminded her quietly. She'd changed into slim-fitting jeans and a hooded sweatshirt pulled over a turtle-neck sweater, and with her hair all tousled and her cheeks flushed and damp from the shower, she looked about sixteen.

She cupped the glass between her hands and stared down into the amber liquid. "I...uh...I've acted pretty badly tonight. If you hadn't come along, that man would have..." She drew in an unsteady breath and shuddered, looking up at him. "I'm sorry."

Her eyes were almost violet in this light, deep enough to drown in, and for the second or third time that evening Trey found himself consciously fighting their spell. "Anytime," he said easily. Then he gave a snort of laughter. "On second thought, forget I said that. Either my fists aren't what they used to be, or I've forgotten how damned much it hurts to smash your bare knuckles against some drunk's teeth."

He rubbed the bruised knuckles on his right hand, smiling reminiscently. He was going to regret that impulsive swing at Rolfson's concrete jaw, but by God, it had felt good at the time! There had been a lot of frustration pent up in that one punch, and even if it meant typing with one hand for the rest of the week, it had been worth it.

He suddenly realized that Linn had been watching him, her expression thoughtful. "You're very good at *that*, too," she said quietly.

"I have my moments." He rubbed his knuckles again and glanced up a moment later to find her still watching him, "If you're planning on continuing these after-dark walks, you might consider learning a few moves yourself."

She smiled faintly. "I've learned my lesson. No more nighttime walks." She stared into the glass, brows pulling together. "It was just dumb, blind luck that you came along when you did. If you'd come out twenty minutes earlier or later, or if you'd gone the other way instead of..." She shivered again, not bothering to complete the thought.

"It wasn't luck. I followed you."

She shifted her gaze slowly. He could see the sudden doubt in her eyes, the beginnings of what might be fear. "I'd seen Rolfson hanging around the beach earlier," he said quietly. "When you and the boy didn't come back from your walk at your usual time, I decided to check things out."

There must have been something in his expression that reassured her slightly, because after a moment or two she nodded. Her eyes were still shadowed with worry, but of a different sort now. "I didn't realize I'd fallen into such a predictable routine," she said, perhaps more to herself than to him.

"Predictable enough." He held her gaze evenly. "The best routine to follow when you're on the run, Mrs. Stevenson, is no routine at all."

She caught the faint stress he put on her name and frowned, obviously annoyed by the jibe. "It's Linn," she said sharply. "And what do you mean, on the run?"

She was damned good, Trey found himself thinking. A bit *too* blasé, maybe, and she'd have to learn to do something about that worried little frown that settled between her brows, but those were things that only an expert would catch. She'd learned to control the fear; that was good. And she had a mind like a whipsaw, always assessing and analyzing and checking the exits.

"Why don't you tell me?" he asked bluntly.

For a moment he thought she was going to bluff her way through it. But at the last instant her gaze faltered and slipped away. "It's nothing," she whispered. "Just a...domestic problem."

He gave a snort of disbelief. The only kind of domestic problem that would put that kind of fear in a woman's eyes was a crazed husband with a gun and a court-bruised ego.

Which wasn't impossible, he reminded himself thoughtfully. She wouldn't be the first woman to take her kid and hightail it. Diane had done it. His eyes narrowed slightly. Except Diane hadn't been running scared, like this woman was. She hadn't flinched at every sudden noise or touch, hadn't looked at strangers with terror in her eyes.

He found himself thinking of Rolfson. He'd had the advantage of height and weight and drunken bravado, yet Linn had fought him like a wildcat, protecting the boy as well as herself.

And she'd held up better afterward than he'd expected. Although he knew that was just another kind of fear. Fear of him, this time; of what he might do to her or the boy should she show the slightest weakness or vulnerability.

I don't know who you are, Linn Whatever-Your-Real-Name-Is, he mused, but you are one tough lady, "I don't like the idea of leaving you here alone tonight. Is there someone I can call who can come and stay with you?"

She shook her head. "No," she said in a soft, hoarse voice.

Her tousled hair was starting to dry in the heat of the fire and he watched the flames play across it, bringing the highlights out. Abruptly he shook himself free. He finished the last of his drink in one swallow, then set the glass on the wide mantle. "I'm going to leave Murphy here tonight."

Linn blinked, Trey's voice working its way through a thousand whirling, muddled thoughts and bringing her back to the present. "You don't have to do that. I'll be all right."

"I'm sure you will be," he told her calmly, "but I'm not leaving you alone."

"But you already said you don't think Rolfson will—"

"It's either Murphy," he said flatly, "or me."

His eyes met hers directly, and Linn bit back the rest of her protest. He had the same expression on his face that Jack used to get when he was convinced he was right about something. Arguing with him when he'd been in that mood had been like trying to shift a mountain with a teaspoon, and what she did or did not want didn't seem to have much effect on *this* man, either.

She nodded, swallowing her annoyance. Having Murphy underfoot all night was one thing; having his tall, gray-eyed owner here was quite another. She'd already let him get closer than she could afford.

Trey walked to the glass door and slid it open, and she followed him thoughtfully. Friend, Mr. Hollister, she asked him silently, or foe?

The question was redundant. Until this business with Santos was over, she had no friends. And everyone, even Trey Hollister, was suspect.

She stepped into the salt-scented night and took a deep breath of the cold air. Moonlight glinted off the restless surge and ebb of water beyond the beach, and the air was filled with the distant boom of breaking waves.

Trey suddenly remembered the borrowed shirt and slipped it off, handing it to her. "Lock the door behind me."

She nodded, hugging the shirt against her. In the months after Jack's death, that shirt had been her magic talisman, protecting her, keeping her from going crazy with grief. It had been the first thing she'd reached for when they'd called from the hospital that night, and in the weeks afterward she'd worn it to bed, able to sleep only when swaddled in its comforting folds. It had still held the scent of him, and even now, four years later, she felt so close to him when she was wearing it that she'd often find herself laughing at some remembered thing he'd said, half expecting to feel the touch of his hand on her arm or the warmth of his breath on her lips.

But its magic didn't seem to be working tonight. For one thing, the shirt carried Trey's scent, not Jack's, and although she couldn't say it was unpleasant, it *was* disconcerting. It still held his body warmth, too, but even that didn't keep the night chill at bay. The wind had picked up and was sighing through the big cedars that sheltered the house, making them moan and creak. The boughs moved restlessly against the moonlit sky, casting ragged shadows across the deck and the steps down to the beach, and she hugged the shirt a little tighter.

"Are you sure you're going to be all right here by yourself?" Trey's voice was quiet. "You had a hell of a scare tonight, and I still think you should call someone to—"

"I'll be all right." She spoke much too quickly and could see both impatience and disbelief play across his face.

"I wrote my phone number on the pad by your phone. If anything strange starts going on, I want you to use it."

"Okay." She nodded again, her voice a subdued whisper.

"And you know where I live." He inclined his head; a corner of his beach house was just visible through the trees, silhouetted against the sky. He looked down at her seriously. "I mean it, Linn. Don't take any chances. Independence is great, but there's such a thing as carrying it too far."

For some reason it nearly made her smile. He thought he knew what was going on, but he didn't. He thought it was about a drunk and a woman on a lonely stretch of beach, but things were a lot more complicated than that, a lot more dangerous. If he had any idea of the secret she was hiding, of the real reason she and Nathan were out here, trying to

disappear into the crowds of summer people, he'd wish he
had never ventured off his sun deck to play hero tonight.

An owl hooted in the darkness and she started slightly.
Trey lifted his head like a stag scenting the wind and gave the
moon-silvered beach and trees a sweeping look. He didn't
seem in any hurry to leave and Linn found herself half
wishing he wouldn't.

She shook off the thought, realizing he was once again
gazing at her thoughtfully. His face was hard-edged in the
darkness and moonlight cascaded across his bare shoulders, making his long, wind-tangled hair gleam blue-black
and catching the glint of gold in his left ear.

For half an instant it wasn't Trey Hollister standing there
at all, but someone out of a different age, a Barbary pirate,
who had just come ashore seeking a resting place for himself and his weary crew after months at sea. In that moment it wouldn't have surprised her in the least to look
beyond him and see his ship at anchor in the bay, to imagine her decks stained with blood and her hold fat with
plunder. He'd have brought some of it ashore to barter for
food and drink and weapons: gold coins from kingdoms to
the south and west, jewels, spices, fine silk and perhaps even
a woman or two, virgin doe-eyed daughters of kings to be
ransomed for whatever live flesh would bring.

And he was gazing down at her, Linn realized uneasily, as
though he wouldn't mind adding her to his booty.

He shifted slightly, eclipsing the moon, seeming to draw
closer without moving at all, and Linn stiffened, certain for
one bizarre moment that he was going to try to kiss her. His
eyes were very dark, full of tangled emotions she couldn't
decipher, and once more she became very aware of the
warm, male scent of him through the essence of sea and
pine. There was an odd tension between them that hadn't
been there moments before, another level of awareness so
unexpected that it took Linn a moment or two to recognize
its subtle but unmistakable sexual undertones.

It took her so by surprise that she simply stared up at him,
more amused by the absurdity than alarmed. It had to be
simple shock, she decided. Maybe there was some genetic
synapse in every woman, automatically triggered by acts of

masculine bravery, which produced a flood of hormones that would send her swooning into her hero's arms.

But she didn't have the time for swooning these days. Even if she *could* risk the chance that Hollister was indeed the hero he appeared to be and not a devious and all too charming dragon in disguise.

Just for a moment, for the tiniest heartbeat of time, she almost wished...

A black, furry presence suddenly squeezed by her and Linn gave a violent start. But it was just Murphy, coming out to see what they were doing.

Trey took a deep breath and shrugged his shoulders as though relaxing tight muscles. Murphy looked up at him questioningly and Trey dropped onto his right knee, wincing. "You're staying here tonight, old fella," he said firmly. "Stay, Murphy. And guard. Understand?" The dog whined and aimed a wet lick at Trey's face that he deftly avoided. He looked up at Linn. "Give me your hand."

Linn held her hand out and Trey meshed his fingers with hers. "Guard Linn, Murph. Stay with Linn and guard her." He drew Linn's hand down and Murphy sniffed at it damply, then licked her fingers and looked up at her with a sharp bark. "Guard, Murph. Guard Linn and Nathan. Got it?"

The big dog threw his head up and gave a series of deep-chested barks, then rubbed his face against Linn's blue-jeaned leg with a soft whine. Trey nodded and got to his feet. "Nobody's going to get near you two tonight," he said with quiet assurance. "Or at any other time, if he's within shouting distance. He stays on my sun deck or within the perimeter of the yard, but I don't keep him chained. So if you ever need him, just sing out and he'll be on an intruder like a terrier on a rat."

Murphy gave her free hand a nudge with his nose and Linn scratched between his ears. He leaned against her leg with a sigh, tail thumping on the wooden decking. Trey was still holding her other hand and to Linn's surprise, Murphy reached out and took his master's wrist between his huge jaws and gently but firmly pulled.

Trey gave a snort. "Murph, you bonehead, you're supposed to be protecting her from *bad* guys, not from me."

"Maybe he knows you better than you think," Linn said dryly, her fingers still tingling from his warmth.

Trey turned his head to look at her, his eyes catching the moonlight, and for an instant he reminded Linn of that Barbary pirate again, dark-eyed and dangerous. "Maybe he does, at that," he said very softly, his eyes holding hers long enough to let her know that he, too, had felt the subtle electricity that had passed between them.

Then he turned away and walked across the wide deck. "Just turn him out in the morning and tell him to go home. He may want to hang around and play with Nathan, but if you're firm enough with him, he'll get the message."

"Does that work with his master?" Her words seemed to hang in the night air, and Linn regretted them the instant they were out. She should have ignored what had happened, or pretended she hadn't recognized it for what it was. Acknowledging it only heightened the unwanted intimacy between them.

Trey paused on the top step and glanced around, his gaze holding hers for a long, still moment. Then one corner of his mouth tipped up. "Good night, Linn Stevenson, or whatever your name is. Sleep well." He turned and padded down the steps and into the darkness.

"Good…night," Linn replied slowly, frowning as she ran one of Murphy's silky ears between her fingers.

What *had* just happened, anyway? She was so out of touch with the intricacies of sexual politics these days that she could have simply misread the entire incident and imagined something that wasn't even there. Were all the subtleties and rituals the same as when she'd been dating? Had everything changed during the three years that she and Jack had been married, or the four since his death?

Odd, she'd never given it much thought before tonight. She'd simply never been *interested* in knowing.

She still wasn't interested, she reminded herself firmly. She smiled at Murphy and gave him a pat. "Do you need to go for a stroll before bedtime, big guy? Because this door is going to be locked tight all night."

He seemed to understand exactly what she was saying and bounded back into the house with a wag of his tail, pausing to look around as though making sure she locked the door securely behind them. Then he put his nose to the floor and trotted into the kitchen, looking very businesslike. Linn followed him and put a bowl of water down, but it took her only a moment to realize he was just checking his perimeter, as every good guard should do at intervals.

He gave the door leading from the kitchen to the carport a thorough sniff, then continued his patrol, making a quick circuit of the living and dining rooms before heading for the bedrooms.

A sudden wave of exhaustion washed over Linn and she yawned, quite content to let Murphy do the rest of his patrol on his own. To her surprise, the horror of Rolfson's attack was starting to fade. It was amazing how resilient the human mind was, she mused as she checked the fire, closing the damper and making sure the screen was tight. Either there was a limit to how much terror one person could absorb, or she was getting better at handling the fear.

She yawned again as she walked down to her bedroom, pausing to glance in at Nathan. He was sound asleep, one arm thrown around the furry neck of the big dog stretched out beside him. Murphy lifted his head as she peeked in and she smiled at him, winning a wag of his tail. Then he put his head back onto his paws and closed his eyes, seemingly relaxed, although Linn had no doubt those big ears were listening to every sound within a quarter-mile radius.

Feeling safe for the first time in weeks, she smiled and went to bed.

It was the hammering that wakened Linn. And the sound of someone softly whistling.

She was out of bed and into her jeans and sweatshirt in one motion, and in the next had slipped silently into the corridor and across to Nathan's room.

He wasn't there.

Linn fought rising panic as she stared at his rumpled, empty bed. She was going to stay calm, she told herself forcefully. It was late—nearly nine—and he'd just gotten up to play. And Murphy was with him. Nothing would happen to him as long as Murphy was there.

The hammering started again. Linn looked swiftly around Nathan's room, then snatched up the tall lamp sitting on his desk, giving the cord a wrench to pull out the plug and discarding the shade. It was one of a pair of living-room lamps, solid brass and heavy as sin, and it settled into her palm with satisfying solidity as she moved silently down the corridor toward the kitchen.

There was a man there. He was standing with his back to her, dressed in filthy jeans and a ragged blue pullover, his stringy gray hair curling around his shoulders. He was bent over the kitchen table, seemingly engrossed in whatever he was doing, and Linn padded a little nearer, brass lamp at the ready.

"What the *hell* are you doing in my kitchen?"

A tape measure went flying across the room as the man shot into the air with a startled oath. He whirled around to skewer her with a hostile glare. "Damn it, lady, you don't go creeping up on a man like that!"

Linn stared at the clutter in her kitchen with a growing sense of unreality. The pane of glass in the window above the sink that Trey had broken had been taken out, and there were tools scattered across the table and floor. "Who *are* you?"

"Toomey," he replied with some annoyance, eyeing the lamp in her hand suspiciously. "Don't need that. Got enough light. Just fixin' the window."

Linn stared at the mess on the table, then at him. "How did you get in?"

"Key, a' course." He gave her a look that said more clearly than words that only an idiot would have to ask the obvious.

"Key? What key?"

"The key *he* gave me," he said acerbically, turning his back on her and picking up the tape measure.

"He?" Linn echoed thinly.

"Hollister, a' course." He pinned her with one impatient eye. "You gonna stand there yammerin' all day, or can I get back to work?"

Linn took a breath and set the lamp down carefully, resisting the growing temptation to pitch it at him. "Have you seen my son?"

"Boy's outside."

Linn gritted her teeth, wondering if Hollister had inflicted this man on her out of revenge or just as some macabre joke. The door leading to the carport was open and she walked outside, looking around for Nathan and Murphy. They were nowhere to be seen, and she felt the familiar panic starting to build, but refused to give in to it.

She walked around to the deck and stood on the top step, staring intently through the trees to the beach. The tide was out and the pale sand seemed to run on for miles, glinting damply in the hot morning sun. And then she saw them—a small boy and a big dog, playing in the sand near the high-tide line.

Her heart gave a thump of relief and she ran down the steps lightly, pausing for a moment under the big trees at the bottom. It was cool in the shadows, and it took her eyes a moment to adjust to the sudden dimness as she made her way along the short, root-strewn path to the sand.

The wide beach was hot and bare and completely empty, except for Nathan and Hollister's big dog. They were racing around in ever-widening circles, involved in some game that seemed to involve a piece of driftwood and a good deal of wrestling and shouting and running. Nathan's cheeks were flushed and he was laughing, the sound of his young voice rising above the muted roar of the surf.

How long had it been since she'd heard him laugh with such happy abandon? Damn Guillermo Santos!

And damn Rodrigo Valencia, too, she found herself thinking with unaccustomed heat. What had ever possessed him to play the hero, anyway? And why couldn't Kathy have married a banker or an accountant or some other peaceful, sane man instead of the dashingly handsome Latino who looked more like a border bandit than the Miami vice cop he was?

It was Rod's single-minded dedication to law and order that had put them all in this danger: his wife and himself in hiding, literally running for their lives, their son smuggled out of Miami to Linn's Fort Lauderdale home. And from there to a wild, windswept beach on Vancouver Island, still in danger from the Colombian drug lord who was trying to kill both his father and Kathy.

Linn caught the anger and swallowed it. Rod couldn't help being a good cop—she knew all about that, being a cop's daughter herself. And she *had* volunteered to take Nathan; it wasn't as though she'd been coerced into it. All she had to do was keep him safe until Santos's court date, when Rod's testimony would put him away for good. Then the danger would be over.

Murphy's excited barking distracted her from her brooding, and she shook the mood off. She smiled as Murphy snatched up the driftwood and took off with Nathan in hot, noisy pursuit, and for half a moment she was tempted to let them continue playing. It had been too long since she'd seen Nathan so carefree and happy, the constant fear momentarily forgotten.

But she couldn't afford to get careless. One slip, that was all it would take. Santos's men could be anywhere....

She was just going to step into the sand when the tall form moved out of the shadows in front of her; a strong hand gently encircled her wrist.

"Leave him," a quiet voice said. "He's all right."

Linn recoiled so violently that she stumbled over a loop of exposed root and would have fallen if the hand holding her wrist hadn't held her upright. She snatched instinctively for support and grabbed a handful of soft chambray shirting, and in the next instant found herself in the circle of Trey Hollister's very competent embrace.

Chapter 4

D-damn you!'' she managed to gasp, her heart cartwheeling with shock. "You scared me half to death!"

"Sorry," he murmured. "I thought you saw me standing here."

"Well, I didn't!" She closed her eyes for an instant, trying to catch her breath, then realized she was still clutching his shirtfront. She released the fabric and stepped away from his supporting arm. "What are you doing here, anyway? And why is there a perfectly horrible little man in my kitchen who says you let him in with a key?"

"That's Toomey—sort of a local jack-of-all-trades." Trey let his fingers slide from her wrist and stood looking down at her, his dark, handsome face thoughtful in the shadows. "He's replacing the glass in that window I broke last night."

"Why didn't you warn me you were sending him around? And what are you doing with a key to my place, anyway?"

"I have a key," he said calmly, "because the owner gave me one—I keep an eye on the place when it's empty. And I didn't wake you this morning to tell you Toomey was coming in because I figured you needed the sleep."

"So you sent him in to scare me to death instead," she said with annoyance.

He smiled faintly. "I told him to wait for a couple of hours, but I guess he just got impatient. I'm sorry."

Linn found herself even more irritated by his sudden and unexpected civility. In daylight, she realized that his dark hair was shot with silver, the effect emphasizing his rugged good looks. And his eyes were the oddest color she'd ever seen, more pewter than gray, with darker flecks of what might have been blue in a different light. They were still private, watchful eyes, but they lacked the underlying savagery she'd seen last night, indeed were almost amused as they held hers; he obviously knew damned well he'd taken the rug out from under her.

"Excuse me," she said with precision, stepping by him. "I've got to get Nathan."

The sand was hot and dry and she curled her toes into it as she walked down to where the boy and dog were playing. "Nathan!" Her tone was sharper than she'd intended, and Nathan's head shot around in alarm. "Nathan, you know you're not supposed to be out here by yourself."

"But I'm not by myself," he protested. "Murphy's here."

"You know what I mean. Come on back to the house. You've got plenty of toys there to play with."

"But, Aunt Linn, we're just—"

"Nathan!" Her voice snapped across the sand, warning and rebuke both, and she saw him pale slightly at his slip. The fear was back on his face again, extinguishing the laughter and joy, and Linn ached with sudden guilt.

He was just a little boy, she reminded herself wearily, and little boys and big dogs were *made* to play with each other. It had been weeks since he'd had anyone's company but hers—and twenty-seven-year-old aunts, no matter how loving or well-intentioned, just weren't the same as a large, rowdy dog.

"Being a little hard on him, aren't you?" Trey suddenly appeared at her elbow. His voice was mild enough, but his eyes were narrowed slightly as he watched Nathan walk slowly toward them, feet dragging, face forlorn.

"Mother's nerves," she replied calmly, only half lying. "I guess I'm still a little shaken up by what happened last night, that's all." Which wasn't quite a lie, either. Although it was getting harder and harder these days to tell truth from fiction, so adept was she becoming at swathing every word in distortion.

"That stands to reason." He watched Nathan for a moment, then looked down at her. "Let him play out here for a while longer," he said quietly. "A kid that age can stay cooped up only so long. And nothing's going to happen to him. I've been watching over him."

"What do you mean?" she asked sharply.

"I mean," he said gently, "that I've been babysitting while you've been catching up on your sleep. I looked out about seven and saw him sneaking down to the beach with Murph, and I figured it wouldn't hurt to keep an eye on him."

He spoke as though it were the most natural thing in the world, but it left her momentarily speechless. It was like something Jack would have done, the kind of thoughtful gesture that was all the more precious for its honesty and spontaneity.

The rest of her anger was defused, and she looked up at him with a faint smile. "You must be getting awfully tired of coming to my rescue every time you turn around."

"I don't think keeping an eye on Nathan for an hour or two this morning constitutes a rescue."

"Maybe not, but last night did." Linn gazed across the sand, rubbing her arms. Nathan had stopped to play with Murphy and Linn opened her mouth to call him again. Then she sighed instead, and looked up at Trey. "I never did thank you for that. Properly, anyway. In fact, I behaved pretty badly, all around. You had every right to be angry with me."

"No." He eased himself onto the stand, wincing slightly. The scar across his thigh was reddened by the chill morning air and he kneaded it slowly, as though it was aching. "I was rougher on you than I needed to be."

She watched his fingers massage his thigh, remembering that swift, clean martial arts kick that had sent Rolfson

flying. Remembering the way Trey had been limping afterward. It had been pain as much as anger that had made him
lash out at her, she realized suddenly. The pain of scar tissue torn too far too soon, of damaged muscles and tendons
pushed past their limits.

Sighing, she sat down beside him. "I'm sorry about that,
too," she said quietly. She reached out without even thinking and placed her hand on Trey's. "Did you hurt it seriously last night?"

He seemed to go very still. She could feel the tension and
latent power in his hand, as though he was forcing himself
not to pull it away, and Linn very carefully withdrew her
own.

"No," Trey said roughly, not looking at her. The unexpected touch had unsettled him more than he wanted to admit, and he massaged the deep ache in his thigh angrily. It
wasn't her fault he'd ripped into Rolfson like some high
school football hero last night. Hell, he knew better! The
doctors had told him it would be months before the leg was
sound, and not a night hadn't gone by since he got out of the
hospital when he wasn't reminded of how close he'd come
to losing it.

Maybe that had been part of his anger last night. He'd
taken on Rolfson with a recklessness he'd hardly recognized as his own, luxuriating in the tear of healing muscle,
in the crunch and pain of bone against bone. His right hand
was swollen and stiff this morning, his knuckles cut and
bruised from where he'd landed that punch on Rolfson's
jaw, but even that had been worth it. He'd relished the sheer
physicality, the violence, as though he'd been lashing out not
only at Rolfson but at all those months of pain and anger
and bad memories.

And in some strange way it had worked. He'd awakened
this morning feeling better than he had in weeks, the gloom
that had been hanging over him all but gone. It was like this
after every tough assignment; the physical and mental exhaustion, the letdown that always followed weeks of in-
tense physical activity and danger. It had been worse this
time simply because the *job* had been worse. A few more

weeks of R and R on this beach and he'd be back up to fighting trim again.

If he didn't wrack himself up first, keeping his mysterious new neighbour out of trouble, that was.

What the hell was it about her that had resulted in this sudden—and uncharacteristic—urge to play hero? Those eyes, probably. She had the bluest eyes he'd ever seen, so wide and clear a man could get lost in them. Or maybe it was just that stubborn way she had of looking at you head-on, just daring you to confront her on the obvious lies. Even last night, so damned angry that he could have strangled her, he'd had to admire her, too. A woman who'd fight that hard to protect her child deserved a man's respect.

He gave her a sidelong look and found her staring across the sand, a frown creasing her forehead, shoulders slightly hunched. She looked small and vulnerable, almost lost, and again he found himself thinking of something wild that had been chased and harried and hunted. She'd been holed up here with her son like a fox in a den, licking her wounds and catching her breath but never relaxing, ever vigilant for the hunter with the gun she knew was out there somewhere.

Suddenly she gave her head a shake, as though breaking free of whatever she'd been thinking about. "I've got to go in."

She stood up and started brushing sand from her jeans. Well-fitting jeans, Trey couldn't help noticing, the soft, worn denim hugging her in all the right places, in all the right ways. As she bent over, he also couldn't help noticing that she wasn't wearing a bra. The heavy wool sweater she was wearing almost but not quite disguised the contours of an unrestrained breast as she brought her arms forward.

Of course, Trey mused: she'd just gotten out of bed. The first thing she'd have done was check on Nathan, and when she couldn't find him she'd pulled her clothes on and raced outside to look for him. That was why her hair was still uncombed, her milky complexion still devoid of makeup.

There was something subtly erotic about it, as though she'd just come tumbling out of *his* bed, all naked and warm and tousled. It took no effort at all to imagine her still in that bed, thick hair spilling like water across the pillow, those incredible eyes almost sapphire in the shadowed dimness of the room. And God, she smelled good! Even from here he could catch the scent of warm female skin and hair, knew instinctively what she'd feel like against him, every inch of her like satin. Satin and sin....

He caught the rest of the thought with rough impatience. Cool down, Hollister, he told himself irritably. The last thing you need is woman trouble. And son, you'd better believe that's what she is! One look at her, that's all it takes. Just one look and a man knows . . . trouble, gift-wrapped in satin and sin....

He shook himself free of it again and stood up, wincing at a jolt of pain in his thigh. He'd ripped something loose in there last night, sure as hell. It would mend, of course. They always did. But it was going to be reminding him regularly and painfully for the next few days that he was getting too damned old for this kind of abuse.

He knew Linn was watching him with faint concern and forced himself not to limp as he walked back along the beach beside her, smiling grimly at himself. They made a good pair, one of them refusing to give in to age, the other refusing to give in to fear.

Linn paused at the bottom of the steps leading up to her rented house, waiting for Nathan to catch up.

Trey had followed her, was standing looking at her now. "You know where I live. If you need a hand with anything, don't be too shy to sing out."

Linn nodded, slightly bemused. He was still gruff and abrupt today, but she had the distinct impression that he was making an effort to be civil to her. It touched her for some reason, and she found herself suddenly contemplating asking him in for breakfast. Or even just coffee. Nathan would love it, and she . . .

No. She caught the impulse in time, unnerved by how easily it had sneaked up on her. Loneliness was perhaps the worst part of this nightmare with Nathan, the one thing she'd never anticipated. It made her vulnerable and it could make her careless. She couldn't take that risk. She'd kept Nathan safe this long through luck, guile and not taking a damned thing for granted; it was silly to start taking chances now, just because she was hungry for the sound of another person's voice.

He was still looking down at her, a curiously thoughtful expression on his face. Even standing on the bottom step, she barely came to his shoulder, and he seemed much broader through the shoulders and chest than he had last night, much more solid. A real flesh-and-blood man this time, not a swashbuckling hero conjured up out of moonlight and desperation.

He was so close she could smell the heathery scent of his after-shave. His cheeks and square, hard jaw were cleanly shaven, the tanned skin silky and smooth, and she could see a faint scar running diagonally across his chin. It ended just under his lower lip and she found her gaze riveted there. His mouth was full and sensuous—remarkably so, she found herself thinking idly, for so rugged a man.

Trey damned near kissed her then and there. The urge came right out of left field, hitting him so solidly that it took every ounce of willpower he had not to cup her upturned face in both palms, turn her mouth toward his and kiss her so deeply and thoroughly that it would have left them both reeling. She was so close he could *taste* her, knew exactly what her mouth would feel like under his, could anticipate the first startled hesitancy, the slow yielding. And it wouldn't be any formal, chaste little kiss, either, but deep and slow and deliciously erotic, an enjoyable prelude to the loving they both knew would have to follow.

But he managed somehow to resist that tempting little mouth and everything it promised. "I wouldn't stay out here in the sun too long, if I were you," he said quietly, daring to brush a tangle of dark hair off her cheek. Her skin was as warm and soft to his touch as he'd known it would be. "You can pick up a wicked burn before you realize how hot it is."

She put her hand up as though to touch the spot where his fingers had lingered, but checked the movement halfway. "No," she whispered, her eyes wide and dark. "I...won't."

"That was a damn fool thing to do." Toomey nodded toward the kitchen window, fastening one faded blue eye on Linn. "What 'cha go do a silly thing like that for?"

"*I* didn't break the darned window," Linn said heatedly. She was still shaken by what had happened on the beach a few minutes ago, could still feel Trey Hollister's gentle touch on her cheek.

"Not talkin' about the window," he grumbled, opening a vast tool chest that looked as though it weighed more than he did. "Talkin' about losing your key. Woman should know better than to be careless with her house key. Just invitin' trouble. Never know *who* might pick it up."

"Mr. Toomey, will you please just fix the—?"

"Just Toomey," he snapped. "I'm not no mister!"

Linn, to her surprise, managed to restrain herself. Nathan was sitting at the kitchen table, supposedly eating his lunch, wide-eyed in wonderment at the stranger's colorful vocabulary.

"Well, it makes no never mind," Toomey muttered as he rummaged through the toolbox. "About the key, I mean. I'll be changing all the locks, anyway."

"Changing the locks?" Linn looked at him sharply.

"Says they're bad, the lot of them. Easy as cheese to get through. Went into town this mornin', he did, and bought a bunch of good ones." He nodded knowingly. "Need a blowtorch to get through these ones. Knows his work, Hollister does."

"Hollister?" Linn's voice rose slightly. "Damn it, he can't just—" She stopped, breathing heavily. "Just what is it that Hollister does for a living that makes him so knowledgeable about locks?" *And so handy at running other people's lives,* she almost added.

Toomey beamed. "Writes them Steele books."

"Steel?" Linn blinked. "He's in construction?"

Toomey gave her a pitying look. "Steele: Man of Action," he explained scornfully. His estimation of her, not high to begin with, had obviously dropped another point or two. "Must have about eight out now, and all bestsellers. *Steele Connection* is the best, I figure. 'Course, there's *Hot Steele*, and *Steele Vengeance*, and—"

"I get the picture," Linn said quickly. "Men's action-adventure, aren't they? Espionage, mercenaries and mayhem?"

Toomey gave her a sharp look. "Bestsellers, all of 'em," he repeated, as though nothing more needed saying.

"So our Mr. Hollister is a novelist, is he," Linn mused aloud. Strange, that didn't fit the image she had of him at all. He'd struck her as the kind of man more comfortable behind the controls of a fighter jet or a race car than a typewriter. Hollister, man of action. Yes, he definitely *was* that, all right.

"Wouldn't plan on going over there and botherin' him about it. Keeps pretty much to himself, he does." He eyed her with mild hostility. "Can't remember him *ever* letting a woman inside. House is kinda his private domain. Off limits to them of the female persuasion, as it were. Not," he added hastily, "that he don't like women. Fact is, he likes 'em a lot. Just not at *his* place."

"I *get* the picture," Linn repeated frostily. "How much longer are you going to be with that window?"

"As long as it takes," he replied tartly. "Window's as good as fixed already, and it won't take long to replace the locks." He speared her with a speculative look. "Whatever it is you want to keep out, I wouldn't worry about it now. Not with Hollister watching over you."

Linn just nodded, biting back her irritation. She was, quite frankly, getting a little tired of hearing about Trey Hollister and everything he could do.

Old Toomey might not know a great deal about women, Linn had to admit that evening, but he certainly knew what he was doing when it came to house repairs. She'd spent most of the afternoon out on the beach with Nathan, and when they'd come in, Toomey and his gigantic toolbox were both gone.

He'd done a perfect job of replacing the broken pane in the kitchen window. As well, it and all the other windows in the house had been outfitted with heavy-duty catches that looked strong enough to keep out bears. The three exterior doors not only sported new locks, but safety chains you could haul logs with. And to top it off, he'd even installed wide-angle peepholes in both the front door and the one leading from the kitchen to the carport.

"I don't believe that guy," she whispered as she tested the new lock on the sliding door to the deck.

"Who, Aunt Linn?" Nathan peered around her, munching a peanut butter cookie. "Mr. Toomey?"

"Our new neighbor." She put her arm around Nathan's shoulders absently as she gazed at the beach. There was a man down there, dark-haired and deeply tanned, walking just along the edge of the water. There was a big German shepherd bouncing along beside him and as she watched, he picked up a piece of driftwood and flung it down the beach. The dog exploded after it and the man continued walking, limping slightly, alone and thoughtful.

Suddenly restless, Linn drew the grass cloth drapes. She'd lighted the fire earlier and it crackled and muttered comfortably on the hearth; now she added another piece of pine to it, then wandered along the well-filled bookcases built into one wall. The man who owned the beach house was a psychology professor at the University of Victoria, and although he'd left the place filled with reading material, most of it was too technical to be of much interest to the layperson.

There were a number of novels, as well, book club bestsellers for the most part, but Linn had already worked her way through the few that interested her. She'd noticed the shelf of hardcover political thrillers and mysteries before, but hadn't paid too much attention. They caught her eye tonight, though, and she wasn't surprised when she spotted a familiar name. Smiling, she reached down and pulled the book from the shelf.

The cover was dramatic, black profiles on silver: a man's face, a smoking gun, a beautiful woman, a file dossier stamped Top Secret. The title, _Steele Connection,_ ran across the top in black, no-nonsense square letters, and under it, in smaller print, the author's name, T. C. Hollister.

Well, well. She opened it curiously, not surprised to discover Trey's name scrawled across the inside below a dedi-

cation to someone named Paul. She flipped the book over
and found herself face-to-face with Hollister himself.

It was a good picture, head and shoulders, shot head-on.
He seemed to be staring right into her eyes, as though it
wasn't just Hollister's likeness in her hands but Hollister
himself. And the effect was slightly unnerving. The pho-
tographer had somehow managed to perfectly capture that
essence of power and danger and raw sex appeal that was as
much a part of the man as those odd gray eyes. It occurred
to Linn that in trying to get a picture designed to appeal to
as wide a range of readers as possible, he had probably come
closer to portraying the real man than anyone had intended. Trey Hollister radiated competence and the kind of
self-confidence that is often mistaken for arrogance, and
there was enough sensual promise in his half smile to make
even her heart give a little thump.

The bio blurb inside didn't tell her much she didn't already know. Famed writer T. C. Hollister, author of seven
bestselling Steele: Man of Action novels, was born in Lub-
bock, Texas, and although an American, had made his
home for the last six years in the isolated Canadian West
Coast fishing village and tourist resort of Tofino.

An ex-marine who had brought home an impressive collection of medals from two tours of duty in Vietnam, he'd
disappeared into the mystique and shadows of something
called military intelligence for nearly ten years. His first
novel, *Steele Gambit,* had hit the stands seven years ago,
and after whetting the reading public's thirst, he had been
writing ever since.

She looked at the back cover again. His eyes seemed to
lock with hers, looking right through the lies and the fabri-
cations to every secret she'd ever had, and she subdued a
little shiver. You're good, she told him silently. You're
damned good. But there's nothing T. C. Hollister, or even
Steele, both men of action, can do to help me. I'm on my
own.

She carried the book to one of the love seats bracketing
the hearth and sat down, tucking her feet under her and
drawing the knit afghan, the one her mother had made last
Christmas, around her shoulders. Nathan was stretched on

his stomach in front of the fire, playing with a complicated array of toy trucks, and she watched him for a moment, then opened the book at the first page.

Linn didn't know what woke her up. One minute she'd been sound asleep and the next she was wide-awake, every sense alert, ears straining to hear something in the stillness of the night. Frowning, she sat up and looked around the dark room. The wind had picked up and she could hear the cedars whispering outside the window, all but drowning the pervasive pounding of the surf. She tossed back the covers and slipped out of bed, reaching for her robe, and made her way to Nathan's room.

He was sleeping soundly, brows tugged together as though he was dreaming about something that worried him. Not surprising, Linn thought, tucking the blanket more securely around his shoulders. He was probably going to have nightmares for the rest of his life, thanks to his father's obsession with putting Santos away.

She made her way down the dark corridor and into the kitchen, checking the living-room door and windows on the way just from habit. Moonlight flooded the kitchen, and she didn't bother turning on a light as she ran herself a glass of water and stood by the sink for a minute or two, drinking it slowly. The cedar just outside the window cast a grotesque shadow on the far wall as it moved in the wind and she watched it only half consciously, idly thinking about Hollister's book.

It was good. Incredibly good, actually. The writing was much like its creator, blunt, hard-hitting and vitally alive, yet with a gentleness and poetic beauty in places that had left her breathless. His characters, too, were fantastically drawn, every nuance of human behavior revealed with a magician's skill. It was his hero, Steele, who troubled her. Steele, the man with one name who never seemed to linger too long in one place, the lone-wolf righter of wrongs who could handle any weapon, drive any vehicle, love any woman better than she'd ever been loved....

The shadow on the wall shifted suddenly, seeming to coalesce into a finite shape, and Linn froze, glass poised against her lips as she stared at the unmistakable silhouette of a man.

The boughs of the cedar shifted in the moonlight, running the patterns together like ink, and when they stilled, the shape was gone. Linn dropped the glass into the sink and spun from the window, her heart hammering so hard that she could scarcely catch her breath.

Don't panic!

She closed her eyes, fighting the terror clawing at her throat. As long as she didn't panic, she had a chance. How many times had she heard her father say that? *Don't panic....*

Soundlessly she slipped across to the carport door and leaned toward it, listening intently. All she could hear was her own heart pounding. But then, very faintly, she heard something else. Footsteps, maybe. Soft, cautious footsteps, betrayed only by the rustle of the dried leaves and pine needles that had blown inside.

Something moved again outside the door, so softly she couldn't be certain it was even real. She eased herself nearer and put her eye to the viewer. All she could see was part of the carport and the tail end of her rental car, both distorted by the lens.

Then, suddenly, someone stepped in front of the viewer. Linn recoiled so violently that she hit her hip on the edge of the counter, and she gave a gasp of pain, clasping one hand over her mouth to stifle the sound. Her heart was pounding against her ribs so hard that she felt light-headed, and she had to struggle to catch her breath, staring numbly at the doorknob as it started to turn.

That was what finally galvanized her into action. She wrenched the nearest drawer open and snatched up the big butcher knife, then headed for Nathan's bedroom. Astonishingly, he was still asleep. For a moment she contemplated waking him, then decided against it. Toomey had installed double catches on his window, which, because of the way the house was built on the sloping hillside, was itself a good twelve feet above ground level. For the moment he was safer here.

She pulled the drapes tightly across the window, then quickly went across the corridor to her own bedroom and the nearest telephone. She'd jotted Trey's number on the pad beside her bed and she dialed frantically, swearing with frustration as she misdialed and had to start over.

Her hand was shaking as she held the receiver to her ear and she prayed silently for him to pick it up as the phone at his end started to ring. "Come *on*," she whispered urgently. "Please be there. Please, *please* ... !"

She could just see a corner of the house through the trees, rising solid and reassuring against the moonlit sky. So near, yet so impossibly distant. "Please answer ... please. ..."

She heard a noise, a twig snapped by a careless footfall, perhaps, or a branch hitting the side of the house. Then, with no warning, someone stepped in front of her.

It was a man, and he rose tall and solid on the other side of the glass, looming against the shadows and sky like something out of a nightmare. He reached toward her and Linn flung herself backward with a soft cry, sending the phone and the knife, her only weapon, flying out of reach.

Chapter 5

Linn!"

The urgent voice, even through glass, was familiar. The tall figure leaned forward and gestured impatiently for her to open the window, and in that moment she was able to see his face as the moonlight fell across it.

"Damn you!" She pressed the back of her hand to her mouth to stifle a sob and managed to get across the room and fumble with the unfamiliar catches to release them.

But she was shaking so badly by then that she couldn't lift the window. Trey did it from the outside and eased himself in through the narrow casement like a dark, lithe shadow. "Damn it," he breathed, reaching for her, "I didn't mean to scare you. I thought you'd seen me out there...."

It was the most natural thing in the world to find herself in his strong embrace, his arms wrapped tightly around her. He was bare to the waist and his skin was smooth and hot and scented with sea air and clean sweat; his masculine warmth wrapped around her like a cocoon. He was breathing quickly and she could feel the fast, rhythmic beat of the pulse in his throat against her cheek, the taut, hard lines of muscle in the arms holding her so closely.

Those strong arms tightened and he buried his face in her hair. For a moment all the fear and the horror vanished and there were just the two of them, man and woman in a long, aching embrace that encompassed all that words never could. It was apology, forgiveness, comfort, understanding and a hundred other things; just two people reaching through the darkness for the touch of another.

Linn drew in a deep breath, feeling her heartbeat finally start to slow, and Trey stirred slightly. The pressure of his arms eased, and in that instant something subtly changed. It wasn't just a pair of arms around her, holding out the night, but Trey Hollister's arms.

And it was Trey's hands on her back, so real that she could feel the pressure of each individual finger through the filmy fabric of her robe and nightgown. She could feel the slick film of sweat on his chest, the rough pressure of the waistband of his jeans against her stomach, could even feel the hard, cold band of his wristwatch.

And it was a good feeling, Linn realized with surprise. It was solid and real and incredibly masculine; it had been too long since she'd been all wrapped up in a man's embrace. Much too long.

But this wasn't the time. Nor, perhaps, the man.

She drew back almost regretfully. She heard Trey draw in a deep, careful breath, running his hands lightly down her arms as though reluctant to let her go. "Are you all right?"

Linn managed a rough laugh. "You need a new opening line, Hollister. You ask me that every time you see me."

"Usually with reason." He glanced around the room swiftly, his expression preoccupied and frowning. "You don't have company tonight, do you?"

"Company?" Her voice held a tremor of laughter until she realized he was serious. "Of course not. It's after midnight."

"I meant all-night company." He was still looking around the room assessingly, then his gaze swung around and locked on hers. "You're a big girl. It's allowed."

For some reason it annoyed her. "Is there a local ordinance about overnight guests or something? And have you been appointed to peek in bedroom windows to make sure none of the local women are entertaining someone they shouldn't be?''

Ignoring her, he walked to the bedroom door and looked into the corridor. His back was swathed in moonlight, strong and well-muscled, a sweep of smooth, tanned skin that was marred by only one thing.

Linn stared at the grip of the small revolver tucked into the back waistband of his jeans. ''Trey, what are you doing over here? And why are you carrying a gun?''

He glanced around, then reached behind him to check the gun. ''Sorry. You weren't supposed to see that. I didn't want to scare you.''

''Damn it, Trey, you've already done that! What's going on?''

His eyes met hers again and held them for a fraction of a second, then he padded across the hallway into Nathan's room. He checked the window swiftly, pausing to look down at the sleeping child for a moment, then he was on the prowl again. He moved through the darkness like something wild and stealthy, gliding from shadow to shadow, his moccasined feet soundless on the hardwood floor. Linn followed him silently, watching as he checked every window and door, tugging the new locks, testing the latches on the windows.

Jack had been like that. A perfectionist himself, he'd never entirely been able to trust anyone else's workmanship, and he'd driven her crazy by insisting on double-checking things she knew perfectly well were all right—only to discover more often than not that they weren't all right at all.

Finally he stopped, standing by the sliding glass door in the living room and staring intently at the beach. Linn went over to stand beside him, rubbing her arms lightly, chilled. ''All right. You've checked every window and door in the place. Now would you like to tell me what's going on?''

He eased a noisy breath between his teeth and flexed his shoulders, looking very large and dangerous in the dim light. ''Murphy woke me up a few minutes ago, barking and carrying on. I got up to have a look around. There's a car parked up on the road, halfway between your place and mine. Lights off, doors locked. But the engine's still warm, so it hasn't been there for more than twenty minutes, half an hour at the most. It's a rental—no ID inside."

"Inside?" Linn looked up at him. "You said the door was locked." His eyes met hers, curiously flat in the moonlight, and she realized very suddenly that she didn't want to hear an answer to that. "And you thought . . . ?"

"I thought I should drop by to see if you were all right," Trey said quietly. Her eyes were very wide and dark and her hair spilled around her face and shoulders, gleaming like black satin in the moonlight. She was wearing something filmy that wafted around her like mist, and he remembered how it had melted around his hands, what her skin had felt like through it.

For an instant he was tempted to reach out and draw her back into his arms, wanting to touch her again, but he fought it down.

"It may just be someone going down to the beach."

It took him a moment to realize she'd said something. He shook himself free of his wandering thoughts and forced himself to look out into the night, away from that upturned face so temptingly near. "Could be," he said doubtfully.

"Or kids. Looking for a place to . . . well, you know."

He had to laugh, looking down at her in amusement. "What does a nice girl like you know about things like that? I can't imagine you sneaking down to a cold beach to . . . you know."

Her mouth curved in a smile. "You're right. But it wasn't prudishness. I just never got asked." She gave him a sidelong look. "When your girlfriend is the police chief's daughter, hormones are no match for blatant fear."

Trey looked down at her curiously. "So. You're a police brat." That explained a few things.

She was frowning very slightly, as though regretting having said anything, and Trey decided not to push it. He looked back toward the beach, very conscious of her standing beside him. The moonlight was behind her and it was hard not to notice the slender, naked form silhouetted against the window. He could see the long sweep of her legs, the curve of a hip, the indented curvature of her back and shoulder. And the clean, perfect outline of one breast, full and lush under the loose folds of her night clothing, so perfectly detailed that he could see the thrust of the small nipple against her nightgown.

His mouth went dry and he forced himself to look away. "I . . . uh . . . think I'd better go." She looked at him in surprise, probably hearing the hint of desperation in his voice, and he managed a careless smile. "It's late. If anyone was around, Murphy would have flushed him out by now."

She nodded and gave him a faint, wry smile in return. "I hope you're not going to feel obligated to tear over here for a bed check every time Murphy spots a squirrel or woodchuck."

"I was in the neighborhood," he said easily, smiling down at her. Then he drew in a deep breath and headed back toward her bedroom. "I may as well go out the way I came in—saves messing around with the door locks."

"Thank you, by the way," she said quietly, following him down the corridor. "For the locks and everything."

"Self-preservation," he said carelessly. "I'll be able to sleep nights, now."

"Like tonight?" she asked dryly.

He had to laugh. "Tonight was a . . . test run. Now I know you're locked in tight, I won't be worrying about you." Which was a damned lie. Who was he trying to convince, her or himself?

Her bedroom was dark and silent, the curtains wafting gently in the breeze coming in the open window. The bed was rumpled, and he could see the shallow indentation in the pillow where she'd been lying, swore he could catch the faint perfume of her hair. In fact the entire room seemed filled with her scent, sweet and evocative, and he looked around curiously, taking in the cut glass bottles on the dresser, the laundry basket by the door filled with small, lacy things. There was something about a woman's bedroom he always loved, and this one was no different, filled with intimate secrets and female mysteries that no man could ever fathom.

The phone, beeping madly, was still lying on the floor where she'd dropped it. He picked it up and put it on the wicker table beside the bed, noticing his own phone number written on the pad of paper. It pleased him more than it probably should have and he gave himself an impatient mental shake, reaching down and scooping up the butcher knife lying near his foot.

He tested the blade against his thumb, then flipped it around and held it out to her, handle first. "You... uh... always greet your gentlemen callers with one of these?"

"My gentlemen callers normally use the door."

His eyes caught hers. "I tried the door," he said softly. "It was locked."

He heard her swallow. "I thought you wanted it that way."

Her voice was just a whisper, caught with something halfway through. The silence grew, enveloping them, and Trey found it difficult to breathe. "I don't know what I want," he murmured truthfully, his eyes locked with hers. "But locked might... be best."

"Yes."

It was a whisper of sound, almost lost beneath the whisper of the curtains in the breeze and the whisper of silk as he reached out and brushed the robe from her shoulders. She started slightly, not from cold or fear but from something else, standing very still as he drew the filmy fabric from her and let it fall. He ran his palms lightly down her arms and tugged her closer, putting her hands on his own waist, then ran his hands up to her shoulders.

Her skin was like hot satin and he slipped his fingers under the thin straps of her nightgown and drew them over her shoulders, lowering his mouth to the nectar of her skin. She flinched at the first touch of his tongue and he heard her breath catch over a tiny groan, felt her fingers flex spasmodically on his hips. He started kissing her shoulder and the long curve of her throat, sucking gently at the sweet, perfumed flesh, and she shivered as he drew his tongue up the side of her throat to her ear. Her breasts brushed his bare chest and he could feel the tips of them puckering, felt a responding surge of pure desire race through him.

It was crazy, taking it even this far, but Trey could no more have stopped himself from touching her than he could have stopped the moon's pull on the great oceans. He'd been going out of his mind for days now, dreaming about the touch and taste of her, knew instinctively that she'd sensed it, too. It was as though each had recognized something within the other that first night on the beach when their eyes had caught and held in the moonlight.

And maybe, he thought dimly, that was what all the anger had been about that night. Maybe they'd been fighting it even then, both terrified, for their own reasons, of what they knew had to happen. Was happening now....

He moved his mouth across her cheek and found her lips with delicious ease. They parted instinctively, welcoming him, and he ran the tip of his tongue along her upper lip. She captured it, drew on it gently, her own tongue touching, seeking. Trey felt reason start to slip and spin away.

He wanted her in that moment more than he'd ever wanted a woman in his life. Wanted to ease her back across the bed, slide his legs between hers and plunge himself so deeply into her that he wouldn't be able to tell where he stopped and she started. It would be exactly what they both wanted, what they both needed: pure, raw sex, with no apologies, no explanations, just hard and deep and driving, the kind of spontaneous, high-octane passion that explodes between two people with no warning at all.

It would have been effortless. She was as ready as he was, woman enough to recognize the moment for what it was, woman enough to enjoy it. She wouldn't expect a damned thing from him when it was over, no more than he'd expect from her, and they'd both face tomorrow with the knowledge that it had been a one-time thing, never to be repeated, never to be mentioned. Never even to be remembered, except for the occasional secret smile.

And, damn it to hell, it wasn't what he wanted at all.

He'd never dreamed he had the willpower it took to ease himself away from her, but somehow, in the end he did. Teeth gritted so hard they ached, he drew in a deep breath and stepped back from her, tugging the straps of her nightgown back over her shoulders. She grabbed his arm as though suddenly afraid of her knees giving away, and Trey slipped his arms around her and cradled her gently against himself, feeling the raging need within him slowly ease.

After a long, long while, he was able to unclench his jaw. "Damn it." It was just a harsh whisper and he drew in another deep, uneven breath. "That would be too easy, wouldn't it?"

He heard her swallow. "Much," she whispered unsteadily.

He drew back far enough to look down at her. Her eyes were still slightly heavy and her mouth, that incredibly kissable mouth, looked swollen and lush. "It would have been good," he said very quietly. *Still could be....*

Even in the moonlight he could see the blush spread across her cheeks. She lowered her lashes, managing to look both shy and provocative at the same time. "I...suspect it might have been," she whispered.

There was still time. It would be different now, slower and more sensual, probably even better. He could see the pulse at the base of her throat racing and ached to lower his mouth to it, to taste her, to feel her heartbeat against his lips.

But it was too late. Done now, their lovemaking would be something altogether different. Not less satisfying physically, but fraught with questions and expectations and a whole complicated array of social rituals. It would still be sex, but of a different kind. The kind he didn't want anymore. The kind he suspected she'd never experienced but would hate fully as much as he. The kind, he reminded himself wearily, that left you avoiding your own eyes in the bathroom mirror the next morning, knowing that if you looked too closely, you'd see something there you didn't particularly like.

He whispered a weary, profane oath, then picked up her robe and draped it carefully around her shoulders. "Somehow, Mrs. Stevenson, I think I'd better go home."

"Stevens," she said in a voice so soft he almost didn't hear her. "My name is Linn Stevens."

"And...Mr. Stevens?" he heard himself asking, his voice very casual.

She looked up at him, her eyes filled with a tangle of emotions he couldn't even begin to decipher. Then, very softly, she said, "there is no Mr. Stevens. Not...anymore."

Trey eased his breath between his teeth, not realizing until that instant how important the answer had been. He smiled at her, then lowered his face and kissed her gently—and briefly—on the mouth. "Good," he said with quiet conviction.

Then he straightened and tugged the robe more tightly around her shoulders. "I'm going home before I get myself into serious trouble, and I want you to lock that window behind me." He turned away and stuck his head out the open window, giving a piercing whistle.

Murphy appeared a moment later, tongue lolling, panting hard. Trey pulled back and snapped his fingers, and the big dog leaped effortlessly in through the window. He stood in the middle of the room and looked expectantly from one to the other of them.

"I'm leaving him here tonight," he said in a tone that brooked no argument. "And in fact, I'd sleep easier if you kept him over here every night."

Linn shook her head impatiently. "Trey, don't be ridiculous. I'm perfectly safe over here—my God, Toomey rigged the place up like Fort Knox. I half expected him to dig a moat around the place and stock it with alligators."

Trey gave a snort of laughter. "We thought of that, but good alligators are hard to find these days." Then he let the smile fade. "I'm serious, Linn. Murph's been dying to get back over here to play with Nathan, and I'll lay odds the kid feels the same way. I can bring his food and—"

"No." Linn said it firmly, with enough steel in the one word to tell Trey that she meant it. "You've done enough for me already." Too much, in fact, she advised him silently. It was just too dangerous to let him get any more involved. If Santos's men found out Trey was helping her, they wouldn't think twice about killing him.

"I'll keep Murphy tonight, but I'm sending him home in the morning and I don't want to see him—or you—again." He drew in a deep breath to protest and she held up her hand, stopping him in his tracks. "If I need help, I promise

that you'll be the first person I'll call. If I see anyone suspicious hanging around, or if I wake up in the night and
need—" A slow smile brushed his strong mouth and she felt
herself blush. "If someone tries to break in and wakes me
up," she corrected, "I'll be on that phone so fast the wires
will smoke."

"Promise?"

"Cross my heart and hope to—die." Bad choice of words.
She frowned, swallowing a sigh. "I know you're just trying
to help," she said softly, "but the most help you can be is
none at all."

His eyes held hers intently and for a moment she thought
he was going to argue, then he just nodded. He turned back
toward the window, but something caught his eye and he
paused, then reached out and picked up the book lying on
her night table.

"Slumming?" He glanced around at her with a faint
smile.

"Don't fish for compliments. It's good, and you know
it."

"Good enough. But not what most women look for in a
book. Especially for bedtime reading."

"I'll admit it's a bit gory in places, but no worse than
prime-time television. Why didn't you tell me you were the
world-famous T. C. Hollister, creator of the equally fa-
mous Steele, Man of Action?"

"The topic never came up." He stared at the cover for a
moment or two, then tossed the book down. "I'm glad
you're enjoying it," he told her quietly.

"He's...lonely, isn't he?" Trey glanced around at her,
and Linn nodded toward the book. "Steele. There's always
a lot going on in his life and he doesn't lack for adoring fe-
males, but underneath it all he strikes me as being a very
lonely man."

He shrugged. "Typical loner, I guess. Happier by himself than with people. Finds it hard to open up."

"Like I said," she told him with a faint smile, "lonely."

"Aren't we all, at some time or another?" he asked softly.

"Well, yes," she admitted doubtfully, "but—"

But she was talking to herself. Trey had slipped through the open window and vanished, appearing a moment later to look in at her. Murphy had leaped to his feet, but Trey held up a restraining hand. "Murphy, stay. Guard." The big shepherd whimpered once, then sat down again and gazed expectantly at Linn, tongue lolling. "Lock this window after I've closed it."

"I'd rather leave it open a bit. I hate sleeping with the—"

"Lock it." He bit each word out, and Linn swallowed the rest of her protest and nodded. He pulled the window down with a bang and waited impatiently for her to flip the latch closed and lock it, then he rattled it fiercely. It didn't budge, and he nodded in satisfaction. Then in the next instant he was gone.

Linn stared out the window for a long while after he'd left, trying to convince herself that the hollow little emptiness she felt was just the residue of fear. And embarrassment. My God, she'd come apart in his hands tonight like a poorly knitted sock. She'd been her usual collected, well-controlled self one minute and a sex-starved nymphet the next, ready to toss upbringing and personal standards right out the window for one explosive night of sheer, uninhibited lust.

And he'd been right—it would have been good. Better than good. There was something about Trey Hollister that made her think he would be the perfect lover, as strong and fierce and uninhibited as she needed, yet gentle too, caring, even tender. He was the kind of man who would make damned sure his women left their bed satisfied, skilled and knowledgeable and self-confident enough to spare no effort to make their time together mutually enjoyable.

It was tempting, no doubt about it.

Yet there was no way she could fulfill even one of those fantasies. She couldn't afford the distraction, for one thing. How could she ever face Kathy and Rod or even herself if something happened to Nathan while she was indulging herself with her next-door neighbor? And there was Trey to think about, too. God help him if Santos found out he was helping her. Being on the run was bad enough; endangering innocent bystanders was unthinkable.

Just stay away from me, Trey Hollister, she whispered, resting her forehead against the cool glass. I'm more trouble than you need, believe me. More trouble than any man needs....

Somebody was watching the house.

Linn turned away from the window, rubbing her bare arms. She was sure of it now. That dark brown Chevy had driven by three or four times, cruising slowly along the gravel road that was the only access to this part of the beach.

It could have been tourists, of course. There was a path leading down to the beach just beyond her house that attracted the occasional carload of picnickers. Except that the weather today was anything but conducive to beach walks. One of the classic West Coast fog banks had crept in during the night, and the entire coast was cloaked in a pale batting as thick as flannel.

For that matter, it could have been sightseers. The expensive beach houses along this road drew realtors and would-be buyers and the simply curious like flies. But there was something about that car that set her teeth on edge. And then there had been that man yesterday. Just standing on the beach, staring up at her. He'd started toward the steps leading up to the house, but at the last moment had changed his mind and had wandered away. But she'd seen him much later, sitting on a gray, weathered log sticking out of a pile of driftwood, apparently enjoying the view but glancing at the house now and again.

She'd seen him again a few times over the past couple of days, never coming close or attempting to speak with her, but watching. Just watching.

Either she was under surveillance, or she was imagining things again. It wouldn't be the first time she'd panicked over nothing. But then again, she'd rather panic when she didn't need to than become complacent at just the wrong time. In fact, yesterday she'd been contemplating packing up and leaving. She'd even gone so far as to haul their suitcases out of the closet, but in the end she'd changed her mind.

Nathan loved it here, for one thing. Of all the places they'd been in the past month, B.C.'s Long Beach area was the nearest thing to home, with its wide expanses of sand and sea. The town itself was a plus, too, small enough for suspicious strangers to stand out like the proverbial sore thumbs, yet busy enough in tourist season for Nathan and herself to blend right in.

She glanced at Nathan. He was playing beside her on the deck, but not very happily. They'd had an argument not long ago over his going over to Hollister's to play with Murphy, and he still hadn't entirely forgiven her for saying no.

She should have let him, she supposed. It couldn't do much harm. She was certain by now that she could trust Trey, and it seemed cruel to keep Nathan cooped up here with her when there was a large, energetic dog right next door and a beach full of tidal pools and piles of driftwood to be explored. But again, there was that danger of becoming complacent and careless. And besides, if she let Nathan play with Murphy, she was going to wind up seeing a good deal of Trey. And there was a whole lot of reasons that wasn't a good idea.

Not that she didn't see him now. In fact, she saw so much of him that she was beginning to wonder how he ever got any writing done. There were the long romps on the beach with Murphy, the two of them tearing around on the beach right in front of her house. He'd glance up at the house now and again, and sometimes if she was on the deck he'd even lift his arm in silent greeting, but to her relief he never showed the slightest interest in joining her.

At other times she'd see him on his own sun deck, sometimes just sitting reading, chair tipped back, long legs braced on the railing. In the early morning he'd be out there doing some complicated exercise routine, a slow, graceful series of moves that was half ballet, half martial arts. T'ai chi, perhaps, or something similar that he'd brought back from his tour in the Far East. It looked both beautiful and deadly, his lean body wheeling and turning, long muscular legs arcing up and around in acrobatic kicks that always reminded her of that night on the beach when he'd brought Rolfson down with one.

There were times when she could have sworn he was actually watching over her. It had annoyed her at first. Kathy had always been the one who turned to the first man she could find when things went wrong, not her. And there was something irritatingly patronizing about a man who automatically figured no woman could handle trouble on her own. But after a few days she started to find it almost comforting.

"Aunt Linn?"

Linn looked around to find Nathan standing beside her, arms crossed on the deck railing, chin planted on the back of his hand. He was staring longingly at the beach, his face wistful and sad.

"Can't we go for a walk, Aunt Linn?" he wheedled gently. "There's nobody down there. And it's been *forever.*"

Linn had to smile. "Nathan, the reason no one is on the beach is because the fog's so thick you can taste it."

"I think it's neat. Kinda spooky and stuff. Like the Everglades, almost."

She smiled again and smoothed his hair with her hand, knowing exactly how he felt. They hadn't left the house since the afternoon Toomey had been over to fix the windows, nearly a week ago.

It was utterly still. The only sound was the constant patter of water dripping from the big fog-wreathed cedars, their lacy boughs heavy with the drizzle that had been coming down on and off all morning. Now and again she could hear the high, thin cry of a gull and, muffled by the mist, the far-off boom of breakers.

"Oh, hell, why not?" she suddenly asked aloud. Much more of this exile and both she and Nathan would need straitjackets.

That brown Chevy had undoubtedly just been sizing up property values, and Nathan was right, there wouldn't be a soul on the beach on a day like this. They didn't have to go far—just down to the water, where Nathan could putter around collecting tidal debris and she could stretch her legs and shake loose some of this nervous tension.

"You mean it, Aunt Linn?" Nathan's face lit up.

"Yeah, why not? Let's get into warmer clothes and grab some plastic bags for shells and stuff." Nathan's enthusiasm was infectious, and Linn felt her spirits lift for the first time in days. She walked across and pulled open the sliding door into the living room, Nathan bouncing along beside her.

"Hey, Aunt Linn, I got a *great* idea!" He looked up at her, eyes bright with excitement. "Let's go 'n' ask Mr. Hollister if Murphy can come with us!"

"Oh, Nathan, I don't think that's a good idea," Linn replied automatically. But as she slid the door closed behind them, she suddenly wondered if Nathan wasn't on to something. Murphy would probably love going with them, Nathan would be in heaven itself, and there was no doubt that *she* would feel a lot safer with the big shepherd playing escort. She hadn't seen Hollister around for a couple of days, but he was probably just busy with the book.

"On second thought, maybe it's not such a bad idea." She dropped an arm around Nathan's shoulders and gave him a quick hug. "It can't hurt to ask, can it?"

"Great!" Nearly vibrating with sudden energy, he shot down the hallway to his room.

Linn followed at a slower pace, changing into jeans and sneakers and a fleece-lined sweatshirt, then pulling on a heavy wool sweater-jacket. She tied her hair back into a loose ponytail, then grabbed up the paperback novel lying on her bedside table and shoved it into her pocket and went back outside, where Nathan was already waiting for her impatiently.

There was a path that led through the pines to Trey's place, but Linn took one look at the heavy, wet grass lining the trail and the puddles of rainwater lying on the mossy ground, and took Nathan along the beach instead.

Like her place, Trey's beach house had a long flight of steps leading up from the beach. As they trudged up, trailing sand, Murphy suddenly appeared at the top. He uttered a bay of alarm that rose to a series of formidable barks and then, suddenly realizing who it was, he bounded down toward them, wriggling with embarrassed pleasure.

He shoved his broad head under Linn's hand for a pat, then swarmed over Nathan with a yelp of delight. Laughing, Linn squeezed by them and climbed the last three steps to the deck.

Trey was standing in the sliding door leading into the house, almost as though he'd been expecting her. He was leaning comfortably against the frame, one arm braced against the open door, the other holding a coffee mug. Barefoot, his hair gently tousled as though he'd just run his hand through it—or had just gotten out of bed—he was dressed in old jeans and a sloppy grape-colored sweatshirt with University of Texas written across it. And he looked, she thought idly, like every woman's fantasy come true.

"So. It *is* really you." He gave her a half smile. "When I looked out and saw you at the bottom of my deck, I thought I must be dreaming."

"Yes, it's really me." She smiled and tucked her hands into the pockets of her jeans, suddenly self-conscious. "I . . . uh, hope I didn't interrupt your writing or anything. I guess I should have called first . . . ."

"I wish all my interruptions were half as attractive," he told her with that same lazy half smile, "and half as welcome."

It was ridiculous, but Linn swore she could feel herself blushing. Trey eased himself away from the door frame and motioned her inside. "How about a cup of coffee?"

Linn shook her head, recalling what old Toomey had said about Trey never inviting people into his home. "No, really, I can't stay." She gestured a bit awkwardly. "Actually, I just dropped over to ask you a favor."

"Ask away."

"Nathan and I are going for a walk and . . . well, it was Nathan's idea, really, but we wondered if Murphy might enjoy a romp."

Trey nodded slowly, eyes thoughtful as they held hers. "A little wet for a walk, isn't it?"

"A little. But Nathan's got cabin fever, and I thought a walk would do us both good. Besides," she added, looking out over the fog-shrouded beach. "I love a day like this. It's so peaceful and still."

And deserted. It was as though he'd said it aloud, and in the moment his eyes caught hers, Linn knew they were both thinking the same thing. *Rolfson.*

"Taking Murphy is a good idea," he said quietly, his eyes holding hers. Then suddenly he smiled. "But how about a two-for-one deal? Could I talk you into taking me for a walk, too?"

"You?" Linn blinked in surprise.

"Nathan's not the only one with cabin fever. I just got back from two days in New York and could do with a romp on the beach myself."

Linn looked at him suspiciously. "You're not suggesting this just because you think I need protecting or something, are you? Because if you are, you—"

"Hey." Trey held up his hand, gray eyes serious. "There are no ulterior motives at work here, trust me. I've just spent two days with a literary agent and my publisher, hammering out a new contract. And I've spent the entire morning sorting through sixty pages of fine print and legalese, trying to figure out who's got who by the throat. Believe me, I need a break. If you don't want me to come with you, just say so."

Linn actually had her mouth half-open to tell him just that when she suddenly realized she'd be lying. "No," she said quietly. "It's all right. I just didn't want you wasting time keeping an eye on me when you should be working, that's all."

"Keeping an eye on you is *anything* but a waste of time," he said very quietly.

Linn's heart gave a peculiar little leap. "Are you flirting with me, Mr. Hollister?" she asked lightly.

"Absolutely," he said with a raking grin. "Though I don't know why I bother—it doesn't get me anywhere but in trouble."

"Which is exactly where it's going to get you this time if you're not careful," she advised him with a careless laugh. "And if you're serious about coming with us, you'd better hurry up. The natives are getting restless." She nodded toward the bottom of the steps where Nathan and Murphy were playing, obviously impatient to be underway.

"Five minutes. Come in and wait."

She wrinkled her nose, pointing to her wet, sandy feet. "I'd better not."

Trey laughed. "The reason they call this a beach house is because it's built on a beach. And a sandy floor is the small price I pay for the view. There's fresh coffee in the kitchen if you'd like a cup."

He disappeared into the house, leaving the door open, and after a moment of indecision, Linn kicked off her wet shoes. She slapped as much sand from her cuffs as she could, then stepped through the door and pulled it closed behind her.

Chapter 6

The first thing she saw was the raven.

Perched on the back of a wooden chair on the far side of the room, it was huge and glossy black. It glared at her malevolently and stomped back and forth, then opened its huge beak and gave a raucous shriek.

A combination of living and dining room, the space was huge, a full two stories high at the front, with open beams and a loft across the back. The entire front of the house was glass, and opposite the windows was a massive, free-standing fieldstone fireplace that separated the living area from the large kitchen that Linn could see beyond. It was rustic and comfortable and overwhelmingly masculine, upholstered in leather and tweed, with lots of tables and lamps and bright Navaho rugs.

The walls were covered with oil paintings and watercolors, many of which were the work of local artists, by the look of them. There were other pieces of artwork as well: stone carvings, a big wall hanging of woven leather strips decorated with fur and feathers and a collection of native wood carvings that would have fitted comfortably in any museum in the world.

There was a sudden whisper of wind right above her head and she recoiled as the raven glided past on huge, silent wings. It banked sharply and landed lightly on the mantel above the fireplace, fixing her with a beady stare. She eyed the creature mistrustfully as it clacked its huge, razor-edged beak, then it stretched its neck and gave a couple of loud, shrill caws.

"I see you've met Poe," came an amused voice from behind Linn. "I should have warned you about him. He can be a little unnerving at first."

Linn uttered a peal of delighted laughter and turned to look at Trey. "My mother used to keep budgies, and I had a friend years ago who had parrots, but you are the only person I've ever met with a pet raven!"

"Poe's not a pet," he said with a smile. "He's a watch bird. If I'd thought you could handle the racket, I would have sent *him* over to stay with you the other night instead of Murphy." He reached out and stroked the big bird's glossy head. Poe preened himself like a cat, clacking his beak softly. "Actually, he's a damned fraud. Bribe him with an oatmeal cookie and he'll let you strip the house bare."

As though to prove Trey's point, Poe hopped over to sit on his shoulder, trilling like a pigeon. Linn very tentatively reached up and he ducked his head toward her outstretched fingers, then clacked in pleasure as she stroked the smooth, glossy feathers.

"I found him in a pile of driftwood last spring with a broken wing and a half dozen BB pellets in him—some damned idiot had been taking potshots at him just for target practice, I guess. He surprised both of us by surviving, and he's been hanging around making a nuisance of himself ever since."

"I hate to sound unadventurous," Linn said with a laugh, "but is he housebroken?"

"Absolutely. I leave a kitchen window open and he comes and goes—usually to eat Murphy's food, but I think he enjoys dropping in now and again just to see what he can steal." He glanced at her small gold stud earrings. "Watch those earrings, by the way. He loves anything shiny. He'll rob you blind and leave a pinecone or a dead beetle in return."

"Oh, terrific," Linn said with another peal of laughter. She was stroking the downy feathers on the underside of Poe's throat and beak and the big bird was crooning like a baby, eyes closed.

"That's nice," Trey said softly. When Linn looked at him questioningly, he smiled. "Hearing you laugh. It's the first real laugh I've heard since we met."

That flustered her, for no particular reason. She avoided Trey's eyes and concentrated on petting Poe. "I guess I've had a lot on my mind," she said carelessly. No need to tell him the rest, she decided: that there was something about Trey Hollister that made her feel safe and out of danger. That when she was with him, she could feel the leaden cloud of constant worry lift, feel *able* to laugh.

She gave Poe one last pat on his broad head, then looked at Trey. "Ready?"

Murphy and the boy were waiting for them at the bottom of the steps. As Trey and Linn started down, Poe spread his shimmering black wings and sailed off Trey's shoulder to dive-bomb Murphy. The shepherd made a futile leap, jaws snapping on empty air, then yipping in frustration, stood watching the raven sweep through the trees.

"What a great crow!" Nathan exclaimed in astonishment.

"Almost," Trey said with a smile. "Poe's a raven. Do you know anything about Indian legends, Nat?"

"I know some stuff," Nathan replied happily, hopping a little to keep up with Trey's long strides. "But not about ravens."

As they started across the sand, the fog curling around them like dragon's breath, Linn smiled. She wasn't the only one who found Trey Hollister easy company. Nathan missed his father terribly, and although Trey certainly wasn't any Rodrigo Valencia—at least in Nathan's eyes—he was adult and male and plenty of fun. And he had a dog, which in itself is pretty wonderful when you're five years old and your world has been turned upside down.

"The local Indians call the raven the Jokester," Trey was saying. "And that describes Poe down to the last pin-feather. He spends his days thinking up new ways to torment Murphy, stealing his food, sneaking up when Murph's asleep and nipping his tail or ear. And that dive-bombing routine is a favorite, although he usually glides in from behind and startles the daylights out of poor Murph. I swear you can hear Poe laughing as he flies away."

"I think he's neat!" Nathan gazed up at Trey worshipfully.

"So do I," Trey told him confidentially. "The raven's an important figure in West Coast Indian myth. He's sly and crafty and he loves nothing better than to cheat and steal and play tricks—that's why they call him the Jokester. Or the Trickster. And he's supposed to have supernatural powers. Another name for him is the Transformer, because he can transform or change himself into other shapes, pretending to be something he isn't. According to the legends, the Raven created the world, then he put the sun and moon in the sky, filled the rivers and sea with fish, then changed the people into various animals."

Nathan grinned with delight, and galloped off ahead. "Hey, Murphy! Let's go see where he went!"

"Nathan, don't you go too far," Linn called after him. "I don't want you to get lost in this fog!"

"Murphy'll look after him," Trey said quietly. "This is supposed to be a relaxing walk, remember?"

She laughed quietly and shoved her hands into her pockets, taking a deep breath of foggy air. "You're right," she said with a grin. "Time off. It seems like forever since I've wandered down to this end of the beach."

You've been afraid of getting too far from home, he told her silently. *Afraid of turning around on a lonely stretch of beach and seeing whoever you're running from standing behind you. Afraid of getting trapped out here.*

She looked so relaxed and happy that Trey found himself smiling for no particular reason, glad that he'd decided on the spur of the minute to come with her.

He hadn't been entirely lying when he'd told her he needed a few hours off. He, his agent and his publisher had spent two days slogging through the intricacies of his new contract. There had been dozens of trick clauses to be ironed out, compromises to be made, a little bit of old-fashioned horse trading to be done. In the end it had probably been worth it. But at the moment he was wrung out.

He flexed his shoulders to loosen the muscles across them and took a deep breath of fog-damp air, feeling it curl down his throat, as thick as candy floss. The tide was full and there was a strong surf running, the water surging in, then back out again like the inhalations of some giant beast. Massive gray breakers roared toward them out of the fog to pile up on the lower beach and send cascades of foaming water hissing within inches of their feet.

They walked in companionable silence. Nathan and Murphy hurtled back and forth like two juggernauts, half-wild with the excitement of sudden freedom.

"It's hard to tell which of those two gets more enjoyment out of the other," Trey said with a lazy smile.

"Poor Nathan's got a lot of energy to run off. He's been bottled up all week."

He avoided asking the obvious question, knowing damned well she'd clam up tight if she thought he was probing. He gave her a teasing sidelong glance instead, then bent and scooped up a handful of water as another wave broke beside them. "And what about his mother?" he asked, grin widening. "Does she have some energy to run off?"

"What are you—? Don't you *dare* throw that on me!" But she was laughing as she said it, already backing away, her eyes sparkling. And in the next instant she'd wheeled with a fresh peal of laughter and was pelting down the beach.

Trey took out after her with a whoop, sore leg and weariness forgotten, not surprised to discover she could run like a deer. Startled, Nathan and Murphy both stopped dead to stare after her as she tore by them. Then Nathan uttered a yell and started after her, Murphy leaping and barking and practically turning himself inside out with excitement at the lunatic behavior going on around him.

She'd have gotten away if he hadn't resorted to trickery.
He moved between her and the water, and when she dodged
behind him and into the deep, soft sand, he had her. He
caught her easily around the waist and swung her to a stop,
both of them nearly falling as they staggered through the
loose sand. She was laughing and out of breath, cheeks
glowing with the cold and damp. The clip holding her hair
back had come loose and without even thinking about what
he was doing, he reached up and pulled it free.

The rest of her hair spilled into his hands, as glossy as a
raven's wing, and he ran his fingers into the thick tangles.
They'd come to a panting stop, still clutching each other,
and Trey looked down to find her face only inches from his,
her eyes laughing up at him. Her mouth was red and lush,
lips parted slightly, and he felt something pull wire-tight
within him.

There was that momentary tension that always precedes
a kiss, the awareness of each other that was half awkwardness, half anticipation. He could feel her breath against his
mouth, the flex of muscle in the slim thigh pressed against
his as she steadied herself in the loose sand. He tipped up her
face and lowered his mouth.

He kissed her lower lip, the corner of her mouth, small,
lingering kisses that were undemanding but incredibly sensuous. He moved his cheek against hers, his skin smooth yet
undeniably male, then kissed her again, still gently, lightly.
A slow, syrupy heat went spilling through Linn, so achingly familiar yet half-forgotten, the first hot tendrils of
desire.

How long, she wondered dizzily? How long had it been
since she'd been kissed—properly and thoroughly kissed by
a man whose very touch made her blood take fire? How
long since she'd felt a man's arms around her, had been
drawn between silken sheets and into a demanding yet gentle
embrace, had felt strong, male flesh cleave and...?

"Please...." She felt breathless and dizzy and turned her
face away, too confused to even think straight. "I—I'm not
sure I'm ready for this...."

She could feel the tension in Trey's arms, the fight he was
having to hold himself back. Her heart was pounding errat-

ically and she felt weak and drugged, knew that if he made even the slightest effort to persist that she'd be helpless to stop him. Wished, down deep, that he would...that he'd just take decision and choice away from her completely. It would be so easy to just let go, to let this strange, erotic magic run its course and to hell with the consequences.

"Damn," he breathed against her ear, his own heart rate more rapid than normal. "Something's happening here. Something neither of us counted on."

"I...know," she managed to whisper, praying he wouldn't step back and let her go without warning or she'd fall flat on her face. "I'm...oh, brother!" She drew in a deep breath, wishing her heart would stop that insane pounding. "I'm not sure this is a good idea."

He gave a throaty chuckle, his arms tightening around her. "Actually, it's a hell of a good idea." He nuzzled the side of her throat. "I could make it good for you, Linn. However you want it, sweetheart. I can give you whatever you need...."

"Trey, it's not that simple." She turned her face toward his, let her lips touch his lingeringly, aching for the taste of him. "It...just isn't a good idea at all."

"Not here, and not now," he murmured huskily. "But sometime soon, Linn. Sometime soon."

"No," she whispered doubtfully.

He heard the lack of conviction in her voice and laughed very softly, his eyes locking with hers, filled with erotic promise. "Yes," he told her quietly. "Oh, yes, Linn. This is definitely something you can count on...." Then, eyes still gently teasing, he let his arms fall away and stepped back. Smiling, not saying anything, he held out the clip he'd taken from her hair.

Just as silently, not even daring to meet his eyes, Linn took it and pulled her hair back again, her hands shaking so badly that she had trouble securing the clip.

This was crazy! She'd never fallen apart at the mere touch of a man's hands before...not since Jack, anyway. In fact, during the past four years, she'd found even the thought of being kissed repugnant. She'd forced herself to date a few times, more to keep her mother and Kathy off her case than anything, but they'd nearly all been disasters. Yet she seemed to turn into a puddle of overheated hormones every time Trey Hollister even looked at her the right way.

Or the wrong way, she thought with a sudden giddy urge to laugh. Whichever way he was looking at her, Trey was doing things to her that no man had ever done but Jack. And to think she'd almost convinced herself that all those old, magical feelings had gone for good....

She drew in a deep breath and finally managed to fasten the clip, then bent to brush sand from her legs just to have something to do. What she was feeling wasn't real. She was just vulnerable, that was all. Alone and lonely and frightened half to death most of the time. And Trey was...very special. You didn't have to know him any better than she did to realize that. And to know he could handle just about anything that came his way, which added to her feeling of security when she was with him.

Jack had been like that, the type of man who always knew what was wrong with the car when it wouldn't start, who knew exactly the right thing to say and when to say it, who could walk away from a fight and never leave a doubt in anyone's mind that he could have won. And, just like Jack, Trey radiated that kind of rugged masculinity that made a woman *feel* like a woman.

And it had been a long, long time since that had happened.

Small wonder she was having trouble keeping things in perspective.

Sometime during the last few minutes Trey had braided his fingers with hers, and Linn marveled at how natural and comfortable it felt to walk hand in hand with him. She glanced at him just as he looked at her, and they traded a wordless, sharing smile.

There were two huge pieces of driftwood wedged in the sand well above the high-tide line, and they strolled over and found a sheltered spot between them, where the sand was soft and dry.

Linn glanced around to check on Nathan. He and the dog were digging industriously in the sand only a few yards away; she sat down and leaned against one of the massive logs with a sigh. Trey dropped beside her, wincing slightly as he straightened his left leg.

"It's bothering you, isn't it?" Linn asked quietly.

Trey smiled grimly, kneading his thigh with his fingers. "No more than usual. The walking's good for it, but this fog and rain don't help much."

"An old war wound?" she teased gently.

"Something like that." He smiled again, dryly this time. "Let's just say I zigged left when I should have zagged right. Story of my life, in a way—always in the right place at the wrong time."

Like being here with me now, she almost said. *In another place, Trey Hollister, and at another time, I could fall for you in a very serious way.*

She shook off the thought, smoothing tendrils of damp, wind-tangled hair from her face as she stared at the water. She felt exhilarated and at ease for the first time in weeks, and as she watched Nathan rummaging through a pile of pebbles and shells, she smiled. "It's beautiful out here. Thank you."

"For?"

"For coming with me today. For showing me this." *For making me feel normal and happy and alive again, even for a little while.*

"Even if I did it for purely selfish reasons?"

"Well, you deserve it, too, after two days in New York."

"That's not what I mean." He reached out and brushed a wisp of flyaway hair from her cheek. "I did it because I like to see you laugh. And," he added more seriously, still massaging his thigh, "because when I'm with you I forget the ache in this damned leg, and forget I have a deadline coming up, and forget... well, just a lot of things."

Linn's heart did another one of those peculiar little cartwheels as his fingers touched her cheek and she forced herself to smile carelessly. "Speaking of deadlines, tell me about your new contract."

Trey had to laugh. "Basically it just says that my publisher is going to pay me an improbable sum of money to sit in my loft and tell a bunch of even more improbable lies about a guy who doesn't even exist."

"I hope that means I'll have lots and lots of new Steele novels to look forward to."

"Five, anyway. Don't tell me you're getting hooked."

"You'd better believe it!" Linn smiled at him, her eyes sparkling and warm. "As a matter of fact," she added, pulling a paperback copy of *Steele Horse* out of her jacket pocket and holding it up with a flourish, "I picked this one up in town last week. The woman in the bookstore assured me it's your best yet."

Trey smiled, shaking his head. "You're knocking my publisher's demographics all to hell and gone, lady. I spent three hours listening to his marketing wizards explain that my average reader is male, college educated, between the ages of twenty-six and forty-seven and probably, but not necessarily, with military service. They *don't* do well with women of any age."

"So sue me," Linn told him with a laugh. "Maybe knowing his creator makes it easier to be sympathetic, but I like Steele. I think he's lonely, and I think he deliberately keeps people at a distance because he's afraid of being hurt, but I still like him. The man has possibilities."

"Possibilities?" Trey arched a doubtful eyebrow.

"Steele's big problem," Linn said matter-of-factly, "is that he needs a good woman."

Trey gave a snort of laughter. "Sweetheart, Steele has nothing *but* good women."

She didn't let his words faze her. "*One* good woman, Hollister. Not a baker's dozen of gorgeous but deadly blondes...he does have a problem with blondes, doesn't he? They're either spies or double agents or in cahoots with the bad guys, and they spend the first half of the book trying to get him into bed and the second half trying to shoot him or stab him or blow him to bits."

Again Trey had to laugh. "I didn't realize I'd gotten so predictable."

"Trust me. He needs a woman."

"There was Sabrina in *Steele Connection*."

"Who got shot in Chapter Nine. That's the other problem with Steele's women—they never last long. I mean, this guy is the kiss of death! The bad guys kidnap them for bait to get Steele, or they step in front of a bullet meant for him, or—like poor Ashley in *Steele Maneuvers*—they just conveniently die of unrelated causes.''

''I had to get rid of her before the next book.''

''Like Dresden in *Steele Gambit*? She loved him, Trey! And Steele just walked out.''

''She walked out on him,'' he reminded her gently.

''Because he'd made it obvious they had no future. He loved her—it was as plain as day. But at the end, faced with admitting it, he took the easy way out and cut and ran. Dresden may have left *physically*, but Steele had already left emotionally.''

Trey looked at her for a moment. Then he smiled again, faintly, and looked out across the fogbound bay. ''Maybe you have to believe in fairy-tale endings to be able to write them.''

''Love isn't a fairy tale,'' Linn said quietly. ''Love is the strongest, most real thing there is. Sometimes it's the *only* thing there is. It can get you through just about anything.''

She frowned slightly as she said it, her eyes focused on something far away, and Trey found himself suddenly thinking of the expression on her face that first night, when she'd come into the room and had seen him in that old plaid shirt.

''He must be pretty special,'' he said quietly.

''He?'' She looked at him, puzzled. ''Who?''

''Whoever owns that shirt I was wearing the other evening.''

A hundred emotions crossed her face in that split second: surprise, pain, love, hurt. Then finally, just an aching sadness so deep that it made something within him twist. ''He was,'' she whispered, looking down at her hands. ''Very...special.''

''Was?'' He said it very casually, hating himself for needing to know.

She nodded, still not meeting his eyes. He didn't think she was going to say anything, and then she took a deep breath and looked up. ''His name was Jack, and I loved him so much I was dizzy with it. But he died. Four years ago.''

Trey winced. He had a few memories of his own he pre-
ferred to have left undisturbed. "I'm sorry."

"So am I," she said softly. She was staring at the water,
seeing something in another place, another time. "We'd
been married for only six months when he got sick. We
thought he'd get better, at first—I guess you always do." She
smiled faintly, looking at him now. "It was harder on Jack
than on me, really. It took him two and a half years to die.
It's not...pleasant, watching someone you love waste away
in front of your eyes, knowing there's not a damned thing
you can do. But it's worse on the other end of it, slipping
away a little more every day from everyone you love,
knowing what kind of hell you're putting them through."

She smiled again faintly, her dark eyes shadowed with old
pain. "I learned one thing, though: there are no atheists in
the chronic care ward of a hospital. Everyone there is too
busy making deals with God. You promise everything you
can think of. Offer to trade places if He'll just make some
of the pain go away. But . . ." She shrugged, letting her gaze
fall again. "In the end you just live through it. One day at
a time."

"Two and a half years," Trey murmured. "My God, how
did you do it?"

Linn looked up at him as though the question surprised
her. "I loved him," she said simply. "I'd married him for
better or worse, had promised to love and honor in sickness
and in health." She managed a wry smile. "Mind you, no
one ever counts on having to make good on promises like
that. But I loved Jack too much to turn my back on him
when he needed me the most." She frowned slightly then
and looked down at her hands. "But I'll admit there were
times I wondered how I'd ever get through another minute
of it. Especially near the end when he was in such terrible
pain and the doctors couldn't do anything. I'd listen to him
screaming for something to stop the hurting, and wonder
how I'd ever get through it sane."

Trey whispered an oath, fighting a shudder of horror. "I
don't know how you managed it, either," he told her quietly.

"I probably wouldn't have if it hadn't been for my family. My parents and younger sister were there for me every minute of those two and a half years."

She was, he found himself thinking, an extraordinary woman. How many young wives, six months married, would have found that kind of inner steel? And still be able to speak of the man four years later with such love in her voice?

A man would be damned lucky to find himself on the receiving end of love like that. It was the kind of love he'd only read about, had thought never existed anywhere but between the pages of a novel. Yet here it was, sitting beside him.

"I shouldn't have brought it up," he said quietly. "It can't be easy to talk about."

Linn smiled. "You didn't bring it up, I did. And I don't mind talking about him. Not now." Her smile widened, sweet with love. "It took me a long while, though."

Trey nodded, rubbing his thigh absently as he watched Nathan and Murphy playing nearby. "So Nathan's never known his father," he said thoughtfully. He found himself thinking of his own son. He, too, had never known his father, had never...

He shook it off and looked at Linn again. "Although it had to help you through some bad times, too. Having Nathan, I mean. At least you still had him."

Linn looked at him blankly for a moment, as though not understanding what he was talking about, then she flushed slightly and looked away. A frown pulled her brows together and she drew in a breath as though to say something, paused, then eased it out again with a little shake of her head, still not looking at him, the frown deeper.

And, suddenly, Trey understood. He cursed his own clumsiness, wondering how he'd possibly missed seeing it: Linn's dying husband hadn't been Nathan's father! By that time he'd probably been too ill to father a child, based on the few details she'd told him. So there had been someone else. Someone who had perhaps offered some sympathy and kindness when she needed it the most.

Trey glanced at Linn thoughtfully. She wasn't the type of woman who would turn willingly to another man to help ease the pain of watching her husband die. So whatever had happened, he'd be willing to lay odds it had happened only the once. And she'd have felt both betrayed and betrayer afterward, would have spent every day from that moment on filled with guilt.

But one thing was certain. Whoever that man had been, he had something to do with why she was here now, running scared and jumping at shadows. Why she never let Nathan out of her sight. Why he was going to wake up one day and discover that she had vanished into the night without a word, without a trace, gone from his life as mysteriously and silently as she'd appeared.

Trey found himself gazing at her, letting his eyes follow the curve of her cheek. What the hell was he going to do with her? She was going to vanish out of his life in a few days or weeks, so it was pointless starting something that could only end in disappointment. And yet there was something within him that didn't want to lose her. Something within him that cried out in the silences of his nights for her touch. For the kind of love that could go through two and a half years of nightmare and come through unscathed.

"Uh-oh."

Trey shook himself free of his meandering thoughts to find Linn looking doubtfully at the sky. Then he felt it too, the first cold drop of rain on his cheek, and he swore under his breath. He eased himself stiffly to his feet, holding out his hand to help Linn up.

"We'd better head back," he said with real regret.

She slipped her hand into his and he lifted her to her feet, found himself tugging her that one step farther into the circle of his arms. She stood there very quietly, gazing at him with those calm, sapphire eyes that seemed to draw him, tumbling, into their depths, and the next thing he knew he was kissing her.

Chapter 7

Her lips were wind-cooled and tasted faintly of salt, but her mouth was warm and moist and deliciously sweet. She opened herself to the first probing touch of his tongue as though, like him, she'd been anticipating this kiss all day. There was none of the awkwardness that sometimes happens, no holding back, just a slow, drugging kind of kiss that is usually the kiss of lovers or soon-to-be lovers, an erotic entanglement of tongue and breath and want.

He reached up and this time deliberately unfastened the clip holding her hair back, dropping it as her hair spilled around his hands, and once again he ran his fingers into the satiny mass. Her arms were around his neck now and her tongue moved in sinuous, silken swirls against his, drawing him deeper, promising more. Wanting more. Her fingers were in his hair, holding him fiercely, and he could feel the pounding of her heart, could hear the tiny whimper she made low in her throat as he thrust his tongue against hers and his kiss grew more demanding, more urgent.

He drew his mouth from hers and ran his lips down her throat and she arched her body against his, letting her head fall back, and Trey could feel the already thin threads of his control near the snapping point.

"I want you," he growled roughly. "I want inside you, lady, so deep I'm part of you. I want to lose myself in you!"

"Trey!" Her voice was a soft, breath-caught plea, more assent than denial; she brought her head up and started kissing his neck and throat, her mouth like flame against his skin.

He pulled her knit jacket open and slipped his arms around her, pulling up her sweater impatiently, wrenching her blouse out of her jeans. Her skin was velvet against his roughened palms and she gave a soft gasp as he cupped her breast, let her head fall back again as she pressed herself into his hand, the nipple sensitive and hard. He rubbed his palm against her, feeling the friction of the lace of her bra arouse her even more.

"I want to make love to you," he groaned against her mouth. "I want to fill you up with it, Linn. I want to feel you moving against me, taking what you want, touching me.... Touch me, Linn." He caught one of her hands and drew it down, cupping her palm around himself.

She whispered something in that breathy little voice and moved her hand slowly, knowledgeably, and he groaned, responding to her touch. It was driving him wild but he couldn't stop himself, couldn't stop her.

"I want you all wrapped around me, naked and soft and warm. I want you moving on me, melting around me. I want you...." He went on, whispering now, the words erotic and explicit as he told her exactly what he wanted and how he wanted it, made her whisper the same words back to him.

He eased his leg between hers and pressed his upper thigh against the softness between hers, bracing his other leg for balance in the loose sand.

She flinched, breath catching yet again, then caught her lower lip between her teeth and buried her face against his neck.

"It's been a long time, hasn't it," he murmured gently, kissing her throat, her ear.

She nodded, not looking at him, and he heard her swallow. "Four years," she whispered. "Longer even." She managed a tiny sob of laughter. "I feel so clumsy and awkward and out of tune with myself. I've forgotten how to...you know."

"Like riding a bicycle," he whispered. "If you've done it once, you never forget."

She gave another gasp of laughter, daring to glance up at him. "I don't mean...well, *that*! I mean I've forgotten all the social bits—the rituals of dating, all that stuff."

Trey looked down at her, holding her gaze. "This isn't a date, Linn," he told her softly. "We're way beyond that."

Her eyes widened slightly and he smiled, then drew her against him once more and nuzzled her cheek, moved his face into the soft curve of her shoulder. "Don't be shy with me, Linn," he whispered. "I want it to be good for you again. I want to show you what it can be like."

"But it's so fast..." she whispered, breathless.

"Because it's right," he murmured reassuringly. "Just let go, Linn. Let me take you there.... Just let yourself go and feel it all happen. Let me make you happy..."

He felt her fighting it and rubbed his thigh gently, firmly, between hers. "It's all right," he whispered, reaching again for her breast. Hard-tipped and lush, it filled his hand, and he heard her groan softly as he caught the nipple between the V of his spread fingers and gently massaged it. "There's nothing to be shy about. You're an incredibly alive woman, with all the responses and needs and wants of a woman. Just listen to yourself, Linn. Listen to what you need...."

"N-Nathan!" she gasped, putting her hand on his wrist as though to pull his hand free. But she pressed it against herself instead, the muscles in her inner thighs tightening urgently around his. "W-we mustn't. Nathan—"

"Is about fifty feet away," Trey murmured, watching the boy over the top of her head. "He and Murphy are digging clams. Just relax and let it happen, sweetheart. You're so close...."

"N-no! Oh, please...!"

Was she fighting him or herself or the memories of a man called Jack? Trey wondered. And if he took her the full distance, if he made her face those long-denied passions fully and without inhibition or holding back on this wild, windswept beach, would she ever forgive him?

"Help me," she sobbed against his throat. "Oh, Trey, I want you so badly. It's been so long...." She moved helplessly against him, arching, straining as she sought release.

Trey put one hand on the driftwood beside him and braced his leg in the loose sand for balance, moving rhythmically against her. "Just let go, angel," he whispered against her ear. "Just go with it...let me take you there. Just let go...."

"I can't! It's been so long and I...oh!" She clutched his shoulders suddenly, her eyes widening with shock.

Trey rocked his thigh between hers, watching her eyes widen even more, seeing the shock turn to sweet surprise, the surprise to wonder. Then she arched back with a soft, shuddering groan, her fingers clutching his shoulders. He felt it run through her, a deep, cresting tremor that made her throw her head back, eyes closed, as she strained against him. The second tremor was even stronger; it tore another cry from her and she clamped her thighs tightly on his, her pelvis flexing in tiny, convulsive thrusts.

Then she collapsed against him, sobbing for breath, and buried her face in his throat. Trey held her tightly, feeling the last of the little shudders work their way through her, feeling her slowly, slowly relax. She drew back after a few minutes, her cheeks flushed, unable to meet his eyes.

Trey gently lifted her face, lowered his mouth to hers and kissed her, slowly and lazily, reveling in the special intimacy they'd just shared. It had been incredibly erotic, holding her in his hands and watching her respond to his caresses and whispered, coaxing words. His own body was so aroused that it hurt just to breathe and he groaned as Linn's small hand reached down to touch him, half-tempted to let her bring him to the same cataclysmic completion she'd just experienced.

But he found himself wanting to hold back, relishing the near pain of it, the anticipation. He caught her wrist and drew her hand gently from him, eyes locked with hers. "I want to stay like this," he said in a gritty whisper. "So ready for you I'm half out of my mind with it." He pressed her palm against himself again, watched her eyes grow heavy-lidded, felt her breath catch slightly. "We're going to go home and we're going to have supper and put Nathan to bed, and then we're going to go into the bedroom and lock the door. Then I'm going to make love to you."

Linn closed her eyes for an instant, trying to breathe. As impossible as it seemed, she could already feel herself starting to respond to the promise in his eyes, his voice, his body. Passion had only been whetted, not quelled, and she wondered if it was possible to lose one's mind with sheer desire. "Trey..."

"The first time's going to be deep and hard and fast, and I'm going to set you on fire, sweetheart, like you've never burned before." Trey's eyes glittered, his husky voice more erotic than anything she could have imagined. "But the second time, Linn...the second time, I'm settling in for the long, slow haul. The kind that takes hours and only gets better." He lowered his mouth and kissed her lightly, his eyes never leaving hers. "I'm going to take you places you've only dreamed of, lady. And then I'm going to bring you back and we're going to start all over again."

"My God, Trey!" Linn sagged toward him, so weak-kneed she'd have fallen if he hadn't been holding her. She felt dizzy and breathless and shaken right to the core of her being; knew, too, that there was no way she was going to be able to deny him everything he was promising. It was wild and dangerous and completely crazy, but it was what she wanted, what she needed. She would worry about Santos tomorrow. Tonight there was just Trey Hollister....

Somehow they got to her house, although the walk back was just a blur to Linn. A light, steady drizzle started coming down about halfway there, but all she could remember was the pressure of Trey's hand around hers and the way he looked at her now and again, his eyes smoldering with erotic promise.

Nathan wore out about the time it started to rain, and Trey laughed quietly as he lifted him up and carried him. "I think he's out for the count."

"Poor little guy." Linn smoothed Nathan's hair from his face as she followed Trey up the steps from the beach. The boy was sound asleep, arms locked around Trey's neck, his face serene and happy. "I feel guilty for having kept him cooped up in here so long. It's just that every time I thought of going down to the beach with him, I thought of Rolfson, and . . ." She shrugged, unlocking the big sliding door into the house.

That was only partly true. She'd thought of Rolfson now and again over the past week, but mostly it was Santos who filled her days and nights with fear.

"Do you want him in here or in his bedroom?" Trey turned to look at her.

"Bedroom, I guess. I'll just let him sleep for now and make supper when he wakes up. It seems silly to wake him now."

Their eyes held for a fraction of a second, then Trey nodded. Linn followed him silently, wondering what on earth she was doing.

Some tiny part of her mind kept telling her she was asking for serious trouble, getting involved with this man. Now. That until Santos was behind bars and her family was safe, she had no business losing herself in any man's arms.

But the need was too real to be denied. It had been four years since Jack had died. Almost five since they'd made love for the last time. She'd just turned off all the switches, and until now, until Trey, had all but forgotten what it was like to love. To be loved. Physically, at least. The deeper kind she didn't want to even think about right now. Couldn't afford to think about. When the nightmare was over, she'd sit down and sort through her feelings and find out what was going on. If it truly was love, she'd deal with it then. And if it wasn't . . . well, no one was going to get hurt.

She pulled back the covers of Nathan's bed and Trey laid him down gently. He sat on the other side of the bed and tugged the boy's shoes off, setting them aside, while Linn removed Nathan's windbreaker and heavy knit sweater. He snuffled and muttered but didn't wake up, and she smiled as she took off his socks and jeans, spilling sand. "I think he's gone for at least three hours."

"Good." Trey's eyes caught hers in the dim light, and he eased himself to his feet. "Don't take too long. I'll be waiting for you."

Linn swallowed, a little shiver of anticipation tingling through her. She brushed the sand from Nathan's bed and drew up the covers over him, pausing to rub a smudge of dirt from his chin. Murphy had ambled in behind them and was standing beside the bed, looking up at her, his tail wagging slowly.

"Do you want up here?" He barked softly and leaped onto the bed with surprising lightness, then lay down beside Nathan and stretched his head along his paws with a huge sigh, eyes already closing.

Linn pulled Nathan's door almost shut, leaving a wide enough crack so she could hear him if he called out, then walked across to her own bedroom. The drapes had been drawn and the bedside lamp was on, but Trey wasn't there. She slipped her jacket off and hung it over the back of a chair to dry, then took a towel from the linen closet, sat down at the dressing table and started rubbing her hair dry.

It was the click of the door lock that made her look up. Trey stood at the door behind her and their eyes met in the mirror. He smiled. "I told you it was a little wet out there for beach walking."

"It was perfect," she said quietly, trying to ignore the way her heart was racing.

"Almost," he said very softly, his eyes locking with hers. "*This* is going to be perfect." He moved slowly toward her, large and dangerous and male in the lamplight. He reached out and took the towel from her hand, dropping it onto the floor, and drew her gently to her feet.

He was still standing behind her and Linn watched their reflection in the mirror as he slipped his arms around her. He smiled, kissing the side of her throat. "Nervous?"

"Terrified!"

"Four years is a long time."

"Four years is forever," she managed to whisper.

The eyes in the glass held hers, serious now. Searching.

Linn held his gaze steadily. Then slowly, very slowly, she reached down and grasped the lower edge of her sweater,

drawing it up and over her head. She gave her head a shake
and her hair spilled around her shoulders, but Trey nuzzled
it aside and kissed her just under the ear.

He started unbuttoning her blouse, his eyes never leaving
hers, and when he'd slipped the last button free, he pulled
the blouse from her shoulders and started kissing her,
drawing moist little swirls with his tongue that made her
melt inside. He slipped the blouse down her arms and let it
drop, then slowly undid the hook on her bra.

Linn stiffened very slightly and he murmured something
to reassure her, kissing her shoulder as he slowly nudged off
one strap, then the other. Swallowing, she let the bra fall,
baring herself to the waist, and she saw Trey's eyes narrow
slightly as he studied their reflection. His hands were large
and sun-browned against her pale skin; she watched them
move slowly to the waistband of her jeans and part the metal
snap and then, even more slowly, draw the zipper down.

He moved his hands back up, slowly, slowly, and cupped
her breasts, and Linn had to fight to catch her breath. Seeing
his hands touching her was somehow even more erotic than
the sensation of roughened palm on already sensitive flesh.
The chocolate tips of her breasts were full and slightly
swollen and she flinched slightly as Trey brushed his thumbs
back and forth against them. As she watched, the nipples
grew hard, aroused as much by the sight of his caress as by
his touch.

Trey's eyes glittered behind the half-lowered lids, and as
he ran his palms down her belly, Linn swallowed again. He
folded back the flaps of her jeans and started to ease them
over her hips, revealing the narrow, blue bikini briefs she
was wearing under them, and she closed her eyes as he knelt
behind her and drew the jeans down.

He ran his mouth down her bare back, settling a little nest
of warm kisses at the base of her spine, then starting to work
his way up again as he straightened. The touch of his tongue
sent little shivers through Linn and she let her head fall forward to bare the nape of her neck to his mouth.

She sucked in her breath as he cupped one of her breasts
again, teasing the nipple with his thumb, and she arched her
back very slightly, mesmerized by the sight of his hand as he

caressed her. He slid his other palm down her stomach and eased his fingers under the elastic waist of her briefs. Linn stiffened and looked away.

"You don't have to be shy with me," Trey murmured. "My God, you're so beautiful, Linn. Don't be shy...."

She looked once more into the mirror, meeting his eyes. Trey's gaze moved down her body and she arched her back again, smiling, and reached up and behind her to rest her hands on his shoulders. The motion lifted her breasts as she offered herself to his hungry gaze, loving what she saw in those burning, silver eyes.

He inched the briefs over her thighs and Linn leaned back against him with a soft moan, catching her lip between her teeth as he ran his hand across her stomach and then down, fingers slipping into the shadowed place where her thighs met. She moaned again, her voice catching on his name, and arched back against him as that questing, gentle touch moved inward, touching the secret places he sought, leaving silken fire in their wake.

"Trey...!" The sensation was indescribable, so exquisite that she cried out a second time, remembering too late the sleeping boy in the other room. Trey's hand moved with wondrous skill and she relaxed against him, shyness gone, wanting only more of the magic.

She was only half aware of turning in his arms, of lifting her mouth for his hungry, urgent kiss as she unbuttoned his shirt impatiently. He helped her finally, wrenching off the shirt and flinging it aside, then struggling out of his jeans and briefs, all pretense at restraint gone.

"Hurry," Linn whispered, reaching for him, touching him. "Oh, Trey...hurry. Please...don't make me wait any longer." She slipped her arms around his neck and returned his kiss eagerly, cupping him between her thighs and pressing herself along the silken length of him again and again.

Trey's breath left him with an explosive groan and he kissed her hungrily, his mouth hot and urgent on hers; he lifted her against him, rotating his pelvis. He took one stride forward and reached out to sweep everything off the dressing table, then eased her onto the smooth, cool wood.

Panting, Linn tried to pull him down to herself, but he just smiled and ran his hands up her thighs, lifting her knees so that she was gripping him by the hips. Then he grasped her hips and pulled her firmly toward him; at the same instant he thrust himself forward, and Linn gave a moaning cry as he sank fully and deeply into her.

It was, as he'd promised, deep and hard and fast. Standing between her thighs, forearms braced on the dressing table on either side of her head, Trey made love to her with the driving, fierce passion they were both ready for, each strong thrust of his hips bringing them together as deeply as their bodies would allow.

As though a floodgate of desire had suddenly opened, Linn responded with joyful abandon, moving greedily under him, taking with the same enthusiasm as she gave. Her dark hair spilled across the table like water and she moved her head from side to side, lower lip caught between her teeth as she strove to catch the elusive wave he could sense building inside her.

He gritted his teeth, praying he could hold out long enough to carry her all the way. He'd been so ready for her that he'd nearly lost it all at the first silken plunge into her welcoming warmth, and at each long, cleaving thrust he was that much nearer. He concentrated on timing his movements to hers, sensing even before she did when that uprushing wave was ready to break. The rhythmic flex of her hips suddenly became erratic and she uttered a tiny inward moan, drawing up her legs and tightening her thighs on his hips. He moved inward and down, holding himself there, rocking his pelvis against hers, and she sobbed his name as the crest caught her and swept her away.

He straightened and gripped her hips firmly in his hands and moved against her in a series of sharp, deep little thrusts, and a moment later everything around him simply exploded.

"Is Trey Hollister livin' here now?" Nathan peered suspiciously into his glass of orange juice, then extracted a floating seed with his fingers. Lifting the glass to his lips, he looked at Linn over the rim. "He's sure been here a long time."

"No, honey," Linn replied casually, "he's just visiting."

There was a movement at the kitchen door just then and Linn glanced up as Trey strolled in, looking very man-about-the-house in nothing but a pair of jeans, a good tan and a lazy, self-satisfied smile. His hair glittered with water from his shower and he'd obviously managed to shave, probably using one of her disposable razors and a can of foam that the previous tenant had left behind, she thought to herself. He ruffled Nathan's dark hair with his hand as he walked by the table, then slipped one arm around Linn's waist as he looked over her shoulder to see what she was doing.

"Blueberry *waffles*?" He drew her loose hair back with his fingers and kissed the side of her throat lingeringly. "Mmm. Not only is she beautiful and fabulous in bed...but she can cook, too. I think I've just died and gone to heaven."

Trading a private, sharing smile with him, Linn slid two waffles onto a warmed plate and handed it to him. "Eat. Nathan, do you have room for another one?"

"Yep." Licking orange juice off his upper lip, Nathan held his plate out and Linn slid half a waffle onto it. "If you an' Aunt Linn...I mean, if you an' Mommy get married, does that mean I can play with Murphy anytime I want?"

"Nathan, for heaven's sake!" Linn looked down at him in astonishment. "Trey is just a friend." Linn absolutely refused to look in Trey's direction.

"If your mother and I got married," Trey said quietly, "that would make me your father. And yes, you could play with Murphy any time you wanted to."

Nathan looked up, frowning, his fork poised over the waffle. "But I've already got a father," he said, obviously confused. "My real daddy's coming back, isn't he?" he asked Linn, suddenly looking upset and frightened. "Y-you promised he was coming back!"

"Nathan, it's all right." Linn put her plate down quickly and knelt by the boy's chair, giving him a reassuring hug. Brushing a cowlick of tangled hair from his forehead, she gave him a kiss, then looked down at him very seriously. "Honey, your daddy *is* coming back. Everything's just very complicated right now, but it will all work out, I swear it." *And if I'm wrong?* she asked herself brutally. If Santos finds Rod and Kathy and—?

She refused to let the thought even form, closing her eyes as a sudden, sick feeling washed over her. *Oh, God, Kathy, where are you? Be safe! Please, just be safe!*

She was aware of a touch on her shoulder and glanced up to find Trey squatting on his heels beside her. "Is something going on here that I—"

"No." She shook her head vehemently, refusing to meet his eyes. "Please, Trey, don't ask me any questions."

"I think," he said very carefully, "that I have a right to know at least one thing." He reached out and put his hand under her chin, turning her face so she was forced to look at him. "Are you married, Linn?"

She pulled away from his grasp. "Nothing's what it seems to be, Trey. I . . . I can't tell you about it. Not . . . yet."

"Damn it, Linn," he said with quiet intensity, "after last night, if you can't—" He stopped short, glancing at Nathan. He stood up, breathing heavily. "We'll talk about this later," he said shortly. "And Nathan, I didn't mean I was trying to replace your real father. Nobody could do that. But can we at least be friends?"

Nathan looked at him for a thoughtful moment, obviously still not certain he believed what he was being told. "Okay," he finally allowed doubtfully. "But my daddy's goin' to be back soon and then I'm going home."

Linn stared at her plate, knowing Trey was looking at her, his eyes filled with questions she just couldn't answer. She started eating mechanically, not tasting a thing, and the silence around the table grew steadily deeper. Nathan, seemingly oblivious to the sudden tension around him, started humming, eating happily and occasionally slipping a piece of waffle to Murphy, who was sitting beside his chair. There was no sound but the click of cutlery, overly loud in the uncomfortable stillness, and the foreboding heaviness of Trey's impatience.

Justifiable impatience, Linn reminded herself. If anyone in the world deserved to know what was going on, it was Trey.

Last night had been...magical.

There was no other word for it. He had touched something within her that hadn't been touched in years, loosing a passion so earthy and abandoned and reckless it had surprised both of then. Those few tempestuous minutes on the dressing table had just been the start, when she'd wrapped her legs around him and had simply given herself over to the pure physical pleasure of her own body.

They'd fallen into bed not long after that and had made love again, slowly this time, Trey being true to his word that he was going to take her further and higher than she'd ever gone before. They'd made love in the soft glow of the lamp for a long, long time, letting it build sweetly and naturally until at the end, when she'd arched under him with an indrawn moan of sheer ecstasy, she'd felt the chains around her heart break and fall away and had lain in Trey's arms afterward, swallowing tears of happiness while he'd murmured her name over and over.

Finally they'd gotten up and Linn had made supper, and after Nathan had gone back to bed, Murphy in tow, she and Trey had sat by the fire with brandy and had talked for hours. Until their eyes had caught in the flicker of the firelight and he'd reached for her hand and they'd walked down to the bedroom, saying nothing, turning to each other in the darkness of her room.

He'd slipped her robe off her shoulders and had made love to her on the big goatskin rug on the bedroom floor, then later making love to her again, in bed this time, teaching her things about her body and his that she'd never dreamed possible. Teaching her things about love she'd never known before, even with Jack.

And all the time the lies had been between them.

She hadn't meant it to happen that way. But the magic that had exploded between them had happened too fast and too strong to be denied, and she'd just never had time to tell him.

Damn! Why had she ever thought it was going to be easy?

"...finished. Can I go out and play with Murphy now?"

Linn looked up blankly, then gave her head a little shake. "Yes, Nathan, go ahead. Just stay within sight of the house."

He nodded and leaped to his feet, grabbing his sweater from the back of his chair. Murphy went bounding after him and then there was silence again. She started to cut another piece of waffle, then put down her knife and fork, knowing she couldn't swallow.

Trey stood suddenly. He took his plate to the counter and set it down, then poured himself a cup of coffee and came back to the table, swinging the chair around and straddling it. He crossed his arms on the back, toying with a spoon.

"I was thinking of taking a couple days off from writing," he said quietly. "A friend of mine's got a big cabin cruiser that I can borrow. We could go down the coast for a few days. Get away."

Linn took a deep breath. "I—I can't, Trey." In one way it would almost be ideal. But she couldn't afford to be away from the telephone for longer than a day. Her one and only contact, Detective Don Rasky from Miami vice, had to be able to reach her at all times, in case there was news about Kathy and Rod. And she called him daily to let him know that she and Nathan were all right. He was the only link she had with her sister and Nathan's father. The only touch with reality.

Trey didn't say anything, but she could see a muscle pulse along his jaw. "How about camping, then? A couple of days up in the mountains, away from everything. No newspapers, no phones, no—"

"I can't." She just whispered it, staring at her hands. "Trey, please don't make this difficult. I'm just asking you to trust me."

"Trust you?" The words were clipped. "Trust is a two-way street, Linn. Why the hell can't you trust me with whatever's scaring you half to death?"

"Trey, please!" Linn got to her feet abruptly and walked to the sink, staring out at the cedars. She could *not* tell him. For Nathan's sake. For hers. And maybe, most of all, for his. "It's too dangerous," she said softly. "You have no idea what's involved, Trey. None at all!"

"Then tell me, damn it!" He reared to his feet angrily and raked back his damp hair with his fingers. "You can make love with me but you can't tell me what's going on, is that it?" He caught her arm and pulled her around to face him. "What the hell can be so bad you can't tell me, Linn? This is *me*, remember? The man you trusted enough to let into your bed last night. The man you trusted enough to let into your—"

"Stop it!" Linn wheeled away from him. "Stop badgering me, Trey. I will not—I *cannot*—tell you, and that's all there is to it. All I will say is that it doesn't have anything to do with you and me. I'm not married, I swear."

"You won't go sailing with me, you won't go camping with me. You're too scared to walk on the beach. When you're in town, you don't talk to anyone, you rebuff any attempt at friendliness."

Linn stared at him, feeling herself go pale. "You've been asking the townspeople about me?"

"I asked a few questions." He gave her an impatient look. "You're the original mystery lady, Linn. Naturally I asked around. Although it didn't get me anywhere. No one knows a damned thing about you."

Linn felt light-headed, fear a cold lump in her stomach. "Don't ever do that again, Trey," she told him with quiet intensity. "You could get me killed by asking too many questions."

Trey's gray eyes narrowed. "Who's after you, Linn? Organized crime? The cops? Just who the hell *is* Nathan's father, anyway?"

Linn turned away from him again, unable to face those angry eyes. She felt torn apart, half of her wanting desperately to blurt out the whole story, to lose herself in the safety of his strong embrace, the other half knowing she didn't dare.

There was nothing Trey could do to help her. And she'd already put him in more danger than she had a right to. He had no idea of the things the Colombians were capable of. No idea at all.

"I'm still waiting for some kind of an answer here," Trey said suddenly, his voice vibrant with anger.

"What do you want me to tell you?" Linn gestured impatiently. "I've already told you all I can!"

"Maybe you can start by telling me just what the hell last night was."

Linn just looked at him. "Last night was...what it was. Why do you have to complicate this, Trey?"

"Honey, I'm not the one complicating things," he told her in a soft, precise voice. "I just don't like being used."

"Used?" She looked at him sharply.

"Used." Hands planted on narrow hips, he stared at her from across the room as though daring her to challenge him. "You're scared, you're lonely—and I sure as hell was available. I can see where a pair of warm arms in the night would be hard to pass up. Maybe a few hours of pleasant sex to make you feel safe and cared for." He gave a snort. "Hell, women have *married* men for less security than that."

Linn felt herself pale again. She stared at him, hardly able to believe what she was hearing. "My God," she whispered, "do you really think I made love with you just because you were *handy*? That last night was...was just 'pleasant sex'?"

His eyes locked onto hers. "I don't know what last night was for you, Linn. But I do know I'm not interested in just being some woman's part-time lover. Just a pair of arms to hold her in the night when the nightmares come."

"Damn you, Trey Hollister, don't you *dare* come in here and start making morning-after demands on my life!" The feeling of panic was growing steadily. She couldn't deal with this now! "I didn't play seductress yesterday and entice you into my bed for an evening of frolic and fun—you were *plenty* ready to get me in there. And believe me, you weren't used. You were an active and *very* involved participant!"

His eyes narrowed dangerously. "Just two lonely people who meet on a beach and wind up in bed, is that it? A few kisses, some fantastic lovemaking—nothing more than helping each other through the night." He shook his head slowly, eyes burning into hers. "I don't even know your real name."

Linn recoiled as if from a slap. She turned away and stood at the sink, fists clenched, filled with a sick, empty despair. "I told you my real name," she said in a whisper, trying not to cry. "Why are you doing this to me, Trey? How can you say that after last night?"

There was a long, taut silence. "I've got a book to write," he suddenly said, his voice clipped. "I'll leave Murphy with you. I'm going to be working crazy hours for the next few weeks meeting this deadline and won't be able to give him the attention he needs, and Nathan could use the company. I'll bring a couple of sacks of food over for him. If you leave before—well, when you leave, just send him home."

Linn swallowed at a thick, salty lump in her throat. "You don't have to do that," she managed to whisper. "I can manage on my own."

"I'm damned well aware of that," he snapped. "But I am leaving Murphy—and you are going to keep him without any argument, got that?" His voice was crisp with authority, the voice of someone used to giving orders, used to having them obeyed.

It made Linn look around at him. His eyes met hers, expressionless. "It isn't charity, if that's what you're worried about. Or even maudlin sentimentality. I just don't like the kind of people you're attracting to my end of the beach. And I don't like trouble. Not in my backyard. So as long as you're living next to me, lady, you'll do as I say, understand?"

"Perfectly." Her voice was just as crisp, just as matter-of-fact. It was better this way. The farther away he stayed from her, the safer he was. And last night was—

There was no point in thinking about last night.

Last night, and everything it could have meant, was over.

Chapter 8

> She was raven-haired and blue-eyed, and from the first time he saw her, Steele knew she was the kind of trouble that no man needed. It came like that sometimes, gift-wrapped in satin and sin and long, smoldering glances that kept you coming back for more. The kind of trouble that left good men dead....

Yeah.

Trey drew in a deep breath and impatiently tossed the manuscript pages aside. He was supposedly proofing his draft of the first four chapters of *Steele on Ice*, but his mind kept wandering all over the damned place and he wasn't getting anywhere.

A package of cigarettes lay on the table and he stared at it, then swore savagely under his breath and took one out. He lighted it and drew the smoke deeply into his lungs, then eased it out again, squinting through it as he looked across at Linn's house.

It was quiet over there. Had been all day. He hadn't seen hide nor hair of her or the kid since early the previous afternoon, when he'd watched them walk down to the beach together, Murphy gamboling happily beside them. He'd stared down at her, willing her to look up, but of course she hadn't. Almost as though she'd known he was up there, as though she'd deliberately kept her back to him, straight and stiff. Unbendable.

"Stubborn as hell," he muttered under his breath, taking another drag on the cigarette. Stubborn and independent: admirable traits in the right place and at the right time, but they could get you killed. He'd seen it happen.

And he didn't want to see it happen here. Not with this woman. Because, like it or not, he cared about what happened to Linn Stevens, or whatever the hell her name was. Cared a lot.

Not that the fact pleased him. In fact, it downright depressed him when he thought about it too much. Caring meant worrying, and worrying meant thinking about *her* when he should be applying himself to other things. It didn't matter much right now, but what if he got a call from the field that someone needed Trey Hollister's special kind of services?

He rubbed his aching thigh, brooding. He'd damned near lost his leg on that Central America job. And for the same reason—a woman. A nun, that time. Some sort of social worker down there, caring for the children a particularly brutal little civil war had left homeless. She'd been taken hostage by a group of renegade soldiers-turned-rebels, the same rebels who'd been doing their damnedest to kill the man he'd been down there to protect. And *he*—breaking every rule in his own book—went playing hero!

He kneaded the scarred flesh. He'd been lucky that time. But what would happen if he went on a job like that now, with Linn Stevens on his mind?

Hell, he didn't even want to think about it!

He took another swallow of cigarette smoke, eyes narrowing. It had always been a hard and fast Hollister rule to hire only unattached men for the dirty jobs—the jobs where one slip could mean death for yourself or your client. Men with wives and mortgages and babies just had too much other stuff on their minds. And here *he* was, the ultimate

lone wolf himself, finding his attention drifting at all the
wrong times. Remembering the sweet glissade of flesh on
flesh, the taste of her mouth on his, that special little catch
in her breathing when he'd . . .

No. Trey sat upright with a soft oath, stabbing the cigarette out angrily. By God, he wasn't going to fall into that
trap. He'd always managed to avoid it up to now. Like
Steele, he loved 'em and left 'em, and that was just the way
he liked it.

He reached out and picked up the manuscript, refusing to
give in to the urge to glance at the other beach house again.

Her skin was hot velvet, and when she moved it was like
smoke and flame against him, and he burned. He was
steel and she was fire, he cleaving, she engulfing, both
blazing white-hot. And like the blade of a finely crafted
sword, he felt himself folded into himself and folded
again, strengthening with each layering until he was—

Where *was* she, damn it?

He tossed the pages aside again with a soft oath and gazed
at the other beach house. He'd seen lights last night, so she
was still there. The last one to go off had been the one in her
bedroom, and he'd stood in the darkness of his house and
had stared across, able to see a shadow move over the window occasionally. Remembering the taste and feel of her,
naked and silken in his arms, the husky way she'd whispered his name just before she'd . . .

That was it!

He pulled his feet off the railing with a bang and stood up,
gathering up the manuscript and his notes. The day was a
write-off anyway, so why not make the best of it? Go into
town and do some shopping. Drop by the pub. Maybe catch
a movie. Then stop in at the Loft restaurant and have one
of their fresh crabs with the works, a couple of glasses of
good wine, a bit of innocent-but-not-*that*-innocent flirting
with the good-looking blond waitress who, given the slightest encouragement, could become some pretty serious trouble herself.

He gave a snort as he walked into the living room. Believe that, Hollister, he taunted himself, and you'll believe anything. Like any man, he might try to delude himself now and again that he'd take what he could get, where he could get it, and that fast, easy sex was the best sex.

But that was a damned lie. He'd never been into that scene. One-night stands and empty affairs didn't fill a man's life, they just emphasized what wasn't there. And that one wondrous night with Linn had only proved what he already knew. He wanted what he couldn't have, wanted what probably didn't even exist. And all the pretty blondes and the not-so-innocent flirting in the world weren't going to take that empty ache away....

"Nathan? Nathan, where are you?" Breathing hard, trying to fight the panic clawing at her throat, Linn forced herself to stop and take a deep, calming breath. "Nathan!"

She looked around frantically, trying to catch sight of him through the racks of tourist T-shirts and display cases filled with souvenirs. This couldn't be happening! He'd been right beside her a moment ago, exclaiming in wonder over a book he'd discovered, filled with pop-up figures of whales and dolphins.

"Nathan, this isn't funny!" Her voice wobbled and two women looking through the racks of postcards looked at her oddly.

She glanced toward the window at the front of the store, but the man wasn't in sight. She'd noticed him in the ice-cream shop first, and then again when she'd popped into the post office to buy stamps. The same man who had been watching the house.

Taking Nathan's hand, she'd crossed the street and swiftly walked the other way, finally losing the stranger in the crowd around a street musician. Then suddenly he'd been there again, pretending to be engrossed by the display in the travel office window when she'd looked around. She'd dragged poor Nathan in one door of an antique shop and out the other, but the man had stuck to her like a burr. At last, in desperation, she'd popped into the gift and souvenir shop to gather her wits and come up with a plan to get back to the car without being seen. And now Nathan was missing!

"Excuse me, miss, but is anything wrong?" The soft voice at her elbow made Linn whirl around.

One of the young women who owned the store was looking at her in concern. Linn nodded. "I've just lost my little boy. He was here a minute ago, then I turned around and he was gone."

The woman's face cleared and she smiled. "Dark curly hair and black eyes and a face like an angel? Wearing blue cords and a heavy knit sweater?"

"Yes!" Linn's heart leaped.

"Oh, he's in the other half of the store—I know it's confusing, no one realizes that the men's clothing store next door and this store are really together." She pointed toward the back where Linn could see a wide doorway linking the two sides of the building. "We carry a very good line of product over there if you're—" She laughed quietly. "Don't worry about your son, he's all right. Your husband's with him. I saw them walking toward the door just a minute ago, hand in hand, and—"

But Linn wasn't listening. She sprinted down the narrow aisle between the display cases at a dead run, dodging a baby stroller and the two gray-haired ladies at the postcard rack. There was a handful of people in the clothing store and Linn glanced around in desperation, seeing neither the stranger who had been following her nor Nathan. There was a young salesclerk nearby, talking to a customer, and Linn ran toward them.

"A little boy came in here a minute ago?" she interrupted. "Five years old, dark hair and eyes. There was a man—"

"Pardon me, madam, but I was—"

"Damn it, did you see him?" Linn's voice cracked through the store, turning heads, and she had to fight to keep from grabbing the man's suit jacket and shaking him. "Was he here? Did—?"

"Over there." Eyeing her warily, the clerk inclined his head toward the shoe section, stumbling back as Linn brushed between him and his customer. "Well, of all the rude—!"

She saw Nathan first. He was trotting along unconcernedly, his hand in the firm grip of the man walking beside him. They had their backs to her and were nearly at the door when Linn shot down the nearest aisle to intercept them.

"Nathan!" Her cry resounded like a whiplash and Nathan turned to look at her, his eyes widening as she lunged toward him.

She grabbed the man's arm just as he was turning around, but before she realized what was happening, he'd seized her wrist and had wrenched her back from Nathan so hard that she cried out. Blazing eyes met hers, narrowed and dangerous. Gray eyes that in the next instant widened with surprise.

They simply stared at each other for a stunned moment or two, then Trey let his fingers slide free of her wrist. He gave his head a slow shake, easing a tight breath between his teeth. "Lady, that is a good way to get yourself killed."

"I—" Linn closed her eyes, trying to get her own breath back. "I thought—there was a man, and . . ." She knelt on the floor and hugged Nathan, squeezing him so hard that he gave a squeak of protest.

"He turned up beside me with no warning," Trey said gruffly. "I was just setting out to find you when you bushwhacked us."

"I'm sorry." Linn looked up at him, giddy with relief. "When I turned around, he was gone and the salesclerk said she'd seen him with some man and—" She managed a rough laugh, giving Nathan another fierce hug. "It never occurred to me that it might be you."

He gave a snort of bitter laughter. "Forgotten that quickly."

Her panic had receded enough by now for other emotions to work their way through, and Linn flushed slightly. "No," she said quietly. "There's been a man following me this morning. And when Nathan went missing, the first thing I thought of was—"

"Man?" Trey looked down at her sharply. "What man?"

"I don't *know* what man," she snapped. "Just a man!"

He nodded thoughtfully, looking through the front display window into the street. Then he glanced back at her. Something gentled slightly in those fierce gray eyes. "You're as white as a sheet," he said more quietly. "Come on, I'll take you home."

"No." She glared at him, still not ready to forgive him for the scare he'd given her. Damn it, he should have known better! She reached down and took Nathan's hand. "My car's just across the street."

Trey whispered something under his breath that Linn didn't quite catch but which, judging by the look of admiration on Nathan's young face, must have been fairly colorful. He pushed the door open and held it for her, then followed her out of the store and across the street with a grim, no-nonsense expression that made Linn keep further arguments to herself.

She'd left Murphy in the car and he burst into excited barking when he saw them, tail windmilling. Trey whistled, the dog leapt through the open window, and they wrestled and played for a minute or two. He watched as she got Nathan settled in the passenger seat and secured his seat belt. Then he lounged against the parking meter as she opened her door and tilted the seat forward to let Murphy into the back, then slid behind the wheel herself.

"I don't suppose," he said evenly, "that there's much point in telling you to drive carefully."

"I appreciate the thought," Linn said shortly, starting the car. "But I make a point of driving carefully all the time."

His expression grew even grimmer. "And I guess *that* means I shouldn't bother asking if you'd like to come over for dinner some night."

It surprised Linn, but she managed to keep her expression blank. "That depends on you. If you're asking me over because you'd enjoy our company, I'd like to. But if you're asking because you want to keep an eye on me or you think I'm not eating properly or you're going to start interrogating—"

"Forget I asked," he growled, shoving himself away from the meter. "And drive carefully anyway, damn it."

Linn felt her cheeks blaze with sudden shame at her behavior. "Trey—"

He glanced around, his face and eyes suspicious and angry. *Forgive me,* she wanted to cry out. *I know I'm handling this badly, but I'm scared and I'm alone and I don't know any other way to handle it!* Instead she just sighed, shaking her head. "Nothing," she whispered, letting her gaze slip from his. "And I will drive carefully. Thanks for... just thanks." *Thanks for caring.*

Linn didn't notice the car behind her until she'd turned off the main highway, and even then she didn't pay much attention to it. It was a nondescript vehicle, pale blue or maybe gray, and it wasn't until it had settled in right behind her that Linn really gave it a serious look. There were two men in it, both youngish, she thought, although it was hard to tell, since both were wearing sunglasses. Normal-looking enough. But there was something about them, about the way they were following so closely, that gave Linn a prickle of alarm.

She eased her foot onto the accelerator and her rental car picked up speed. The gap between the two vehicles widened momentarily, as though she'd caught them by surprise, but then they surged up behind her again, even closer. There was definitely something wrong! If they wanted to pass, they had plenty of room and opportunity to do so. And they weren't local kids out for a romp, or they'd have been hooting and hollering and generally making nuisances of themselves.

No. These two were sitting back there for a reason.

She swallowed, tightening her grip on the wheel, and glanced at Nathan. "Is your seat belt good and tight?"

He checked it, nodding. "Yep. How come?"

"We...uh...might be going for a fast ride, Nathan," she said very calmly. "So I want you to hang on really tight, okay?"

But just going fast wasn't going to help. She was a good driver, but could she outmaneuver and outrun them? And where should she go? Home? They'd expect that.

Damn, why hadn't she accepted Trey's offer of a ride? Or better yet, why had he chosen *this* particular day to go into town? If he'd been home she could have gone there. She'd be safe there. Trey would make sure she was safe....

She forced the thought away impatiently, her mind spinning with possibilities. Going back to town was the best idea, but there was no place to turn—not with them two feet off her back bumper. If she could only—

"Nathan, hang on!" Linn almost screamed, barely having time to brace herself before the car behind smashed into their rear bumper. The impact threw her against her shoulder harness and it snapped tight, keeping her from hitting the wheel but knocking the breath out of her. Something struck the back of her seat, there was a yelp of surprise and pain from Murphy and the sound of claws scrabbling for purchase on the rubber floor mats. Nathan uttered a wail of fear.

"Hang on, here they come again!"

The second impact was even harder and the car slewed, half out of control. The rear end skated sideways, sending up a spray of dust and gravel from the shoulder, and Linn fought the wheel. She got back onto the pavement, tires screaming as she floored the accelerator, and glanced into the rearview mirror in time to see them coming again.

But she was ready for them this time. She pulled left and braked hard, and they went flying by on the right. In that instant she whipped the car back to the right lane to give herself room, then wrenched the wheel to the left again and slammed the brake pedal down.

Tires howling, the rear of her car slewed full around, but at the critical instant, Linn released the brakes and floored the accelerator. The car fishtailed, tires smoking, then they got traction again and the vehicle shot down the road toward the highway.

Linn dared a swift glance into her rearview mirror. Her pursuers had turned nearly as quickly, and her heart sank as she realized her maneuver had bought her only a minute or two.

Not even that. Another glance into the mirror showed them right behind her and she braced herself as they pulled closer. But instead of smashing into the rear of her car, they pulled out and around and came up beside her. Linn gasped, realizing too late what they intended to do. She stamped on the brakes, hoping they'd shoot by again, but the driver of the other car was anticipating her this time and braked too, slamming his car into the side of hers.

Murphy was baying with rage in the back, snarling and snapping helplessly at the other car, and poor Nathan was howling in fear. But Linn barely heard them, too busy fighting the wheel to keep her car on the road. The other car plowed into her again and her right front tire hit the shoulder. She tried to get it back onto the pavement, but the other car hit hers again; in the next instant, her car was skidding into the shallow ditch.

It plowed nose first into the steep bank on the other side and Linn was thrown forward savagely. She struggled to get her seat belt undone and Nathan out of the car before the men could reach them. Murphy had been thrown to the floor again but he was on his feet and in full, murderous voice a moment later, practically chewing his way through the side of the car, and the instant Linn flung her door open he was out.

She caught a glimpse of a black and tan missile hurtling up the shallow bank of the ditch to the road as she flung herself at Nathan. She snapped his belt free, opened his door and shoved him out in one frantic motion. He hit the ground, still howling, but Linn was beside him an instant later, snatching him to his feet.

She saw one of the men pull a revolver from his coat pocket and dropped like a stone, covering Nathan's body with hers. The windshield of the car dissolved at the same instant she heard the crack of a gunshot. Hugging Nathan, she started wriggling backward, keeping the car between her and her assailants, praying that Murphy could keep them busy long enough for her to get into the relative safety of the heavy woods.

There was a scream and the sudden sound of a dog worrying something, then another gunshot and a yelping howl of pain from Murphy that went through Linn like a knife blade. There was another scream, human this time, then the shriek of rubber as a brown sedan—the same brown sedan she'd seen lurking by the house—came to a screeching stop right behind her pursuer's car.

Linn didn't quite know what happened next. Nathan was now bellowing in pain and fright, someone was shouting, someone else was screaming and there were more gunshots. The two men who had been chasing her were struggling back to the road, one half dragging the other. He was kicking and swearing at Murphy, who was snarling and snapping at them, seeming fully intent on eating the two of them alive.

Then someone else was there. A bright red Jeep came to a smoking stop right behind the brown car. Her pursuers had managed to get to their vehicle by then, but Linn realized that someone was running toward her. There was a piece of sun-bleached wood lying beside her; she picked it up and swung it at the looming figure, screaming at him to get away, almost blinded by her own hair and the tears that just wouldn't stop.

Someone grabbed her hands and brought them down, then two strong arms were around her, holding her tightly. "It's all right," a familiar husky voice murmured. "It's all right now, sweetheart. They're gone. He's safe—Nathan's safe."

"Trey!" And then, finally, she could cry.

She was, Trey found himself thinking, the most incredible woman he'd ever met. He'd seen that race-car-driver turn she'd pulled back there, had seen the dents and scrapes in her car and knew what they meant. He'd seen the expression of pure, murderous rage on her face when he'd come running toward her. It was the look of someone pushed as far as they can be pushed, that last-stand expression that means they've got nothing more to lose.

She was shivering uncontrollably now and still sobbing, her arms wrapped tightly around Nathan, whose own tears had stopped, although he was still pale and plainly terrified.

Trey rubbed her back and shoulders and after what seemed like a long while, she lifted her face and gazed at him through brimming tears. "W-where d-did you c-come from?"

He smiled, brushing her tear-damp hair from her face. "You're going to be mad when I tell you."

"You f-followed me."

"You got it."

She tried to look indignant, failed badly, and started digging through her pockets. He found a tissue and handed it to her and she blew her nose and dabbed at her eyes, still hiccoughing with swallowed sobs. "They sh-shot Murphy."

"Just grazed his shoulder. He'll be limping around as badly as I am for a few days, but he'll be okay. By the look of that guy's leg, though, he might not be so lucky. Murph really did a number on it."

"Hey, Hollister?" Trey looked around to see Joe Cippino jogging down the slope of the ditch, frowning. "Got a trace on the car plates, but it's like we thought—they rented it under false names. Came into Vancouver three days ago."

Trey nodded. "Okay, that pretty much confirms what we already know. Has Correlis found anything yet?"

Cippino shook his head, his glance drifting toward Linn. "If she is who she says she is, there aren't any warrants or anything on her. Not so much as a fingerprint on file."

Trey nodded slowly, blowing out a weary breath. Linn looked up just then, her eyes still bleary with tears, but when they settled on Cippino they widened with horror and she reared back so suddenly that Trey nearly lost his grip on her.

"That's him!" She tried to scramble to her feet, but Trey held her firmly. "That's the man who's been watching my house! The one who was following me this morning! He—" She stopped at Trey's snort of laughter, looking from one to the other with dawning horror.

Trey sobered instantly. "Hold it, Linn, it's not what you think! Joe's a friend of mine. He does security work for me sometimes and I—well, I..." He winced. "He's been keeping an eye on you for me. When I knew I was going to be in New York for a couple of days, I called him in. Just in case something happened while I was gone and you needed help."

She blinked at him. "You...hired someone to watch me?"

Joe gave a snort and rubbed the back of his neck. "As best as I could. You are damn near impossible to keep under surveillance, I'll tell you! Like trying to catch a gopher—while you're watching one hole, she's goin' out another!"

She closed her eyes, looking suddenly too weary to even stand up. "I want to go home," she said quietly. "Is my car drivable?"

Trey helped her to her feet. "Nat, can you walk up to the Jeep or would you like a hand?"

"I can walk my own self," the boy announced a little unsteadily, reaching for Linn's hand.

His expression of grim determination was a mirror of the one on his mother's face, and Trey had to bite back a laugh. God almighty, what a pair! Any man who decided to take these two on had his work cut out for him!

They got back to Linn's house about twenty minutes later, and Trey motioned for Joe to go ahead while he helped Linn and Nathan out of the Jeep.

They were nearly at the door when Joe stepped out of the house, looking grim and serious. "They must have come here first," he said quietly. "Broke this door in, smashed the big glass door leading in from the deck. Most likely when they couldn't find her and the kid here, they set up that ambush on the highway."

Trey swore. Linn was looking at him blankly, as though she hadn't quite comprehended what had happened. But her confusion didn't last long. Taking a deep breath, she pushed Nathan gently behind her and walked into the house.

The carport door leading into the kitchen had been taken half off its hinges, the frame splintered where Toomey's new lock had held but the wood around it hadn't. Not saying anything, Trey gave a nod to Joe to look around outside, then followed Linn, letting her have a good look at it. Hoping, finally, to shock her into opening up.

She walked into the living room and simply stood there, looking at the smashed patio door. Piles of broken glass lay in drifts across the carpet, glittering in the sun. Nathan leaned against her leg and she reached down almost absently and stroked his head.

"I'll get Toomey to put a sheet of plywood over that until he can order new glass," Trey said quietly.

Linn turned around and walked past him without saying anything, her eyes wide and dark. As she and Nathan headed toward the bedrooms, Trey watched her for a moment, then took a quick, thorough look around the house himself. Murphy had followed them inside, limping heavily, and when Trey knelt beside him he whimpered.

"You did a good thing today, old fella." Trey rubbed the dog's neck and throat. "You're a naturally heroic son of a gun, aren't you?" Gently Trey examined Murphy's wound. The bullet had torn a deep furrow through the muscular flesh of the dog's left shoulder, angling across his ribs. His thick fur was soaked with blood and he was shivering, whining slightly as Trey looked him over for any other injuries.

"How is he?" Joe squatted on his heels beside the dog.

"He'll be okay, but he's lost a lot of blood."

Joe stood up. "I'll get him to the vet and have him sewn up while you're sorting this out."

"Here, put this around him." Linn's quiet voice made Trey look around. She was carrying the comforter off Nathan's bed and she handed it to Joe, then knelt beside Murphy, cupping his broad face between her hands. "I haven't even thanked you, Murph," she whispered, her voice catching slightly. "You saved our lives. If—if you hadn't been there..." Her voice broke and she didn't even bother trying to finish, just slipping her arms around the dog's furry neck and giving him a gentle hug.

Then she stood up, wiping her eyes with the back of her hand; Trey snapped his fingers and led the dog to Joe's car. He got Murphy settled as well as he could in the back, wrapping the comforter around him to fight the danger of shock, then stood there for a weary moment and watched as Joe drove away.

Linn heard Trey come into the bedroom a few minutes later but didn't bother turning around. She scooped up a handful of underthings and stuffed them into the suitcase that lay open on the bed.

"He'll find you again sooner or later, just like he found you here," he said with an edge to his voice. "How long can you keep it up, Linn?"

"Long enough," she replied shortly, folding a pair of jeans and shoving them into the suitcase, too. She caught herself after a moment and took a deep breath. Running both hands through her hair, she straightened and turned to look at Trey. "I'm sorry. For getting you involved in this, for getting Murphy hurt, for... everything." She faltered slightly, turning her attention back to her packing.

"Running away isn't going to solve anything." His voice still had a rough undertone and he started prowling the room, dragging deeply on the cigarette in his hand.

"Running's all I've got." Maybe she'd come back. Maybe, when it was all over, she and Trey would be able to explore what was between them more fully. But not now. She had Nathan's well-being to worry about before she could allow herself the luxury of falling in love.

If it even *was* love, she reminded herself brutally, and not just a bad case of fear, lonely nights and opportunity. Only time would decide that.

"So that's it? You come into my life and turn it upside down, then just leave again without so much as an explanation?" He stared at her and she could see the look on his face that she'd half dreaded, anger mixed with bewilderment and bruised male ego and a hundred other things. But it was useless even trying to explain what was going on.

She recognized his type. Like Jack, he was a born knight errant, as stubborn as he was heroic. If he found out just how serious things were he'd feel duty-bound to protect her—and she'd get him killed. And there was no way she was letting that happen. Trey Hollister, man of action, was going to have to sit this one out.

He strode across and took her firmly by the shoulders, gazing down at her intently. "Damn it, Linn, I can help you. I can—"

"No, you can't," she told him with fierce certainty, pulling away from his grasp and continuing to pack. "Trey, believe me, you don't have even the slightest idea of what you'd be letting yourself in for. The longer I stay here and the more involved we get, the more danger you're in."

"I can handle the danger," he growled. "Trust me."

"No!" It was so tempting to believe him. But temptation made people careless, and carelessness got people killed. "I'm mixed up in something you don't even want to think about. If I stay here, I'm going to get you hurt—or killed. For your safety, for mine and for Nathan's, I have got to leave here and just disappear. Because I—" Her voice cracked and she swallowed, folding a sweater and putting it into the suitcase. *Because I already care too much. Because I think I've fallen in love with you, and I just won't risk getting you hurt because of it....*

He was silent behind her. So silent that for an instant she thought he'd left. Then a strong, tanned hand came from behind her and caught her wrist as she started to pull the suitcase closed. "For how long, Linn?" he asked softly. "If you won't think of your own safety, think of Nathan's—if it's as bad as you're saying, it's not right to endanger the boy."

"Oh, honestly!" She wrenched her wrist from his grip. "Why are you so determined to make this as difficult as possible? We had one night of magic, Trey Hollister, and I'll never forget it—or you. But that does not mean I'm going to let you— Damn it, what do you think you're doing?" Her voice rose in shock as he upended the suitcase and dumped her clothing over the bed.

He flung the empty suitcase violently across the room. "You're staying, lady," he told her bluntly. "I'm not letting you panic and run just because this guy's got you so scared you can't think straight. The only way you're going to be free of him is to make a stand. And I'm going to be right beside you when you do."

"A stand?" The word broke on a harsh, disbelieving laugh. "Trey, have you lost your mind? Do you have any idea of what—"

He gestured impatiently, "Of course I do! Do you think I'm blind? For whatever reasons, you've kidnapped your own son and his father wants him back. It happens all the time. Courts are giving custody to fathers who shouldn't have it, and more and more women just aren't taking it anymore. Hell, there's a new underground railroad running from one end of the country to the other, women taking care of women, sheltering them, hiding them." He caught his anger, looking at her seriously. "But you don't have to do it alone, Linn."

"That's not it." She said it quietly, but there was something in her voice that stopped Trey cold. His eyes narrowed slightly and she sat down on the edge of the bed with a sigh of defeat, shoulders slumping with tiredness and despair. "I wish it were that simple, Trey. I wish..." She shook her head slowly, rubbing at a grass stain on the knee of her jeans, trying to figure out where to start. There was no other place to start than at the beginning.

Chapter 9

Nathan is not my son," she said quietly. "He's my sister's boy. Kathy is three years younger than I am, and she's married to a . . . a crusader!" She smiled faintly, glancing up at Trey. "He reminds me of you, in fact."

She let the smile fade from her lips and stared at the stain on her knee again, rubbing it absently with her fingernail. "Rod is a cop. Miami vice. He's been working under cover for nearly a year now, infiltrating a cocaine smuggling operation run by a Colombian drug lord by the name of Guillermo Santos. The police finally got enough to indict Santos, and they're bringing him to trial sometime later this month. Rod is their key witness."

Trey gave a long, low whistle. "I'm beginning to not like the sound of this."

"Santos's organization isn't the biggest or most powerful to come out of Colombia, but it's growing fast. He's young, mean and greedy—and scared. He got careless and trusted people he shouldn't have, and now he's looking at spending the next fifty years in prison."

"And he'll do anything to stop your brother-in-law from testifying."

Linn nodded. "He's already tried to kill Rod twice, and six weeks ago Santos's men made an aborted attempt to kidnap my sister, planning to use her to force Rod to change his mind." She took a deep breath, looking up at Trey. "But Rod doesn't scare easily. He and Kathy went into hiding, but they decided not to take Nathan with them. For one thing, he'd make them more vulnerable—Santos knows he's looking for a man and his wife and their five-year-old son. For another, he'd slow them down. And most important, they were worried what it would do to Nathan."

"So they asked you to take him."

"I volunteered to take him," she corrected. "It was my idea right from the start to split the family up. Kathy and Nathan aren't the only ones in danger—I am, our father is, anyone trying to help us is. We tricked Dad into going to Ireland for a couple of months. He's retired and Mother died last year, so I convinced him to visit relatives over there just to get him out of the way. Then I took Nathan.

"My original plan was to stay with friends in Missouri, near Lake of the Ozarks. They have a boy about Nathan's age—I figured it would be easier on him with other kids to play with, and lots of fishing and boating to keep his mind off...things."

"What happened?"

Linn shook her head. "I don't know. I left Fort Lauderdale—that's where I live—and everything seemed fine. But after I'd been in Missouri for a few days, I realized I'd been followed. I also realized I was putting my friends in danger and I left."

"So you came up here."

"Not at first. I headed out to California. But it didn't take long for them to find me there, too. So I rented a car and headed north—actually, I wound up touring eight different states, going in so many circles I made myself dizzy. When I was sure I'd lost whoever was tailing me, I bolted up here. Crossed the border on some logging road in the mountains and made my way out here. I figured nobody would *ever* be able to track me down."

"Wrong again."

"Wrong again," Linn echoed in despair. "They want Nathan as blackmail, of course, to keep Rod from testifying."

"Killing you in the process."

"They'll try."

Trey snorted as he strode across to pick up her suitcase where it had landed against the far wall. He tossed it onto the bed and started shoving her clothes back into it. "Where's Nathan?"

"In his room, getting his things together." Linn watched him as he pulled the last drawer out of the dressing table and turned it upside down over the suitcase, mashing everything together and zipping the case closed. "What are you doing?"

"Packing." He tossed the larger case onto the bed and opened it, then started stripping the closet. "We'll take all we can carry now, and Joe and I can pick the rest up later."

"Take?"

"You're staying with me."

"Oh, for—" Linn caught herself, taking a calming breath. "Trey, didn't you hear a thing I just said? This isn't some irate ex-husband we're dealing with here, it's a Colombian drug lord fighting for his life. Do you have any idea what these people are capable of? *Narcotraficantes* determine the way of life down there. They even have their own army, the *sicarios*: paid assassins."

Trey closed the second suitcase, then picked up both and carried them into the corridor. "Have you got your stuff out of the bathroom yet?"

"Did you hear what I said?" Linn's voice vibrated with impatience. "Damn it, taking care of things is my specialty! I've been taking care of things in our family for most of my life. I took care of a dying husband for two and a half years, I took care of my mother for six months before *she* died, and I'll damned well take care of this, too!"

"Not alone, you won't," Trey growled as he walked by her and across the corridor into Nathan's room. "How are you doing, sport? Got everything packed?"

Nathan was pulling his toys out of the cardboard box by his bed and putting them into his suitcase. Tears were running down his cheeks and he had to stop every now and then to wipe his eyes clear.

"You and your aunt are going to be staying with me for a while. How does that sound?"

Nathan shook his head, his lower lip protruding, face set with sullen anger and fear. "Don't wanna," he said in an uneven voice, casting Linn a hostile look. "I wanna go *home*. I want my *daddy*!"

"Well, I can sure understand that," Trey said softly, squatting beside the suitcase. "But we have a little problem. Murphy was hurt this afternoon. Not badly," he added quickly, seeing the expression on Nathan's face, "but it's going to slow him up some. And I was hoping I could convince you to help me take care of him. I'm going to be busy for a few days, and he's going to be feeling pretty down."

"Trey..." Linn's voice was vibrant with warning.

Nathan wiped his face on the sleeve of his jacket, giving Trey a disdainful look. "There's nothing *I* can do."

"Actually there's a lot you can do. Keep him exercising his leg, for one thing. Make sure he's eating and that he's got plenty of fresh water. For the first couple of days he's not going to be feeling very chipper, and I think just having you there will make him feel better."

"Trey, damn it," Linn exclaimed, "don't you do this to me!"

"Really?" Nathan's face brightened slightly.

"Really." Trey smiled and stood up, ruffling Nathan's hair with his hand. "So let's get the rest of this stuff packed, okay?"

"Trey, I am *not*—" Linn snapped her mouth shut as Trey suddenly wheeled around and stepped toward her, his face hard with impatience.

"Yes," he said in a soft, but steel-edged voice, "you are." His eyes locked with hers, intent and hard and utterly implacable. "I don't know how in the hell you've managed to stay alive this long, but your luck's running out fast. Nothing is going to stop these guys until they kill you and kidnap Nathan—and I am not letting you risk your life and the life of that kid in there, just because you can't stand the idea of accepting help, understand?"

"They're killers, Trey! This isn't some novel you're writing. This is *real*."

Trey's face was grim as he glanced around to check the room. "Okay, let's go."

"Trey! You can't possibly protect Nathan and me against—"

"Yes, I can," he said bluntly, meeting her eyes dead on. "It's what I do, Linn. And I do it well."

"But—" But nothing. There was no arguing with him, Linn realized despairingly. Or more correctly, she *could* have argued with him, but if she attempted he'd probably toss her over his very capable shoulder and carry her across to his place.

To Trey's satisfaction, Linn followed him to his house docilely enough. She didn't even protest when he and Joe went back a couple of hours later to bring over the rest of her things. Later she'd come into the kitchen and had wordlessly started helping him with supper, making a green salad while he'd grilled the salmon steaks he'd picked up that afternoon.

Murphy had come through his ordeal at the vet's like the old warrior he was, stiff and bruised and groggy with painkillers, but unbowed. Even Nathan had settled in happily enough. Worn out, he'd barely made it through supper before falling asleep. Trey had carried him into the living room and tucked him under a blanket on the sofa where Linn could keep an eye on him. Then he'd lighted a blazing fire and had poured Linn a glass of brandy and himself a stiff shot of whiskey, and they'd been sitting here in silence ever since.

He took a swallow of the liquor and leaned well back in the easy chair, bracing one foot on the wide hassock and gazing over his upraised knee at the woman curled up in the big armchair across from him. She was subdued and thoughtful, her forehead fretted with lines of worry, eyes shadowed with unease, but he was surprised at how well she'd come through everything that had happened.

No, he decided on second thought. Not surprised. He'd seen flashes of that steely inner strength before. Relieved was a better word. He'd half anticipated an all-out brawl over her staying here, but—for the moment at least—she seemed content to let him run things. Which probably *was* surprising, he thought with a sudden flash of humor. Linn Stevens didn't strike him as being the kind of woman who let anyone run her life.

As though aware of his gaze, she raised her head slowly and looked at him. "Where's Joe?"

"Outside, giving the perimeter alarms a final check."

She smiled very faintly. "You make this place sound like a fortress."

Trey didn't smile. "Close enough."

She nodded, looking at him for a silent while. "I think," she said quietly, "that it's time you told me just who you are. And why you don't even turn a hair at the possibility that Santos could have an army at the back door by tomorrow morning."

"First things first." He lighted a cigarette—his fourth or fifth of the day, but what the hell—and drew on it deeply, eyeing her through the spiraling smoke. "You're not really Nathan's aunt, are you?" She looked puzzled, and he smiled tolerantly. "You're damned good at this kind of thing. A little too good to be just a caring sister-in-law. Where did you learn to handle a car like a pro, for instance? I saw that one-eighty you did on the highway this afternoon. Either you're a cop, or you grew up running moonshine in the Arkansas backwoods."

She looked badly startled for a moment, then her laughter rose through the shadows. "My dad would be grinning from ear to Irish ear if he heard that." Still laughing, she shook her head. "But you're wrong. I am Nathan's aunt, and I'm not a cop. Not that I wasn't *supposed* to be, understand."

Trey looked at her quizzically and Linn smiled. "Right from the day I was born, Dad had it figured that I was going to follow in his footsteps—just as he'd followed in *his* father's. So I was more or less groomed for the job right from the start. He's the one who taught me to drive like a Brooklyn cabbie." Her smile faltered. "Although I was wishing the other night on that beach with Rolfson that I'd paid more attention to my karate lessons."

"So you were the son he never had."

"No, not really. He's just a strong believer in knowing how to take care of yourself—especially if you're a woman. He taught Kath and me how to 'discourage unwanted admirers,' as he put it, before we were even in our teens." She grinned. "*Disable* was more like it. He showed us a whole lot of dirty little tricks that would have scandalized our mother, had she ever found out. She thought we spent all those hours in the basement learning Latin verbs, and really Daddy was teaching Kath and me how to knee an unwanted admirer in the groin."

Trey winced, laughing. "Did you say he's retired?"

"Thank heaven! If he was still on the force, I don't know what we'd have done. As it was, Kath and I knew we didn't *dare* let him in on what was happening. If he had the slightest clue that his baby daughter and his only grandchild were being chased by Colombian *narcotraficantes*, he'd be taking them on single-handed. So we tricked him into visiting his brother in Ireland to get him out of the way until this is over."

"For his safety, too," Trey speculated quietly. "Santos wouldn't be shy about kidnapping your father and using him as collateral, either."

"Exactly. Uncle Rory knows the situation and he and some of his old street-warrior friends are keeping a close eye on Dad without letting him know what's going on." She managed another smile. "Even Santos's bunch are no match for that band of ruffians—old Sinn Fein and IRA types, the lot of them."

"Seems to me," Trey said slowly, "that you might have been smart to have gone over with him—and taken Kathy and Nathan with you."

She gave him an odd look. "Kathy wouldn't have left Rod. And I certainly wouldn't have left Kath. We toyed with the idea of sending Nathan with Dad, but sooner or later Dad would have twigged to the fact that something was going on." She smiled again. "Patrick Duffy O'Connor grew up near the Shankill Road in Belfast and was teethed on car bombs and assassination squads. To hear him tell it, the Colombians are just amateur upstarts in the terrorism department."

Trey gave a snort of laughter. "Sounds to me as though he passed a bit of that Irish orneriness on to his eldest daughter."

It made her smile. "Yeah, well, you wouldn't be the first person to suggest it."

Trey nodded, looking at her thoughtfully. "Your sister is asking a hell of a lot, as I see it. Seems to me she could have gotten Nathan put under police protection, and it would have been easier on everyone."

She looked at him as though she did not fully understand the question. "Kathy's my sister," she said quietly. "I love her. Nathan might have been safe with the police. Then again he might not have been—and who knows the psychological damage he'd have undergone, being left with strangers? If you can't turn to your family for help, who on earth *can* you turn to?"

Trey frowned, staring at the glowing tip of the cigarette. "I wouldn't know," he said with faint bitterness. "My family was never big on...caring." He looked up after a minute or two to find Linn gazing at him curiously and he managed a ragged, careless smile. "My old man drank. A lot. He wasn't around much when I was a kid, which was just as well—he was surly and mean and not shy about taking a swing at anyone who annoyed him. My mother died when I was about eleven and some relative took me in. But they had a bunch of kids of their own, and I was just one more mouth to feed. I took off when I was fifteen. Joined the marines as soon as I was big enough to lie convincingly about my age...."

He was still staring at the end of his cigarette, as though lost in the past, and Linn found herself studying him thoughtfully. *Typical loner... happier by himself than with people. Finds it hard to open up.* He'd been talking about Steele when he'd said it, Linn recalled. But how much was Steele, and how much his silent, introspective creator?

"And from the marines," she coaxed him gently, "to a couple of tours in Vietnam. Then a stint in military intelligence, whatever *that* means. Which, I presume, is where you started doing whatever it is you do."

He looked up in faint surprise, then broke into a quiet laugh. "You have me all figured out, don't you?"

"Not even by half," Linn replied very seriously. "Tell me about it, Trey. Tell me why Santos doesn't scare you. Why your house is rigged up so it could withstand a marine assault force."

He shrugged, still smiling faintly. "Nothing mysterious about it. After I got out of MI I needed a job. Looking over my work skills, I realized they hadn't taught me a hell of a lot, other than how to kill efficiently. And how to keep people from killing me. I figured I could either become a professional hit man, or adapt what I'd learned to some other use."

He took a final drag on the cigarette, then leaned forward and flicked it into the fire. "I took a good look at the state of the world and decided security was a lucrative field to get into. So I put together a list of people with skills like mine and went into business. Antiterrorism, mainly. If a big corporation has a field office in a high-risk country, I go in and set up a security system to keep their employees safe from kidnapping, bombing, that sort of thing. I also work with foreign governments now and again—I designed the security system for the Canadian embassy in France a couple of years ago. And our own embassy in Spain has a few of my touches."

Linn simply stared at him. "That's how you knew. Right from the start you knew I was in trouble."

"I knew you were running scared from something."

"And why you started watching over me."

He smiled. "Some habits are hard to break."

"And your leg? When you zigged instead of zagging, that was business, wasn't it?"

Trey nodded, the laughter leaving his face. "Central America. I was down there trying to keep a peace advisor alive long enough to get negotiations started. There had been a military coup and the place was in chaos, the military on one side and rebel government sympathizers on the other. By the time we got down there, the country was in a shambles. There was this woman—a nun from a local mission. One of the generals had her kidnapped, planning on using her as collateral in the peace negotiations.'' He frowned slightly, staring into the fire. ''I wasn't supposed to get involved, of course. We weren't taking sides, just trying to hammer out a workable compromise both sides could live with.''

His profile was hard-edged against the flames and Linn traced it with her eyes. ''But you did.''

He smiled faintly, slipping her an amused sidelong look. ''Yeah, old Trey Hollister can never keep himself out of trouble!'' Then the smile slid away and he stared into the flickering flames, his face cold. ''I got this sudden urge to play hero. It was crazy—if I'd been caught it would have compromised our credibility and the entire mission would have been in jeopardy.'' He uttered a snort. ''Jeopardy, hell! We'd have been lucky to get out of the country with our skins intact.''

''And?'' Linn urged gently. ''Did you get her out?''

''I got her out.''

''And did they ever find out who did it?''

He shook his head. ''They had their suspicions—particularly when I turned up the next day with my leg half shot off. But I told them I'd done it myself while cleaning my gun, and they couldn't very well come out and call me a liar without jeopardizing their own position.''

Linn gazed at him, shaking her head slowly. She smiled. ''And you had to ask why I volunteered to take care of Nathan? Seems to me you've got a pretty deep streak of caring yourself.''

Trey gave her a sharp look. ''That was business. What you're doing is just plain nuts.''

Like watching over me was business, she felt like adding. But she didn't. You're a damned fraud, Hollister, she told him silently. You may have convinced the rest of the world you're as hard as nails, but I don't believe a word of it.

''So you can believe me whan I tell you that you're safe here,'' he said suddenly, his voice quiet. ''Nothing's going to happen to you here, Linn. I'll make damned sure of that.''

It wasn't until he'd said the words that Trey realized how much he meant it; his voice must have given away more of his feelings than he'd intended, because Linn gave him an odd look.

It was strange how life worked, he found himself musing. You could be going along minding your own business, pretty much doing what you wanted to do and thinking you were happy, and then up would pop a woman with eyes like deep water and a smile that could melt a man's heart where he stood, and suddenly you realized that what you'd thought was happiness was just acceptance.

And maybe habit, too. Sometimes you just got so deeply into your comfortable little rut that you didn't even see it *was* a rut until something came along to jar you out of it.

Nathan stirred in his sleep suddenly, muttering something, and Trey shook off his meandering thoughts. Linn got up and walked across to the boy and Trey, setting the glass aside, did the same. He looked down at the sleeping child and smiled. "Poor kid's had a rough day."

He looked at Linn then, reaching out to brush a tendril of dark hair from her cheek. She was very pale and delicate shadows lay under her eyes like bruises. "So have you. You look beat."

She nodded, smiling wanly. "I am."

He smiled and bent down to scoop Nathan into his arms. "Come on. I think it's time I put both of you to bed."

It was one of those innocent statements so loaded with possibilities that it practically gave off sparks. And Trey knew, by the thoughtful glance she gave him, that Linn was as aware of the underlying tension that had been between them all day as he was. But he forced himself to ignore the growing temptation to simply take her into his arms and kiss her with all the pent-up passion of a man closer to the edge of his self-control than he'd like to admit, and walked toward the stairs leading to the upstairs bedrooms.

Linn followed him wordlessly up the stairs and to the small spare room where he'd taken Nathan's things. She turned down the covers and Trey slipped the sleeping child gently into the bed, watching her as she tugged the boy's sweater and jeans off, then tucked the covers under his chin.

"You do that like a natural," he said quietly. "You and Jack didn't have children?"

She shook her head. "We thought we'd have plenty of time." She looked up at him, smiling wryly. "You always figure bad things happen to other people, and that your life is going to unfold exactly to plan. Jack owned a small local newspaper, and our dream was to run it together—we did, too, for a couple of years. That's how I met him, as a matter of fact, when he hired me as his assistant editor." She gave a soft laugh. "Although on a paper that size, an assistant editor does everything from proofing advertising copy to making coffee."

Her face was warm with memories. "We figured we had forever to do all the things we wanted to do together—having children, building our own home, buying a sailboat and touring the seven seas."

"Then he got sick."

She nodded, her expression pensive. "We didn't think it was anything serious at first. Even when the first test results came in, we didn't really believe them—you never do. But soon it became obvious that Jack was seriously ill and wasn't going to be able to continue working. He wanted to sell the paper, but I flatly refused. Somehow, in my mind, the paper had become the symbol for Jack's survival—if we kept the paper going, he'd *have* to get better. But if we sold it, it was as though we were giving up." She looked up at him again. "Silly games. Sometimes games are all you have left."

"But they didn't work," Trey said softly.

"I tried to hold on to him and that damned paper for two and a half years, and in the end I lost both of them." She was silent for a moment, gazing down at Nathan. "I kept the paper until three months ago. Then I realized one day that it just didn't have the same magic without Jack, and that I was just trying to cling to something that didn't even exist. So I sold it and the house we'd bought, and was trying to figure out what I wanted to do with the rest of my life when this business with Santos came up. I've been on the run ever since."

She gave herself a sudden shake, as though casting off the memories, and smiled at Nathan, smoothing a handful of hair off his forehead. "I learned one thing, though—don't wait for the things you really want. I've always regretted not having Jack's child. It would have been something, at least. As it is, all I have left of him are the memories."

"Most people don't even have that," he said almost absently. He tried sometimes to remember what Diane had looked like, feeling a jab of guilt when he failed. In fact he couldn't even remember what it had felt like to be married. Maybe he'd never really known.

He found himself gazing at Linn, marveling over the kind of love it must have taken to get her through those two and a half years of caring for, loving, a dying man. It was the kind of love that came along once in a lifetime. If a man was very, very lucky.

"I'm sorry about all of this, by the way."

Trey blinked, finding Linn still sitting on the edge of the bed, looking up at him. "For?"

"For everything," she said with a rueful laugh. "I ruined your entire day, for a start. I hope you didn't have anything planned for tonight."

"I didn't."

"And," she added with a deep sigh, "I'm sorry for turning your home into a Gypsy camp, and for getting your dog hurt, and for...oh, hell, just for all of it." Wearily she combed her hair back with both hands. "You had a nice, peaceful life here until I turned up. You're supposed to be recuperating. And finishing your book. And instead you're running around rescuing me—not to mention getting my locks changed, hiring people to keep an eye on me when you can't, playing surrogate father and big brother combined to Nathan."

"Peace and quiet are overrated," he said carelessly. "Trey Hollister, man of action, that's me."

She smiled, as though knowing damned well that he was lying through his teeth, and got to her feet. "Well, Trey Hollister, man of action," she said softly, "I'll never be able to thank you for it."

"If I were an unscrupulous cad," he murmured, reaching for her, "I'd play on that guilt for all I was worth and get a kiss out of it. Maybe even two...."

She stepped into the circle of his arms as though she'd been waiting for his touch all day. "What's a little unscrupulousness between friends?" she whispered, lips already parting.

Her mouth was like peaches and cream, and kissing her was like coming home. It was a welcoming, unhurried kiss, relaxed and deep and rich with sensuous memories. A manwoman kiss, filled with everything they'd been and everything they still could be, as evocative as a glance across a room, as filled with undemanding promise as a smile.

She drew her mouth from his at last and slipped her arms around his waist with a small, contented sigh, relaxing against him as though it was the most natural place in the world for her to be.

Which it was, Trey realized idly. She fitted into his arms and into his life with sublime perfection. It had been strange, seeing her there in the shadows and angles and familiar patterns of his home today. Normally he would have found the intrusion jarring, even irritating, and yet there had been a curious rightness to it that he hadn't even questioned.

He tightened his arms around her and rested his cheek on her hair, breathing in the perfume of her. "I've been wanting to do this all day," he murmured.

"And I was hoping you would," she whispered back, nestled against his chest. "This has gotten much more complicated than it was supposed to, hasn't it."

"Complicated can be nice." He ran his hands down the long sweep of her back. "You feel real good here, lady. As though you belong."

"It's strange, but I know what you mean. There was a long time after Jack died when I couldn't stand having a man even touch me, let alone kiss me. I never dreamed I'd ever be normal and happy again. That I'd ever want a man to make love to me. Yet the other night, making love with you was the most natural, comfortable thing in the world.

As though we'd known each other forever instead of a few days."

"Right place, right time," he murmured.

"Right man," she whispered, her arms tightening around him. Then, before Trey could even fully take in what she'd said, she eased herself out of his arms and looked up at him, smiling wearily. "And thank you for *this*, too," she said quietly, nodding toward the connecting door that led to the other spare room where he had taken her suitcases. "I'll admit that when you first brought me over here, I was uncharitably suspicious about your intentions. But I... well, I appreciate the fact you didn't just *presume....*"

"You've been through a hell of a lot," Trey said quietly. "It might be pushy, but I'd like to think I'm not completely obnoxious." Then suddenly he had to grin. "But I'd be a damned liar if I told you I hadn't thought about it." Linn's mouth curved up at the corners with a responding smile and Trey reached out and stroked her hair back from her face, letting his palm cradle her cheek. "In fact, I think about it a lot. That day on the beach with you and Nathan. Then later, that night, making love to you for what seemed like hours...."

Her eyes had widened slightly, so deeply blue now that they seemed almost black in the dim light coming from the hall, and she turned her face and kissed his palm. "So do I," she admitted softly, her gaze locked with his. "All the time."

Trey drew in a deep, careful breath. "This... could get even more complicated," he warned her in a ragged voice.

"I know," she whispered.

He eased the breath out between his teeth. "My room's down at the end of the corridor, on the right. But I want you to be sure, Linn. I don't want you having any doubts about it in the morning, hating me for making it too easy."

"I know," she whispered again.

Trey nodded, holding her gaze, then he turned and walked to the door. "I'm going to have one last look around." He glanced around at her. "And Linn... I'll understand if you decide not to. You have to be sure, sweetheart. You have to be comfortable with it. I want to make love to you so badly

I ache with it, but I want you in my bed because you *want* to be there, not because you think you owe me something or because you think I expect it. We're both too old for those kinds of games.''

She smiled gently, her eyes glowing in the shadowed light. ''But if I were to be there when you came back ... you wouldn't kick me out or anything, would you?''

''What do you think?''

His voice was just a husky, evocative purr that made Linn melt right to her toes. His eyes locked with hers for a heart-beat of time, then he slipped through the open door and into the shadows beyond and was gone.

Linn suddenly realized she was holding her breath. She eased it out shakily and adjusted the blanket around Na-than's shoulders again, her heart giving a leap as the bed-room door swung inward on silent hinges. But it was just Murphy, limping heavily and moving with infinite care as he made his way slowly across the room. He made an attempt to jump onto the bed before Linn could stop him and fell back with a yelp of pain. Whimpering, he rested his chin on the edge of the bed and looked up at Linn, his tail giving a couple of half-hearted thumps on the floor.

''Murph, you don't have to do this,'' Linn told him softly, her eyes prickling suddenly as she realized he'd made his slow, painful way up the stairs just to be with Nathan. ''He'll be fine, I promise.''

Murphy barked softly, staring at her intently, and she had to laugh. ''No, I am *not* going to help you up onto the bed! If you have to get down during the night, you'll rip those stitches out. But I'll settle on a compromise.'' She gathered up the spare blanket lying on a nearby chair and spread it on the floor beside the bed, making it into a rough nest. ''How's that?''

Murphy eased himself onto the blanket, turning around a couple of times before settling down with a quiet whim-per. He reached out and ran his tongue across Linn's hand and she smiled at him, scratching between his big, bat-wing ears. ''You're as big a sucker for damsels in distress as your owner,'' she told him quietly. ''And you're both too damned heroic for your own good!''

Chapter 10

Trey's bedroom was exactly as Linn had imagined it.

It was a large room, spacious and airy and uncluttered. There was a sitting area at the near end with a fieldstone fireplace, thick rugs and a love seat and matching easy chair of tan leather, worn as supple and soft as velvet. The big built-in bookcases flanking the fireplace were stuffed with hundreds of volumes, and the walls were covered with Indian carvings and paintings.

Like the man who owned it, the room was uncompromisingly masculine. Yet there was a richness there, a complexity of interests that gave away more about his personality than he probably would have been comfortable with.

Maybe that was why he never brought anyone here, she found herself thinking. Because of the fear of giving away too much, the possibility of someone catching a glimpse of the real man behind the armored facade.

Two wide pine steps led to the sunken bedroom, and Linn walked down them slowly. The fawn carpeting was rich and deep-piled, the furniture heavy and solid, the ceiling open-beamed and peaked. The big bed was angled to capture the incredible view of the beach and restless ocean provided by the wall-to-wall windows across the far end.

The en suite bathroom was as spacious and well-appointed as the bedroom, with a multitude of skylights and mirrors and plants. A sunken whirlpool tub stood at one end with twin marble sinks and a huge, freestanding shower enclosure of smoked glass that captured Linn's attention at once.

She rummaged through a couple of cupboards until she found Trey's cache of spare towels, then quickly stripped and, after fiddling with the faucets until they relinquished a deluge of steaming water, stepped under it with a sigh of utter pleasure.

She hadn't realized just how much the day had taken out of her until then. Exhaustion rolled through her in leaden waves and she simply stood under the pounding water and let the heat relax the taut muscles across her shoulders and neck, feeling the aftereffects of terror slowly wash away.

It wasn't until she turned the water off and stepped out of the shower, wrapped in thick towels and wreaths of steam, that she realized Trey had been there. The untidy pile of clothing she'd kicked to one side was gone and in its place was a plush terry robe that she wrapped around herself gratefully.

A small gesture, Linn mused. Yet exactly the kind of thoughtfulness she'd come to expect. Still toweling her hair dry, she smiled and stepped into the bedroom.

Trey was standing by the windows, leaning lazily against the wall and staring out across the moonlit water. He glanced around as she came out of the bathroom and his mouth lifted in a slow, warm smile as his eyes caught hers, held them. "That's nice."

Linn walked across to him and slipped effortlessly into the curve of his outstretched arm. He drew her close and she relaxed against him comfortably. "What's nice?"

"Having you here." He slid his other arm around her and cradled her against him. "Just standing here, listening to the shower and knowing you were in there. Knowing you'd be coming out soon and I could touch you again." He nuzzled her wet hair, lightly kissing the side of her throat. "Knowing I'd be kissing you again. Making love to you again."

Linn laughed quietly and kissed his cheek. "Breaking all your own rules, aren't you, cowboy?" she teased gently. "I thought you made love to your women on *their* turf instead of bringing them up here."

He drew back and looked down at her so quizzically that Linn had to laugh again. "Toomey was filling me in the other day. He made a point of advising me that you didn't like houseguests."

"Toomey talks too much," he said with a scowl. "I suppose he gave you the whole ten yards, did he? The women, the affairs, the private jet, the group gropes in Cannes, the—"

"I think he overlooked those last two," Linn said with mock seriousness. "Group gropes?" She raised an eyebrow.

Trey gave a snort. "Toomey's grasp of reality sometimes slips a cog or two. He's got this fantasy that a writer's life is all hard liquor and fast women, and he doesn't let a little thing like the truth get in the way of a good story." He smiled at her, his eyes as warm as melted silver. "If I indulged in half the mischief he likes to think I do, I'd have died of exhaustion long ago."

Linn reached up to brush a cowlick of dark hair off his forehead. "You don't owe me any explanations, Trey. I'm hardly naïve. Or so insecure I need you to tell me I'm the first and only."

His own mouth curved slightly in response. "Not the first, maybe. But very definitely the only." His smile faded and he gazed down at her, eyes caught with what could have been wistfulness. "It's been a long time for me, too, Linn," he said very softly. "Longer than a man likes to admit. I could give you a hundred high-sounding excuses, but the truth is it's been a long while since I met a woman who makes me feel like baying at the moon. Who makes me feel even close to how you make me feel."

His mouth was on hers, warm and questing, and as she opened herself to his deep, drugging kiss, Linn's firm resolve not to fall too heavily under Trey Hollister's formidable spell all but vanished. She'd made up her mind when she'd come in here tonight that what she wanted—what they both wanted—was a simple and loving affair, uncomplicated by promises or dreams of tomorrow. Tonight—tonight was all that mattered.

And yet as his arms tightened around her, she found herself thinking of what it would be like to spend the rest of her life with this man. Of what it would be like to fall in love and marry again and have all the things this time around that she and Jack had been cheated of. Children. Growing old together. Sharing all the things that can be shared by two people so much in love that it hurt just to imagine it.

"Ohh, honey—I've gotta go." Giving a laughing groan, Trey gave her one last fierce kiss, then eased himself away from her. He rubbed his chin, fingers rasping on a late-day growth of beard. "I've got to get rid of this, for a start, or you'll never forgive me." He grinned at her, his eyes teasing, yet wary, too. "You're not going to get cold feet or something while I'm in the shower, are you? I'd hate like hell to come back and find you'd gone."

Linn reached up to outline his lower lip with the tip of her finger. "I'll be here," she whispered. "Waiting...."

He groaned again, obviously torn between going and staying. But in the end he did go, and Linn, still smiling to herself, walked to the big bed. She tossed the robe aside and slipped between the cool sheets, stretching languorously, loving the feel of the cool sheets against her naked skin. Trey's sheets. Touching her where Trey would be touching her. Caressing her breasts and thighs and belly and...

She shivered in anticipation, her body responding to even the memory of their lovemaking so vibrantly that it made her catch her breath. She could remember with distinct, wondrous clarity the instant he'd brought their two bodies together that first time, that moment of cleaving and acceptance, of taking and surrender.

It had astonished her how easily her body had accepted him, anticipating some last-minute doubt, if not actually discomfort, after all that time. But there had been none. It had been like the first time all over: the anticipation, the complete trust, the certainty of how right it was.

And the . . . love?

Now don't go start making things more complicated than they already are, she warned herself fiercely. She had a million things to worry about right now without tossing love into the equation: getting Nathan safely back to Kath and Rod after the trial, figuring out where she was going to live now that she'd sold the house, deciding what she was going to do with her life. She was at a crossroads, with possibilities and options running in all directions, and the last thing she needed was a major distraction while she was trying to make up her mind. And face it, she reminded herself with a smile, Trey Hollister could become a major distraction.

She was still thinking about that a few minutes later when she happened to turn her head and saw the photograph. It was sitting unobtrusively on the bedside table, just a small oval frame holding the snapshot of a child. A little boy, Linn decided, with wide blue eyes, a shock of black, curly hair and a slightly uncertain expression, as though he was trying to decide whether to laugh or burst into tears.

She rolled onto her side and picked it up curiously. It took her a moment or two to realize that the picture had been cut down from a larger one and that in the original, the boy had not been alone. All that remained of that mysterious other person now was a slender hand cupping the child's shoulder. A feminine hand, Linn couldn't help noticing, complete with wedding band.

A shadow fell across her just then. She glanced up and found Trey standing beside the bed, naked but for the towel draped loosely around his hips. He was looking down at the photograph, his expression a curious blend of anger and pain, and after a moment he reached out and took it from her.

"I didn't mean to snoop," Linn said quietly, "but I happened to see it there and—"

Trey shook his head. "It's all right. I don't know why I keep it there, to tell you the truth." He sat on the edge of the bed and rested his elbows on his knees, holding the picture in both hands and staring at it in thoughtful silence.

He kept his expression carefully blank, yet Linn could sense more than actually see weary despair. Sadness. Regret. She put her hand on his shower-damp shoulder and started kneading it gently. "He looks like you."

He looked at her blankly for a moment, then gave his head a shake as though dispelling the past and smiled very faintly. "He should," he said softly. "He's my son." Then his eyes turned bleak and he looked back at the photograph. "Or . . . was."

Linn felt a chill go through her. "Was?" she asked softly.

"He was born during my first tour in 'Nam. A few months after this picture was taken, my wife—ex-wife—decided that I wasn't the kind of man she wanted to spend her life with. Or the kind of man she wanted helping raise her son. So she took him when she left me, and I haven't seen him since."

"Oh, God," Linn whispered, feeling half sick. "Trey . . . I—I don't even know what to say! How could she just take him away from you? I mean, how could a mother do something like that?"

Trey's expression was haunted in the soft glow of the lamp as he gazed at the picture in his hands. "I can't blame her. Hell, maybe I'd have done the same thing. We got married three months before I shipped out to 'Nam, and when I got back a year later, she . . . well, I'd changed." A muscle in his cheek pulsed and Linn tightened her grip.

"We both had. I was in the marines when I married Diane, and she used to say it was the uniform that had won her over. That it was the uniform she'd really married, and had just taken me as part of the deal." He smiled fleetingly. "When I came back from that first tour, she was wearing love beads and granny dresses and talking about peace marches. She'd let her hair grow halfway down her back and went around with flowers painted on her cheeks, and she had a couple of doped-up, spaced-out hippies camping in the damned basement.

"I'd heard about all the antiwar demonstrations and everything while I was in country, but hell, it didn't make much sense. But I hadn't been home ten minutes when I got my first taste of it. A friend of Diane's came over—I swear he had hair longer than hers—and to say he and I didn't hit it off would be the understatement of the century." He gave a snort of rueful laughter. "He called me a baby-killer and I called him a long-haired freak, and things kind of deteriorated from there. I wound up punching him through the front window, with Diane screaming and crying and the two basement hippies waving incense sticks at me and chanting mantras."

He gave his head a wondering shake. "How I ever got out of there without killing the lot, I'll never know. But I did. I stayed with a buddy of mine that night, and by morning I'd cooled off enough to go back and talk with Diane. But she wasn't in a talking mood. She was packing and waiting for her friend when I got there. I tried to stop her, but it was...well, there was just no point, I saw that quickly enough. The last straw came when she told me she'd legally changed Craig's name to Rainbow SunChild, that she was moving to a commune and that if I ever tried to contact her *or* Craig, she'd have me arrested. She didn't want—as she put it—a baby-killer being anywhere near *her* child."

"Oh, Trey," Linn whispered, "I don't know whether to laugh or cry!"

He gave her a lopsided grin. "Neither did I at first. So I did the only thing I knew how to do—re-upped for a second tour, and went back to fighting Vietcong."

"But when you got home finally, didn't you—?"

"No." His voice was rough and he stared down at the picture cradled between his two sun-browned hands. "I wasn't in great shape when I got back," he said softly. "I spent about ten months in a VA hospital, getting rid of the shakes and the cold sweats and the nightmares, learning how to handle real life again. I'd been wounded just before my tour was up and had some trouble getting off the drugs they were giving me for the pain. Then after I got off that, I had some trouble with liquor...."

He was silent for a long moment, then gave his head a shake and looked at her. "By the time I got myself back together, I realized I'd all but forgotten how to be a husband, let alone a father. I tracked Diane down and discovered that I was divorced. I didn't even remember signing the papers. That was the kind of shape I'd been in." He managed a fleeting smile.

"And . . . your son?"

"Diane had met someone—her pediatrician, as a matter of fact." That fleeting smile brushed his mouth again. "His wife had died and left him with a couple of kids, and he and Diane found they had something in common and started seeing one another. One thing led to another and they fell in love. She'd held off marrying him until she'd talked to me about it—she didn't owe me a damned thing, but she...well, she'd grown up a lot by that time, too."

He was silent for a moment. Thoughtful. "I met Ken—oddly enough, we hit it off all right—and we talked about Craig. Ken wanted to adopt him, but only if I was happy with the decision. Diane had been given uncontested custody, considering the shape I'd been when we were divorced, but they were willing to give me partial custody or visiting rights or whatever I wanted." He stared again at the photograph, caressing the frame with his thumb. "But hell, I wasn't in any shape to take on fathering, even part-time. Ken could provide the two of them the stable kind of life I'd never had—the kind I figured she and the kid needed and deserved. I didn't want my son growing up in a torn-apart family like I had. So I let him go...."

The admission was torn from him, and the pain in his eyes and voice was raw. He drew in a deep, careful breath. "It was better that way—for all of us. Diane said that when he turned eighteen she'd tell him about me, about what happened, and that if he wanted to track me down it would be all right with her. I said I'd leave the decision up to her. And him. And I have."

"So he could turn up one day. Wanting to know all about his father." Linn smiled and ran her fingers through his hair. "When he does, he's going to find he's very lucky to have you in his life, Trey Hollister. You're an incredible man...."

"I abandoned him," he said softly, his voice raw.

"No. You loved him." Linn kissed his shoulder and slipped her arms around him, holding him tightly. "No son would ever mistake what you did for him as anything but love, Trey." Reaching out, she took the photograph gently from his fingers. She laid it on the table and then leaned across and snapped the light off, leaving them in pale, moonlit darkness.

"Make love to me, Trey," she whispered, drawing him around and into her arms. "Let's leave the past back there where it belongs and take tonight for us."

The tide had come in.

Trey stood in the darkness, staring down at the moon-silvered water, seeing and yet not seeing the huge breakers crashing onto the beach. He drew deeply on his cigarette and blew the smoke out slowly, watching it spiral upward. So much for good intentions. He'd sworn he wasn't going to have another.

But then he'd also sworn he wasn't going to let himself get involved with his raven-haired, blue-eyed neighbor.

He smiled in spite of himself and looked toward the bed. She was sound asleep, hair pooled around her face and shoulders, the sweet curve of one dark-tipped breast limned by moonlight.

Involved, hell. He was halfway to being in love with her.

He took another drag on the cigarette, eyes narrowing against the smoke as he blew it out in a thin stream, and thought of what she'd told him about her husband.

Two and a half years! She'd loved a dying man for longer than he and Diane had even been married.

What would it be like, being loved like that?

Linn stirred in her sleep, murmuring something, and he watched the moonlight play across her breasts and flat stomach and felt his own stomach tighten a little in response. Could she ever love *him* like that?

Or maybe the question was, could he ever let her?

He ground his cigarette out in a nearby ashtray and padded back to the bed, covering her lightly with the sheet, then easing himself under it, trying not to wake her. She murmured again and turned toward him and he cradled her against him.

It had been different tonight. There had been passion and excitement and even moments of abandon, but their lovemaking had been sweeter than their first time together, gentler. She'd reached out to him and had enfolded him in such tenderness and caring that it had started unraveling a tightness within him he hadn't even been aware of. It had been a healing kind of love, a filling kind of love, and for a while, lost within the sweetness of her, he'd felt whole for the first time in his life.

And now?

What happens now, Hollister? he asked himself, staring past Linn's shoulder into the darkness. What the hell happens now?

"What happens now?" Linn shoveled a half dozen sizzling slices of bacon onto the plate in her hand, added two eggs and toast, and handed it to Joe. "I can't just hole up here forever."

"Why not?" Trey accepted the next plate and gave her a very warm, very private smile.

Linn's heart gave a foolish little leap that she pointedly ignored; she walked to the big kitchen table with her own breakfast. Nathan, sitting between Trey and Joe, with Murphy at his side, was munching happily on a piece of toast, and Linn frowned. Everyone seemed ridiculously congenial this morning.

"I don't know how you two can just sit here as though everything's normal!" She stabbed a slice of bacon with her fork. "Santos knows I'm here. God knows what he's going to try next."

"Relax," Trey told her calmly. "We know what we're doing. Trust me. And we've contacted the Canadian authorities. They'll be on the lookout for Santos's men at the border."

"I got across without anyone knowing it," she reminded him pointedly. She nibbled on the bacon, distracted and restless. "I've got to call Kath this morning. She'll be half out of her mind, knowing I didn't check in last night."

Both Trey and Joe looked at her sharply. "What do you mean, 'check in'?" Trey asked. "I thought you didn't know where your sister and her husband were."

Linn looked at him. "I don't. Rod's partner is acting as go-between, so we're always in touch with each other in case... well, in case something happens. Rod gave me a special phone number, and every day I call about midnight their time and leave a message, saying I'm all right."

Trey was looking at her intently. "And how do they get in touch with you if they have to?"

Linn glanced at Joe, then back to Trey. "I leave a phone number where I can be reached."

Trey swore under his breath, trading a look with Joe.

"No, you're wrong," Linn put in quickly, realizing what they were thinking. "Only Don Rasky has access to that information. And he wouldn't sell out. They're partners!"

Trey's eyes were hard in the morning light. "Anybody can be bought if enough money's involved."

"Partners don't sell each other out."

"Maybe not, but there's a leak somewhere. Didn't you say that Santos's men have followed your every move?"

Linn nodded grudgingly. "I knew the phone calls were risky," she admitted softly, "but I didn't know what else to do. You don't really think...?"

"I don't know, but we're not taking any more chances. And you're not calling *anyone*, got it? I'll handle it from here on in."

"But—" Linn bit off the rest of her protest as Trey's eyes met hers, as intractable as gray stone. Arguing with him was pointless. He was as bad as her father when he had his mind made up about something. And the irritating part was that they were usually both right.

"Well, I'm going to turn in." Joe swallowed the rest of his coffee as he was getting to his feet, sparing Linn a smile. "That was delicious, Mrs. Stevens."

He gave Nathan a friendly pat on the shoulder as he walked by, moving wearily toward the spare bedroom at the back of the house. Linn watched him for a moment, then looked at Trey. "He was up all night, wasn't he?"

"I spelled him off for a couple of hours," he replied calmly, his mouth tipping in a lazy smile. "You mean you didn't even notice I was gone? That's great for a man's ego."

"I would have slept through an earthquake. And trust me, Hollister—your ego has nothing to worry about."

"Glad to hear it." His eyes glinted with devilry. He finished his own coffee as he shoved back his chair and got to his feet. "Well, I've got a book to write, among other things. Do you want a hand with the dishes?"

Linn shook her head. "It'll keep me busy for a few minutes. There isn't anything else you want done, is there? I'm going to go nuts sitting around here with nothing to do."

"I can think of two or three things I'd like done," he murmured, slipping his arm around her waist and planting a lingering kiss on the side of her throat. "But they'll have to wait until tonight, after somebody's in bed." He glanced meaningfully in Nathan's direction. "Unless I can get Joe to take him for a walk later this afternoon."

Linn gave a throaty laugh. "Your mind just never quits working out all the angles, does it?"

"Nope." He patted her bottom lovingly. "Especially when you've got such *great* angles." His eyes held hers for a long moment, then he put his other arm around her and drew her gently against him, suddenly serious. "I sure do like having you around, lady. And I don't mean just at night, although I'm not complaining about that, either. But it feels good having you here with me, Linn. Damned good."

"It feels good being here," Linn told him softly.

The skin around Trey's eyes tightened slightly. "Don't tell me I might just be in the right place at the right time for a change," he said carelessly, his voice at odds with the sudden seriousness in his eyes. "That would be a first."

Linn felt her heart give an erratic leap. What did he want her to say? That—as impossible as it was—she'd defied all the odds and had fallen in love with him? Or did he simply want her laughing reassurance that she wasn't getting serious at all, and that his precious independence wasn't being threatened?

"I think," she finally said, very carefully, "that the only person who knows the answer to that is you."

His eyes held hers intently. "What would you like it to be, Linn?"

She stared up at him, her mouth suddenly dry. "Trey, what are we talking about here? What—just what are you asking me?"

He went very still, his eyes still locked with hers, and she could feel a sudden tension running through him, as though he were fighting some great inner battle. Then abruptly he uttered a snort of laughter and released her, turning away. "You serious about wanting something to do?"

Linn drew in a deep breath, her gaze following Trey as he strolled across the room to put his plate and cup into the sink. Fight it, damn you, she told him silently. One of these days, Trey Hollister, you're going to discover that admitting you care for someone doesn't hurt a bit! But all she said aloud was, "Yes. What did you have in mind?"

He poured himself another cup of coffee and turned to look at her, his expression carefully noncommittal. "You told me you have a good background in editing and proofreading."

"That's right." Her voice was a little more controlled than it needed to be, and Linn took another calming breath.

"How would you like to take a run through the first eight or nine chapters of this book I'm working on? Ordinarily I do it myself, but I'm really bucking the deadline on this one and I could use the help. And I wouldn't mind someone going over it with a critical eye and pointing out some of the rougher spots—the writing's pretty erratic. I've had a lot of interruptions, between this damned leg acting up and...other things."

"Other things being me," she said with a smile. "I'd love to go through it, but are you sure you want me to? I spent nearly six years editing and proofing a little backwoods newspaper, Trey, and before that I worked with technical books. Fiction, especially men's action-adventure, is a whole different thing."

"I might be on a tight deadline, but I'm not masochistic enough to let someone mess around with my work if I didn't have confidence in them. You've read most of my books, you seem to have a good understanding of Steele and what makes him tick. Maybe a little *too* good at times," he added with a fleeting smile. "And I trust you. It's that simple."

"With an endorsement like that, how could I refuse? When do we start?"

"How about right now?"

Chapter 11

The next two days dragged on interminably.

It seemed inconceivable, but Linn discovered it was possible to be happy, scared and mind-numbingly bored, all more or less at the same time.

The tension was the worst: knowing that Santos's men were out there somewhere, knowing that sooner or later they'd make their move. Every noise made her jump; every time Joe or Trey were gone for longer than fifteen minutes she was certain they'd been ambushed and killed. She found herself wandering aimlessly from window to window, not even realizing what she was doing until Trey would point out, none too patiently, that she was wearing ruts in his hardwood floors and would she for God's sake *sit down*!

Both men seemed unfazed by either the odds that Santos's men could appear at any moment, or by the fact that they were all prisoners to some degree. Trey spent most of his time at his computer, banging out page after page of *Steele on Ice*, and Joe spent the greater part of his waking hours playing endless games of solitaire with a dog-eared deck of cards that went everywhere he did.

To Trey's credit, he seemed to understand what she was going through and tried his best to keep her occupied. He kept coming up with an endless array of things she could do for him: filing, writing out checks for a stack of bills, taking care of updating his business accounts, sorting through seven months of unfiled receipts for his income tax records.

And making love, Linn reminded herself with a secret smile. That was one distraction he took very special pains with.

In fact, it was their nights together that made this whole nightmare tolerable. They'd slip upstairs after Nathan was in bed and Joe had discreetly withdrawn and lie in the dark for hours, making love and talking and laughing and making love again. They even managed to escape a couple of times during the day when Joe, with a knowing wink in Trey's direction, had taken Nathan down to the beach to run off some excess energy.

It seemed impossible, but every time Linn was convinced that it couldn't get any better, it did. Trey was an incredibly skilled, patient and attentive lover, releasing a passion within her she had literally never dreamed she'd ever experience again. It was a part of her nature she'd never even known about until she'd married Jack. And after his death—before, actually—she'd simply closed it off, finding it too painful to remember what they'd once shared physically while watching him waste away a bit at a time, until all that remained was the shell of the vital and passionate Jack Stevens she'd married.

It had stayed closed off. Until now. Until Trey had found the key and given her back the magic of being able to love again.

If only he could find that key for himself, she found herself thinking idly. If only he could just let himself believe in that magic, believe that it *could* be his.

She tossed aside the manuscript pages she'd been proofreading and stretched, yawning and glancing at her watch.

Five minutes later than when she'd looked at it the last time. At this rate, the afternoon was never going to end.

She looked at the pages scattered across the sofa beside her: chapters fourteen and fifteen of what was turning out to be a superb book. Different from his others in a way, although that could simply be her perception of it, based on the way she felt about its creator. But it seemed somehow to be a gentler book, without the bitter edges his earlier ones had. Even Steele was different.

Trey was letting more of his hero come out, for one thing. Tidbits of information about Steele's past that explained so many things, the occasional bit of insightful dialogue that provided clues to a complex and interesting man. Steele seemed to be a little less arrogant, a bit more open to the possibility that he might not know all the answers. His methods were still as brutally matter-of-fact and unorthodox as ever, but this time around he was experiencing some guilt, some doubt. And, just maybe, even some love.

Linn smiled, fingering through the pages until she found the one she wanted.

He watched her walk to the door, feeling something tight and hot spill through his chest. He didn't want to lose her.

For a moment he toyed with telling her what she wanted to hear. What the hell would it matter if he meant it or not? It would keep her here. Telling her he loved her would keep her here.

But for how long? Until she read the lie in his eyes one day and simply turned and walked away? What the hell did a man do then? Invent another lie, then another? When did the lying ever end, once it started?

And if it wasn't a lie? If he really did love her? Would that make it any more certain that she'd stay?

Hell, there were no guarantees. There were never guarantees.

She paused at the car and looked back. He could see the tears on her cheeks, even through the rain. And the tightness, the heat in his chest, pulled even tighter.

Just tell her, you idiot, Linn advised him impatiently. She tossed the page down and got to her feet, shaking her head at Steele's inability to recognize the real thing, even when it was right in front of him.

She walked into the kitchen and poured herself a glass of orange juice, leaning against the counter as she drank it and staring out the big window above the sink. Poe was perched in a half-dead pine and broke into raucous cawing when he saw her. She leaned across and unlocked the window, pushing it open for him. He swooped down and landed on the wide sill, then gave another caw and hopped over to sit on the faucet, tipping his head and eyeing her impatiently until she reached over and turned the water on for him. The moment it started to trickle into the sink he went crazy with delight, screeching and bobbing up and down, trying to catch the stream in his huge beak.

"You're a cheap date, Poe," Linn told him as he finally settled down to drink his fill. His blue-black feathers glistened like coal in the sunlight and she ran her fingers down his back, marveling at the size and strength of him. He murmured with pleasure, then hopped into the sink and proceeded to have a bath, flinging water in all directions as he shook his wings out.

"Hey! That's enough of that!" Linn reached across and turned the water off, whipping her hand back as Poe took a spiteful peck at it. He uttered a loud, angry caw and took off with a strong downbeat of his wings, spraying her with water.

"Keep it up, bird," she called after him, "and you'll be trussed, stuffed and roasted by suppertime!" Swearing under her breath, she mopped herself dry, then picked up her glass of orange juice again.

"You and Poe having a disagreement?"

Trey's quiet voice startled her so badly that Linn's heart very nearly stopped on the spot. The glass went flying out of her hand and hit the edge of the sink, spraying both her and the counter with orange juice, but she just stood there for a moment, eyes closed, trying to collect her scattered wits.

"Relax, Linn," Trey drawled, starting to wipe up the spilled juice. "It's just me."

"Damn it," she whispered through clenched teeth, "will you *stop* sneaking up on me like that! Can't you clear your throat or cough or wear creaky shoes like normal people?"

"Maybe you should just lighten up a bit," he growled. "I told you no one's going to get in here."

Heartbeat still erratic, Linn snatched the cloth from his hand and started blotting orange juice off her sweatshirt. "I know, I know. It's just that this waiting is going to drive me crazy!" She flung the cloth into the sink and leaned back against the counter, taking a deep breath as she combed her hair back with both hands.

Then she sighed and looked at Trey. "I've spent half my damn life waiting and I hate it. Waiting for Dad to come home safe every night—they say that being married to a cop is rough, but it's no joke being a cop's kid, either. After Kath married Rod, it was the same thing—waiting for her to call to say he's been shot or killed or has just gone out on one of his undercover jobs and disappeared. Waiting for Jack to get better, then after the final diagnosis came in, waiting for him to die. Then going through the same thing— the same waiting—with Mother."

"Maybe you just worry too much," Trey told her calmly.

Linn glared at him angrily, then, in spite of herself, had to laugh. "That's what Dad says. He calls me the Official Family Worrier—says it takes the pressure off him because I do enough of it for everyone."

"You and your dad are pretty special to each other, aren't you?" Trey's voice was quiet.

Linn nodded, smiling. "Yeah. A father's bonding with his firstborn and all that. He adores Kath, of course, but they've got more of an ordinary father-daughter relationship. He used to buy her pretty dresses and tease her about boys and stuff like that, but they were never as close as he and I are."

She looked at Trey. "Dad's always treated me like a . . . a friend, I guess. I was still very much his daughter—I had to toe the line and do as I was told, and heaven *help* me if I stayed out too late. But we've always spent a lot of time together, talking about...oh, just things. Politics, religion, the state of the world. And more personal things, too. If I had a problem with a boy, for instance, it was always my dad I went to for advice. I always figured he knew just about everything there was to know.''

Trey smiled faintly, staring out the window at the wind-teased pines, and Linn put her hand on her shoulder, rubbing it gently. "It must have been rough, growing up with no one," she said softly. "I can't even imagine what it would be like, not having someone there you can count on to love you, no matter what. Not having someone to share good news with, or someone who'll comfort you when things get bad.''

She drew her hand down his arm, smoothing the dark hairs on the back of his wrist. "I don't think I'd have made it through those two and a half years with Jack if I hadn't had Mom and Dad and Kathy. There were some nights when all I could do was cry, and Dad used to hold me for hours and hours, not saying anything because he knew words wouldn't help. But just *being* there.''

"You're an incredible woman, Linn Stevens," Trey murmured, slipping his arms around her and cradling her against him. He rested his chin on the top of her head and she felt more than heard him sigh. "I don't know how you did it, either," he said half to himself. "Where you ever got the strength...."

"I loved him," she said simply. "When you love someone, it isn't hard at all—because there are no questions, no decisions, no doubts. It's just all there.''

"I guess I wouldn't know about that," he said almost roughly. Then he shrugged carelessly, smiling. "But you don't miss what you've never had.''

"But your wife loved you once," Linn said softly. There was something in his eyes, his face, that tore at her. "And you must have loved her—enough to marry her. To have a son with her.''

His eyes hardened slightly. "I might have loved her once—or thought I did, anyway. Maybe I was just looking for someone to hold in the night, I don't know. But whatever it was, it didn't last." His eyes met hers, bleak and cool. "It doesn't come with guarantees."

"You're starting to sound like Steele," she teased, thinking to herself that it was probably the other way around. "Life doesn't come with guarantees," she added more seriously. "No one's standing there the day you're born, promising satisfaction or your money back. You take what you're given, and you do the best you can with it. And it's the same thing with love. It's a rare and a precious gift, having someone love you and loving them back. It doesn't come with guarantees, you're right. But if you really want it, you have to simply trust and jump right in. It's only when you stop holding back for fear of being hurt and just open yourself to everything it can be, that it *will* work."

"The ultimate act of faith?" he asked with a faint smile.

"That's right," Linn said softly. "No reservations, no keeping back little bits of yourself, no dipping your toe in the water—it's all or it's nothing."

"Seems to me like a hell of a risk. No smart person jumps into unknown water without checking out the bottom first."

"That's just the point—there is no bottom. Love is as deep as you need it to be. As deep as you want to make it."

He was staring down at her, his eyes troubled, his face pensive. Then he gave a snort and stepped away, reaching for the carton of orange juice. "You're getting too metaphysical for me, sweetheart. Maybe the kind of work I do for a living makes me a little more skeptical—or a little more realistic. But I like to know where the hell I'm going to land before I jump." He lifted the carton and took a deep swallow of juice.

Linn gazed at him, feeling a kind of weary despair drift through her. What was the point? He'd closed himself off too well, had locked the door and tossed away the key, and odds were he was never going to find the way out. She had thought—had hoped—that if he'd just open enough to let her slip through the barricades around his heart she could start the healing process. He needed to accept love before he could give it, but she was beginning to think that maybe he was too far gone even for that.

"What do you think so far?"

She shook off her brooding thoughts. "About what?"

He looked at her with mild impatience. "*Steele on Ice.*"

"I think it's great. Probably your best yet."

His eyes narrowed very slightly. "But?"

"But what?"

"You tell me. There was a distinct *but* in your voice."

Linn glanced at him, tempted to shrug it off. But then she decided to toss caution to the wind. "Okay, you're right. I do have a problem with the end of chapter fourteen, when Steele's lady—and that's something else. Why doesn't she have a name?"

He shrugged. "I liked the idea of this beautiful woman coming into Steele's life and then leaving, and him never knowing her name. So he can't even track her down if he wants to."

Linn looked at him with growing exasperation. "Honestly, you think of everything, don't you! Everything to keep Steele from having to make a choice, that is. Or a commitment. Kill them, leave them or lose them—is that *your* philosophy about women as well as Steele's?"

A look of irritation flickered across Trey's handsome face. "That's the way life works sometimes," he said gruffly. "You said you were having a problem with something in chapter fourteen?"

"A continuation of the same problem. Why does Steele let her go? My God, the man's hopelessly in love with her! Why doesn't he just come out and tell her?"

Trey's eyes held hers for a long, taut moment. "Maybe he just doesn't know how," he said in a soft, rough voice. "Not everybody does, Linn."

"All you have to do is say the words," she replied very quietly. "That's all it takes, Trey—just the words." And with that, she turned and walked back into the living room, knowing that if she didn't leave now, she was going to say something she'd undoubtedly regret. Like *I love you*, for instance. Just to prove how easy it was.

But it wasn't easy at all. Not loving someone who couldn't love you back, anyway.

All *you* have to say...? Trey stared out the window above the sink again, feeling restless and suddenly on edge. Now just what the hell had she meant by that? He took another swallow of the orange juice, not really tasting it. If either of them was having trouble spitting out what they wanted to say, it was her. He'd left it wide open that morning, had stood there *willing* her to say she wanted to stay here with him, that she figured they had a chance together.

But she hadn't. Those sapphire eyes had held his almost accusingly and she'd turned it right around on him, side-stepping the issue as though it didn't even exist.

Damn it, what did she want from him? Sure, he could tell her he loved her if that was what she wanted. But why mess up a good relationship with a lot of words that could some-day come back to haunt them? Words didn't mean a damn thing. Feelings did. Those feelings he experienced every time he looked at her, every time he touched her, every time they made love. The feelings he'd had just that morning when they'd turned to each other in the faint light of dawn and he'd eased himself into her slippery warmth and they'd lain there wrapped around each other.

He'd moved gently, almost freeing himself and then pressing deeply, slowly inside her again, watching her face as that familiar, elusive tension built within her. And he'd sensed a corresponding tension within himself pull sud-denly so tight that he'd thought he might explode. It hadn't been simple sexual tension—that was building, too—but something else, deeper and more profound. And it was still there. Even now, just thinking about her, he could still feel it. A deep, aching *want* unlike anything he'd ever experi-enced. A want so great that he felt torn and shaken apart by it.

He had that to give her. So why were the damned words so important?

He took another swallow of the orange juice, then folded the top of the carton and put it back into the fridge. Words were just—things. He used them every day, was familiar, comfortable with them. He knew their powers and limita-tions.

And he knew only too well the kinds of trouble they could get a man into if he wasn't careful. Words like *love* and *forever*, for instance. Love was something that only hap-

pened to other people, and forever didn't exist. Just more
lies.

Murphy came into the kitchen, hobbling along on three
legs, his ears drooping, tail lifeless. He limped over to his
dishes and started lapping up water, and Trey smiled.

"We make a hell of a pair, Murph. You'd think we'd be
smart enough to keep ourselves out of trouble by now."

Murphy glanced up at him, managing a single waft of his
tail, then turned and limped back into the living room.

They made love that night, as they had each night that
she'd been there, but this time it was different. It was
good—Linn couldn't imagine it being anything but good
with Trey—but there was something subtly wrong. Trey
seemed slightly preoccupied, for one thing, and although he
was certainly there physically for her, she kept having the
feeling that something was weighing on his mind.

For her part, Linn had to admit that she kept thinking
about Steele and his beautiful lover. The lady with no name.
The lady who had captured her man's heart but not the man
himself. Like the chameleon that would shed its tail to avoid
capture, Steele would rather shed his very heart than give in
to love.

She lay in Trey's arms afterward, still brooding about it.
If he noticed, he didn't mention it, appearing lost in his own
faraway thoughts, and after a long while Linn drifted into
sleep.

She didn't know what it was that wakened her. The moon
was up, and the room was filled with a ghostly silver light
that made everything look eerie and unfamiliar.

Trey was gone. It didn't alarm her at first, because he
often got up during the night to check the house or spell Joe
for a few minutes. But then she heard Murphy's deep-
chested bay of rage and, almost lost in the barking, the distant but unmistakable sound of a gunshot.

She was out of bed and into her jeans and sweatshirt in an
instant, and down the corridor and into Nathan's bedroom
in the next. He was there, awake but groggy, and looked up
at her grumpily as she burst through the door.

"Get up, Nathan," she ordered, already tossing the blankets back. "Come on, honey, hurry!"

He gave a sleepy mumble or two of protest, his voice inching toward a whine, and Linn reached down and lifted him bodily onto the floor, giving him a firm shake. "Nathan! Wake up!"

It was her voice more than her actions that got through to him finally. The sleep vanished from his eyes and was replaced by fear. "What's the matter? How come we're gettin' up?"

"Come on—quick!" She took him by the hand and started back toward Trey's big bedroom. "There's someone downstairs."

Murphy was barking almost hysterically now, and she could hear the sound of running footsteps, a shout, another gunshot, nearer this time.

"The bad men after my daddy?" Nathan broke into a trot, his voice wavering. "The men who bumped our car into the ditch?"

"I don't know," she replied tightly, casting a quick glance behind them. "Quick, in here!"

She ran across to Trey's huge walk-in closet and wrenched the double doors open. There was a big cedar blanket box sitting against the back wall, half hidden under jackets and hiking boots and sweaters. She pulled everything off it, then opened the box and started emptying it. "Nathan, I want you to get in this box and *keep quiet*! I'll toss some of this stuff back over it, and I don't want you to move until I come back up here and get you, understand?"

Nathan peered fearfully into the box, and in the single shaft of moonlight coming through the closet door she could see his chin wobble. "I'll snuffocate!"

"You're not going to suffocate," she told him gently, trying to calm him even as she neared panic herself. Murphy's ferocious baying was reaching a crescendo, and there was the sudden crash of breaking glass. "The lid's not that heavy—you can lift it easily from the inside. And I'll prop it open a bit." She urged him forward. "Nathan, get in! I don't have time to argue!"

He gave her one last frightened look, then obediently clambered into the big box and huddled down, and the last thing she saw as she lowered the lid was his pale, terrified face. She propped the lid open a scant half inch with a paperback copy of *Steele Gambit* she found lying on a nearby shelf. Then she tossed a couple of armloads of the discarded blankets and clothing back over the box, praying no one would think to root through the clutter to open it.

Praying no one got this far.

There were more running footsteps downstairs, another shot, then another, both right outside. What should she do? she wondered frantically. Stay there in the moonlight and darkness and wait? Phone the police? Or grab the revolver out of Trey's night table and go down and help?

She wet her lips, taking only a moment to decide before diving across the bed. He'd shown her the gun their first night together, as well as where he kept the extra clip and shells, and had told her it would be there if she ever needed it.

To her relief, it was. She checked it swiftly, then pulled back the bolt to put a shell in the chamber. It gave an evil snick and she shivered slightly, making certain the safety was on, then grabbed the extra clip and tucked it into her pocket.

She hated guns. But hate them or not, she knew how to use them. Her father had spent countless hours teaching her how to handle just about any handgun and rifle on the market, badgering her to improve her accuracy and competence until they'd often wound up in shouting matches. But tonight, as she walked swiftly down the corridor toward the stairs, she whispered a silent prayer to the stubborn Irish cop who'd made certain his daughter could take care of herself in a tight spot.

Because they didn't get much tighter.

She tiptoed halfway down the open stairs, then stopped, listening intently for any sound that would give her a clue as to what was happening. But there was nothing. Even Murphy had fallen silent, although she thought she heard the quick, predatory click of clawed paws on hardwood somewhere in the darkness.

Not even breathing, she eased herself down the rest of the steps, the revolver braced firmly. She swallowed as she reached the bottom, pausing to get her bearings, then she started moving silently toward the back of the house. Trey... where was Trey!

Linn didn't even know what happened next. There was a gunshot—outside, by the sound of it, but very close—then a slim shadow shot by her, so close she could have touched it if she'd had any warning. It vanished toward the corridor leading to the back bedrooms before she could even swing the gun around, and she stepped forward just as another shadow hurtled out of the darkness and as she scrambled after it, another shadowy form came charging toward her.

Her hand closed on the gun and she swung around just as the shadow paused, breathing heavily. Now Linn could see his face. "Trey!"

He whirled, crouching and bringing the gun in his own hands swinging toward her. "Linn?" His voice was a whisper of astonishment and shock. "What the *hell* are you—?"

"Nathan! *Nathan!*"

It was a woman's voice, coming from the back of the house, and Linn went rigid with shock.

Trey straightened with an oath. "Stay down," he hissed. "Murphy!"

The dog surged to his feet with a roar just as the woman called again, her voice rising in panic and desperation. Linn screamed "No!" just as Murphy took a leap toward the shadow that had suddenly appeared in front of them. She caught the big dog by the scruff of his neck and somehow managed to wrench him to the floor.

"Trey, don't fire! Stop, Trey, for the love of God! It's Kathy! It's my sister!"

Chapter 12

There was a split second of stunned silence, then Trey was bellowing at Murphy to get back and someone else—Joe, by the sound of it—was shouting something from the kitchen.

"Linn?" It was a small, shocked voice, and the shadow stepped forward tentatively. "Is it really you?"

Trey snarled something and moved forward, wrenching the small figure into the moonlight. It was Kathy, all right, scared to death, her eyes and mouth dark circles in her small, pale face.

"What are you doing here!" Linn's voice was rough with shock. "Where's Rod? What's happened?"

"H-he's outside," her sister stammered, "S-somebody started shooting and—"

"Is anybody else out there?" Trey snapped.

"N-no." Kathy's voice wavered and she stared up at Trey in wide-eyed fear, trying to pry his fingers from her wrist. "Linn? W-who is this man?"

"Trey!" Now it was Linn's turn to move, her heart pounding. "Rod and Joe are out there shooting at each other."

Trey dropped Kathy's wrist and headed for the door with an oath. He glared at Linn. "You keep her the *hell* inside, got it?" Then he was gone at a sprint, the gun in his hand gleaming wickedly.

"I knew we should have just gone to the police!" Kathy exclaimed with a sob. "I knew we shouldn't have tried to do it by ourselves."

"Kathy, what in God's *name* are you doing, sneaking around like this!" Linn's own voice was unsteady. She groped for one of the small tables and switched on the lamp. "It's a miracle you didn't get shot! My God, I could have killed you myself!"

Two large tears trickled down Kathy's cheeks. "We didn't know what else to do! You'd disappeared, and th-then this man called and said he was holding you and Nathan and—" She swallowed a sob, shivering so badly that her teeth were chattering. "W-we knew it was probably a trap, but—"

There was a shout outside and another, then the kitchen door flew open with a crash. Someone snarled an oath and someone else started shouting; then three voices were lifted in a cacophony of threats and angry cries that was followed by the distinct thud of a fist meeting solid flesh. More crashes, this time of someone falling. Then finally, only the sound of heavy breathing and a few muttered curses.

Rod appeared first, stumbling heavily into the room as though he'd been given a ferocious shove from behind. He was cradling his bloody mouth and chin, and his dark, handsome face was livid with fury. Joe came in next, looking rumpled and out of breath, and Trey brought up the rear, flexing the bloodied knuckles of his right hand as he stalked into the lamplight, his eyes narrowed and glittering. There was a scrape along the side of his jaw, which was already discolored and slightly swollen, and he was probing his lower lip with his tongue.

"Are you all right?" Rod walked across to Kathy and put a protective arm around her shoulders. She nodded mutely and he looked at Linn, his face haggard and gaunt. "What about you? They haven't hurt you, have they? And is Nathan okay? Is he here with you?"

"Yes." Linn managed a rough laugh, giddy with relief at seeing the two of them alive and unhurt. "And he's fine. We're both fine!" She took two steps and embraced Kathy fiercely. "My God, I'm so glad to see you! And I'm sorry for shouting at you, Kath, but you scared me half to death! If I hadn't grabbed Murphy he would have—" She didn't even let herself finish the thought, giving Kathy another fierce hug instead. "I can't believe it's really you. Both of you!"

Relief had eased some of the harsh lines in Rod's dark face and he enfolded Linn in a smothering embrace. "Thank God you're all right. We've been going crazy with worry for the past week."

Linn hugged the two of them tightly, half laughing and half crying with happiness. "How on earth did you find me? What are you doing here? And why are you sneaking around in the dark like two burglars?"

"That," Trey growled from behind them, "is a damned good question. Valencia, what's going on here?"

"That should be obvious," Rod snapped, his eyes narrowing dangerously. He eased himself away from Linn and Kathy and put himself solidly between them and Trey. "It's me Santos wants, not my family. Let them go and we can talk a deal. But hurt one hair on the head of anyone in this family, and I swear I'll get you. Even dead, I'll get you. There'll be a Valencia on your trail before I'm cold, and they'll follow you to hell itself."

"You've got the wrong man, Valencia," Trey replied in the same chill tone. "I don't work for Santos."

"No?" Rod stared at Trey with hostility. "Then just who the hell *do* you work for? Why are you holding my son and sister-in-law here?"

"Rod," Linn said quietly, "Trey's been helping me. And Nathan and I aren't being held here against our will—we're both here very willingly, in fact."

Rod gave her a hard look, clearly skeptical, and Linn smiled and stepped around him, moving to stand beside Trey. "This is Trey Hollister—and if it hadn't been for Trey, Santos would probably have Nathan right now and I'd be dead. He's been protecting us, Rod. And that's Joe Cippino, a business associate of Trey's.''

Rod gave a snort. "Hired thug, you mean. What business are you *in*, Hollister? As though I can't guess. You've got trouble written all over you. And I swear if you've laid a hand on Linn, I'll—''

"Why, you—!" Trey stepped forward on the balls of his feet, fists clenched.

For a fraction of a second Linn thought the two men were going to take each other on there and then. They stood eye to eye, faces hard with anger, and she readied herself to intervene.

"Mommy?" The small, tremulous voice made all four of them swing around. Nathan was standing on the stairs, still in his pajamas, scrubbing at his tear-stained face with his fist.

"Nathan!" Kathy catapulted across the room and scooped the boy up in her arms, and in that instant the tension in the room subsided.

Rod strode to his wife and son and wrapped his arms tightly around them. Linn eased out her breath between her teeth and suddenly realized that if she didn't sit down, her knees were going to give way. She walked to the stairs and sat down harder than she'd intended to, feeling numb.

Trey raked his hair with his fingers, then tucked his gun into the waistband of his jeans, shaking his head wearily as he walked toward her. "What the devil are you doing with that?"

Linn looked down stupidly and discovered she had pulled the revolver out again and was holding it. "I... mmm...thought you might need help.''

Trey swore and reached down to take it from her. "It didn't occur to you that Joe and I might have things under control, did it? That you just *might* be safer staying upstairs with the boy?''

"Don't you shout at my sister!" Kathy gave Trey a furious look. "And why did you hit my husband?''

"I'm *not* shouting at your sister," Trey bellowed, "and I hit your husband, lady, because he was trying to kill me!"

"Hey, buddy, that's my wife you're talking to, not some—"

"*Stop it!*" Linn's voice brought instant, startled silence. Taking a deep breath, she stood up and held out both hands. "Just stop it, all of you! Rod, Kathy... Trey is not a hoodlum or gangster, and in fact he's saved my life a couple of times over the past few days. And he's the one you should be thanking for keeping Nathan safe, not me. And Trey, my sister and her husband have been through hell for the last month, and neither of them are acting rationally. So would you all please just calm down, because you're giving me a *headache*!"

Rod glared at Trey and a taut silence crackled between them. Then he mumbled something that could have been an apology, casting a hostile glance in Joe's direction. Trey mumbled something back, and the two of them eyed each other like strange tomcats, bristling with anger and belligerence and too much adrenaline. Finally Rod shoved out his hand and Trey, after a tense moment or two, grudgingly accepted it.

"I think you have my gun," Rod said with precision.

Trey stared at him for a moment longer and then, even more grudgingly, took Rod's service revolver from the waistband of his jeans and handed it to the other man. "RCMP know you're packing this, Valencia? They take gun control seriously up here."

"*Detective* Valencia," Rod snapped, taking the gun and spinning the barrel, checking it before slipping it into the shoulder holster under his leather jacket. "And I have a carry permit." He looked evenly at Trey. "And you still haven't told me who the hell you are. This place is rigged with more alarms and booby traps than Fort Knox. You're either into something that makes you very nervous, Hollister, or you're one unfriendly son of a—"

"Oh, for crying out loud," Linn interrupted, "It's what he *does*, Rod—security, antiterrorism, specialized alarm systems. Would you both just lighten up?"

"So y-you haven't been kidnapped or anything?" Kathy was still kneeling on the floor, cradling a sleepy Nathan against her shoulder. "We thought—"

"Of course I haven't been kidnapped," Linn said impatiently. She was still shaken, remembering how close she'd come to firing at that slender, elusive shadow that had bolted by her in the darkness. "Do I look kidnapped?"

Kathy glanced at Rod. "I told you we were panicking for nothing. I knew she was all right. Daddy's always said Linn would make a better cop than most men on the force."

Rod snorted, looking at Linn with a faint, wry smile. "It's not that I doubted you could take care of yourself in a tight spot, Linn—hell, you've got three generations of Irish cop in you. But when you just disappeared like that, with no word in three days, we...well, we just assumed the worst."

"And then we heard from some man—" Kathy spared Trey a suspicious glance "—saying you were with him now."

"And you thought it was Santos."

"Of course we thought it was Santos." Kathy shot Trey another hostile glance. "He said the only way we could contact you was through him."

"And you traced the phone number to here," Trey said mildly.

"Eventually." Rod looked at Trey. "You're damned good, Hollister, I'll say that for you. It took every resource I had, legal and otherwise, to track you down."

Trey just smiled.

"So you two came charging up here to rescue me," Linn said in disbelief. "Even though it could have been a trap."

"Rod said we couldn't risk wasting time with paperwork."

"Miami vice cops can't come up here to Canada and start operating as though they're on home turf," Rod explained calmly. "Coming up in an official capacity meant notifying the local authorities, and that would have meant bringing people in at a federal level. The whole thing would have turned into an international incident. And while the bureaucrats were arguing over who had jurisdiction to what, you and Nathan could have been murdered or...God knows what."

"So you decided to cut a few corners and free-lance." The corner of Trey's mouth tipped up with the barest hint of humor. "I like your style, Valencia. I think you're crazy, but

I like your style. If you ever decide to leave Vice, let's talk. I may have a job for you.''

"And speaking of crazy, Kath," Linn said in exasperation, "just what were you doing tearing around here in the dark? I can understand Rod breaking in to look around, but—"

"That's a damned good question," Rod put in. "What *were* you doing up here? I thought I told you to stay in the car and radio for help if I got into trouble."

"I heard shooting," Kathy whispered, hugging Nathan a little tighter. "I couldn't just wait there, not knowing what was happening. I had to find Nathan. I *had* to."

Rod's expression turned grim. "I'd expect a lunatic stunt like that from Linn," he muttered. "That's why I agreed to this entire plan in the first place, because I knew she could handle herself in a rough spot. But, damn it, I expected *you* to know better!"

"Three of the four people I love the most in this world were in this house," Kathy said with conviction, her eyes daring anyone to argue. "I was not going to just sit out there doing nothing when for all I knew, you, Linn and my baby were fighting for your lives in here. You're *family*. And—"

"—family takes care of family," Rod completed with a smile. His eyes were warm as he gazed down at her. "You know," he added softly, kneeling beside her, "there's maybe one woman in a thousand who'd be willing to stick with her man through what I've put you through these past couple of years. Who'd support him in every decision, even when it meant risking her life and the life of their child. I'll never know how the hell I got so lucky, Kath . . . but I love you all the more for it."

Kathy smiled up at him, and Trey felt something tighten in his gut. Her face held the same radiance that Linn's had that first night when she'd walked in and seen him wearing Jack's old shirt. That expression, he knew now, was simple love.

Simple? Trey snorted quietly. There was nothing simple about either of these women—or the love they had for their men. It was the kind of love a man could build a life on, knowing the foundation was strong, the girders unbreakable. The kind of love that could go through hell itself and come out stronger.

The kind of love, he found himself brooding, that a man only dreamed of finding....

He shook the thought off roughly, like a dog shaking off water, and turned to look at Joe. "Everything secure out there?"

"Shipshape." Joe nodded toward Rod and Kathy, his eyes faintly troubled. "What are we going to do with them?"

"Damned if I know," Trey breathed, shaking his head. Linn had moved to stand by her sister and as she and Kathy embraced, with Nathan between them, Rod slipped his arms around the three of them and hugged them tightly.

Family taking care of family. It was a tight little group, strong and self-sufficient, fortified against the world. He looked at Linn's dark head and found himself wondering where he fitted into the equation now. If, in fact, he fitted there at all.

He rubbed the back of his neck wearily, feeling at loose ends for some reason. There didn't seem to be a hell of a lot left for him to do, but in spite of that he felt oddly reluctant to just wrap it up and call it quits. It somehow didn't feel...finished. As though there were still things that needed resolving, bits here and there that needed nailing down.

"So how do things stand now, Valencia?" The three of them were still in a tight little knot that seemed to exclude him and the rest of the world, and Trey felt a jab of irritation. "What's your plan?"

Valencia lifted his head slowly, as though almost too exhausted to make the effort. "Plan?" His voice was hoarse.

"Plan," Trey repeated impatiently. "You *did* come up here with a plan, didn't you?"

Valencia's mouth twisted with a wry smile. "I never thought that far ahead, Hollister. Plans are for people with a future—I've just been living day to day, making it up as I go along." Trey swore quietly and Rod's face darkened. "Don't you worry about me. I'm doing fine."

"I'm not worried about you," Trey replied flatly. "I'm worried about the three people depending on you. You're so tired you're practically sleepwalking, and your wife's out on her feet. I didn't risk my neck keeping Linn and your kid alive just to have you fall asleep at the wheel and put your car over a cliff.''

"I've been tired before. And I can still do whatever I have to do to keep my family safe, you can count on it."

"For how long?" Trey asked bluntly. "The shape you're in, you may as well just turn yourself over to Santos and save him the chase. You need help, Valencia. And you need it bad."

Rod gave an exhausted snort. "Yours, I suppose."

"That's right." Trey looked at him evenly. "I do this kind of thing for a living. And I'm damned good at it."

To Trey's relief—and admiration—Rod didn't refuse outright. He looked at Trey for a long while, as though weighing all the options, and Trey's grudging respect for the man took another leap. It wasn't everyone who could accept help when it was offered, even when it could mean the difference between life and death. Especially when his family was looking on.

But maybe in the end it was concern for his family that made him nod warily. "What did you have in mind?"

"You're safe here—safer than out there on your own, anyway. I've got spare beds and plenty of firepower, and I've already alerted the RCMP to what's going down. They've got extra men out, and a special watch set up on the border for any of Santos's people. If anything starts, they'll know about it."

Rod's eyes narrowed. "We're under Canadian jurisdiction up here. How do we know they'll cooperate?" Trey simply smiled, and Rod eyed him with renewed speculation. "Someday I'd like to hear just what it is exactly that you do, Hollister."

"Does that mean you're staying?" Trey asked blandly.

Rod stared at him for a moment longer, then finally nodded, combing his hair back with his fingers. "As long as you know what you're letting yourself in for. Odds are that Santos already knows I'm up here—he seems to know what I'm doing even before I know it myself. If he does, he's going to be coming in here with everything he's got. And these boys play rough—even with the government crackdown on the Colombian drug cartel, they have enough manpower and arms to outfit an army.''

"I have a few resources of my own," Trey told him calmly.

"I should call Don—Don Rasky, my partner. Let him know where we—"

"No," Trey said flatly. "No calls."

"Now wait just a—"

"If you stay here, Valencia, you do it my way, got that? No calls in, no trips out. As far as anyone out there knows, you've just fallen off the edge of the world."

Rod started to get that look on his face that Linn recognized only too well, and she stepped smoothly between the two men. "Rod, the man knows what he's doing. Trust him. Trust *me*."

Rod glared over her head at Trey, but he subsided after a moment or two, easing his breath between his teeth. "No calls."

"How long's it been since you had any sleep?" Trey asked calmly.

"A couple of days."

"Three," Kathy said quietly, her own face gray with exhaustion.

"Then why don't you catch a little shut-eye? We'll all be looking at things more calmly with a bit of rest under our belts."

Linn looked at Trey, her eyes warm with gratitude, and he felt his breathing catch in that odd little way it always did when she looked at him like that. It suddenly occurred to him that their sleeping arrangements might lead to more speculation than she'd be comfortable with and was just going to suggest that he'd take the living room sofa so Kathy and Rod could have his room when Linn said, "I'll put them in the room off Nathan's. That bed isn't being used."

Her eyes held his for a meaningful heartbeat, making his grand gesture a little superfluous, and he found himself smiling to himself at how easy she made it. He watched as she led Kathy and Nathan up the stairs, then looked at Rod. "Before you turn in, I want to know everything you know about Santos—right down to how he thinks. And then I want to beef up our perimeter alarms and—'' He stopped dead, frowning. ''Which reminds me—how did your wife get in here, anyway?''

Rod snorted. ''Don't ask me, man! As far as I knew, she was waiting in the car, about half a mile up the road.''

Kathy paused halfway up the stairs. ''The kitchen window was unlatched. I just pulled it open and wriggled through.''

''And nearly got yourself shot,'' Linn said disapprovingly.

''But I latched that window myself,'' Trey protested.

Linn winced. ''I . . . mmm . . . that was my fault. I opened it to let Poe in, then forgot to lock it.''

''I need a drink,'' Trey said wearily, rubbing his eyes. ''Or a cigarette. Anyone got a cigarette?''

''Who *is* that man?'' Kathy muttered as she followed Linn upstairs and down the corridor to Nathan's bedroom. ''He just walks in and takes over, as though the whole universe runs on his say-so.''

''Parts of it, anyway,'' Linn said with a smile. ''Okay, Nathan—back to bed.''

Nathan clambered onto the bed agreeably, yawning. ''Mommy, are we going home soon?''

Kathy smiled at her son as she tucked the blanket around his shoulders. ''Soon, honey,'' she said softly. ''We're all going to stay here for a few days first, though. Daddy has some . . . some business to take care of, then we're going home.''

''Is he gonna kill Santos?'' he asked sleepily.

Kathy traded a grim glance with Linn. ''I hope not,'' she told him quietly. ''Killing is never an answer, Nathan. Even when it's someone like Santos.''

''But Daddy's killed bad men before,'' he murmured, already half-asleep. ''I heard him say so.''

''Yes, he has,'' Kathy said after a moment, frowning as she reached out to stroke Nathan's cheek. ''But it's not something he ever *wants* to do, Nathan. It just happens that way sometimes. If he has a choice, he'll arrest Santos and take him to jail.''

"Trey'll help him," he whispered, eyes sliding closed. "Trey an' Murph will help Daddy. And Santos won't ever hurt anybody again...."

Kathy stood up slowly, gazing down at her sleeping son. "My God, what's this doing to him? What's it doing to all of us?"

"Come on," Linn said gently, steering Kathy into the adjoining bedroom. "Don't worry about Nathan—he's handling things just fine. Aside from a couple of bad scares, it's been one long adventure to him. But right now it's *you* I'm worried about."

"I don't know how to thank you for keeping him safe," Kathy whispered, sudden tears welling in her eyes. "I knew you would, but I was so scared. And these last two days have been—'' She shook her head, swallowing a sob.

Linn gave her a comforting hug. "It's all right now, Kathy. You're safe. Trey and Joe know what they're doing."

"I've never met anyone b-bossier," Kathy said through a sob. "Is he really as good as he says?"

"Better," Linn told her reassuringly. She pulled back the comforter and sheet on the big bed and plumped up the pillows, then started rummaging through her suitcase. "I'll give you one of my nighties, and I want you to get into bed and sleep the clock around. You look as though you haven't slept for a week."

"I haven't," Kathy said with a damp laugh, wiping her eyes with her sleeve. "We've both been catnapping in the car, mostly. I don't know how Rod's managed to stay on his feet."

"Well, you can sleep as long as you want now," Linn told her. "With Trey watching over you, we've got nothing to worry about."

"You sound as though you almost like him," Kathy muttered accusingly.

Linn smiled to herself. "I do," she said very quietly, not looking at her sister. *A lot,* she added silently. *In fact, more than a lot....* She found the nightie she was looking for, shook the wrinkles out of it and handed it to Kathy. "The bathroom is across the hall. Do you want shampoo or anything?''

Kathy shook her head, frowning as she looked around the room. "These are all your things in here, Linn. Rod and I can't take your room—where are you going to sleep?"

"I ... mmm ... haven't been sleeping in here," Linn admitted quietly. To her amazement, she felt a blush pour across her cheeks.

Kathy looked at her for a puzzled moment, then her eyes widened. "Oh, my God!" Her eyes widened even more and she sucked in an astonished breath. "You're not—!"

Linn had to smile at Kathy's expression. "'Fraid so."

"Linn!" Kathy looked so sincerely shocked that Linn nearly laughed aloud. "Linn, you can't be serious! Are you telling me that you and...and that...that *man* are—?" She stammered to a stop as though unable to even bring herself to say it aloud.

"I'm a big girl," Linn reminded her dryly. "These things *do* happen."

"Well, I know," Kathy said, still sounding shocked, "but not to you! I mean, in the four years since Jack died I don't think you've even dated more than once or twice. And I certainly never thought you were ... well, doing *that*."

"I wasn't," Linn said calmly. "Don't play the prude with me, Kath. I used to cover for you when you stayed over at Rod's before you were married, remember?"

"That was different," Kathy protested. "We were engaged!"

"You and Richard Cordston weren't engaged," Linn reminded her pointedly. "I used to tell Dad you were staying with Mildred Jones, remember? If he'd ever found out the truth, he'd have killed both of us. Not to mention what he'd have done to Richard."

"That wasn't the same thing and you know it," Kathy said tartly. "Richard and I had been dating for nearly two *years* before we slept together, and besides that, we'd known each other forever. You've barely even met this man. How long have you known him? A week? Two?"

"It seems like I've known him all my life," Linn said quietly. Then she sighed and sat on the edge of the bed.

"Don't give me a hard time on this, Kath, please. I'm as surprised as you are, to tell the truth. I was afraid that—well, after Jack died, all those feelings died, too. I was beginning to think I'd never be...normal again. Then I met Trey, and one thing led to another, and suddenly all those feelings were back...."

She shrugged, not looking at her sister. "Jack was the only man I ever loved, Kath. And that part of the love—the physical part—was wonderful. But it ended long before he died, and I guess I never thought it could ever be as wonderful again. But I've discovered that it can be. Trey's made me feel like a woman again. Alive and happy and...whole." Finally she looked up, meeting Kathy's gaze evenly. "I'm sorry if this has upset you, but I'm not going to apologize for it. And I'm not going to sneak around behind your back, pretending nothing is going on. You're my sister and I love you, but this isn't any of your business."

Kathy was silent for a moment, her eyes searching Linn's. Then she smiled ruefully and sat down beside her. "You're right," she said very softly. "And I'm sorry. I didn't mean to sound like a disapproving mother—heaven knows, I've spent enough time trying to convince you to go out and start living again. It just caught me by surprise. I mean, with all that's been going on, the last thing I figured you'd have time for was...well, finding a man."

Linn had to laugh. "I'm still a little shocked at myself, to be honest. Or at least at how easy it was. I always thought I'd be racked by guilt, feeling unfaithful to Jack and everything, but when things got to...well, to that point, it was the most natural thing in the world. In fact, I swear I can feel Jack's approval. This sounds absolutely crazy, but I just know Jack would tell me it's okay if he could. I know he'd approve of Trey, too."

Kathy nodded thoughtfully. "He reminds me of Jack a little. Not his looks or the way he talks or anything, but there's a bit of Jack in the way he takes control of things." Then she gave a soft laugh. "Mind you, there's a lot of Jack in *Rod*."

"And a lot of Dad in all three of them," Linn added with a mischievous grin. "You don't suppose there's something

Freudian going on here, do you? Daughters falling in love
with their fathers and all that heavy-duty psychological
stuff?''

Kathy laughed again. "I always thought it was just that
we're cowards—just to avoid the fireworks if we brought
someone home who didn't meet his standards." She glanced
at Linn, looking as though she was wondering if she should
ask the next question or not. "Are you in love with him,
Linn?" she asked quietly. "I'm not asking as a sister, now.
But as a woman.''

Linn frowned slightly and rubbed at a grass stain on her
denim-covered thigh. "I don't know," she finally said
thoughtfully. "At times I *think* I am. But at other times I
think that it's just the situation that's brought us together.
He's strong and he's protective and I feel safe with him.''
She smiled faintly and looked at Kathy. "I guess women are
always attracted to men who make them feel protected,
aren't they? It probably dates back to prehistoric times when
our lives, and our children's lives, depended on having a
mate who could keep us safe. But it's more complicated today. And I don't know if what I feel for Trey is really love,
or just hormones and genetics.''

Kathy uttered a peal of laughter and hugged Linn tightly.
"There's something to be said for hormones, sister dear.
And I'm darned glad to see yours are working again!''

"What's this about hormones?" Rod stepped through the
door leading from Nathan's room, thoughtfully rubbing one
side of his jaw.

"Linn's hormones," Kathy said blithely, standing up and
reaching for the nightie Linn had tossed onto the bed. "She
and Hollister are sleeping together.''

Linn yelped in protest, but Rod just nodded grimly.
"Yeah, I know.''

Linn felt her jaw drop, but Kathy just looked at him curiously. "How did you find out?''

"Gut instinct," Rod rumbled, still rubbing his jaw. "So
I asked Hollister straight up. He didn't bother denying it.''

"And he hit you?" Kathy looked at her husband with interest.

"No." Rod's dark eyes flashed. "I told him if he did anything to hurt Linn, I'd kill him—and *that's* when he hit me."

"Good grief," Linn muttered. "As glad as I am that you two are safe, I'm beginning to think life would be simpler as an only child!"

Kathy just grinned at her. "You'd better get some ice for Trey's hand—Rod's got a jaw like cement." She stood on tiptoe and planted a lingering kiss on her husband's cheek. "You and Hollister had better learn to play nice. I think she's serious about him."

"Kathy..." Linn started wearily.

"The man hits like a street fighter," Rod rumbled, glowering in Linn's direction. "Don't tell me you're thinking of marrying a man who packs a gun."

"I am not—"

"I married a man who packs a gun," Kathy reminded him sweetly. "And so did our mother. Are you saying Mom and I made bad choices in *our* men?"

"I am going back to bed," Linn said with precision. She strode out the door and down the corridor to the accompaniment of Kathy's soft laughter, feeling her cheeks burning. But in spite of herself, she felt her mouth twitch with a smile. At least the horror of the past three weeks hadn't dimmed Kathy's spirit—or dampened that irrepressible sense of mischief!

Chapter 13

Trey was in the kitchen when Linn walked in, swearing creatively as he fumbled one-handedly with the ice tray. His right fist—still a little tender from connecting with Rolfson's jaw—throbbed like a sore tooth, the knuckles already swelling, and he didn't argue when Linn took the tray from him. Wordlessly she gave it a twist and spilled ice cubes into the bowl sitting on the counter. Then she wrapped his bruised hand gently in a dish towel and eased it into the ice.

Trey gritted his teeth, breath hissing, and Linn looked at him. "Did you break anything?"

"No," he growled. "That damned brother-in-law of yours just has a jawbone like braised steel."

"He doesn't think much of you, either," she replied mildly. "That's the same hand you used to hit Rolfson, isn't it?" When he nodded, she gave him a look of mild exasperation. "If you're going to continue battling for my virtue, Hollister, you'd better think about learning to punch left-handed."

He grunted noncommittally. "He always that protective?"

"Since Jack died." Linn filled the ice tray and slid it into the freezer compartment. "Actually he started playing big brother about the time Jack was diagnosed as being terminal. Part of it's the cop in him, I guess—making sure the people in his precinct are safe. And part of it's just that he's a really nice guy." Linn's mouth curved into a smile. "A little blunt, maybe. But nice."

Trey grunted again, flexing his fingers experimentally. The ice seemed to be numbing some of the pain and would hold the swelling down, but he was going to pay for that rash punch for the next few days. Valencia *had* been blunt. Damned blunt. He'd looked Trey squarely in the eye and had demanded to know what his intentions were, and when Trey had suggested it was none of his business, Valencia had advised him in a cool, matter-of-fact voice that if Linn got hurt—physically *or* emotionally—Trey Hollister was a dead man.

In spite of the pain in his hand, Trey had to smile grimly. It was hard not to respect a man who cut through to the bottom line like that. He shouldn't have been surprised. It made sense that the fierce loyalty and love that Linn felt for her sister and Valencia ran both ways. Like elephants who pull into a tight, defensive circle when one of their own is hurt or threatened.

Did the herd take in strangers? he suddenly found himself wondering as he let his gaze rest on Linn. Or was he forever cursed to remain on the outside, looking in?

He shook off the idle thought, realizing that Linn was looking at him with an oddly thoughtful expression. "I'm going to get a couple hours of shut-eye," he said gruffly, breaking eye contact. He picked up the bowl with his left hand, keeping his right submerged in the ice. "Everything's locked up tight, and Joe has things under control down here."

Linn nodded, not saying anything, and they walked into the living room together. "Is this going to be a problem?" he asked. "The sleeping arrangements, I mean? Because if it is, I can take the sofa down here."

Linn's smile was mischievous. "Rod making you a little nervous?"

His eyes captured Linn's. "It would take a hell of a lot more than an overly protective brother-in-law to scare me off you, lady. But if it's going to make things hard between you and your sister, I can take a cold shower and bunk down here."

"Kathy's not a child anymore," she said simply. "I might have been a little more discreet a few years ago, but there's no need for any of us to be coy at our ages. She knows the situation between you and me, and I think it would upset her more to discover you were sleeping on the sofa." Her smile turned mischievous again as they started up the stairs side by side. "Kathy is, when all's said and done, an incurable romantic. Don't be too surprised if she starts making noises like a prospective sister-in-law."

Trey's stomach gave an odd little wrench and he looked at her quizzically, something in his expression making Linn laugh quietly. "Oh, don't worry," she teased gently, giving him a sultry, sidelong look, "you're not going to wake up face-to-face with the family shotgun."

"That's…good." It occurred to Trey, even as he said the words, that they didn't sound as filled with conviction as they should have. But he was thinking of the expression on Kathy's face tonight as she'd looked up at her husband, that wordless look of unconditional love that held no demands, no expectations.

"They seem to have beat the odds," he said half to himself. As they walked into the bedroom, he realized Linn was looking at him questioningly. "Your sister and Valencia," he explained. "A lot of women wouldn't have put up with having their lives threatened and their families torn apart."

Linn just shrugged. "She loves the guy. And she knew what she was getting into, remember. She grew up watching Mom pace the floor nights, and has watched a lot of Dad's friends go through divorces over the years. Kath might come across as a bit of a scatterbrain, but she's a realist. She went through a lot of soul-searching before she agreed to marry Rod, wanting to be absolutely sure she could deal with the kind of life she'd be letting herself in for. And once she made up her mind to make it work, she learned to deal with the problems as they came up."

Trey looked at her thoughtfully. "Like you learned to handle Jack's illness."

Linn smiled faintly. "I didn't handle it as well as you seem to think I did. One of the reasons I married Jack—I mean other than the fact I was crazy in love with him—was that he wasn't a cop. I'd decided years ago I wasn't going to put myself through that kind of grief. So I married a nice, peaceable newspaperman, thinking the worst I'd have to deal with was a deadline crisis now and again."

She stood by the dressing table, running the brush through her long, thick hair almost absently, her eyes focused on something faraway. Then she gave her head a little shake and looked at Trey. "There was a while at the beginning when I figured fate had really double-crossed me. Then I realized I didn't have a choice—Jack was going to die, and I could either deal with that or run away from it."

"I can't see you running away from anything."

"I was tempted once or twice," she said very softly, staring into the mirror. "But he needed me. I couldn't leave him to deal with it alone." She was silent for a long while, frowning slightly, then took a deep breath and looked at Trey, as though shaking off the past. "Like I said a couple of days ago, love doesn't come with guarantees."

Again Trey just nodded. He sat on the edge of the bed, nursing his throbbing hand, trying to convince himself that the weariness he felt was nothing but the natural result of being up half the night.

"Thank you, by the way."

He looked up just as Linn tucked one foot under herself and sat down beside him. "For what?"

"For helping Rod and Kathy."

He shrugged, easing his hand out of the bowl of melting ice. "Like I told Valencia, this is what I do for a living."

"True." Gently she started unwrapping the cloth from his swollen hand. "But this isn't the same as being hired to help someone. And bringing us all into your home goes above and beyond the call of duty."

"I have to sleep nights," Trey drawled. "Valencia's in no shape to hold off Santos by himself. If I let him take you out of here, I'll just be helping him get you all murdered. I don't particularly want that on my conscience."

But was that the real reason? he found himself wondering grimly, or did it have something to do with the gaping emptiness he felt every time he thought of Linn leaving? She'd be gone for good once he let her go. She'd return to Florida and pick up the scattered threads of her life and he'd never see her again. He wasn't entirely sure he was ready for that yet. For cutting it off so quickly, so cleanly....

"I feel guilty for dragging you into this mess," she said quietly, not looking at him as she examined his scraped knuckles. "It's not fair, getting you involved in my family's problems when the risks are so high. If anything happens to you or Joe because of me, I'll never forgive myself."

"Hey..." Trey tipped up her face so she was looking at him. "I didn't come into this with my eyes closed, lady. I had a hundred opportunities to back out—I stayed with it because I wanted to."

"But—"

She was frowing and Trey smiled, kissing her lightly on the mouth. "But nothing, sweetheart. Call it pride, call it ego—a man likes to think he's needed. And even though you don't need me now that Rod's here, how about letting me hang on to the illusion for a while longer?"

Her gaze moved across his face like the touch of a moth's wing and he could feel the warmth of her breath on his mouth. "I do need you," she whispered, her eyes soft and warm in the golden lamplight.

Trey felt something inside him pull impossibly tight and he lay back against the pillows, tugging her down and across him. Her dark hair spilled over his face like perfumed silk and he heard her sigh as he eased the sweatshirt over her head and caressed the smooth sweep of her bare back with his hands.

"No more than I need you," he whispered, finding her mouth and kissing her deeply, drugging both of them with that sudden, urgent need. Her hands were at the buttons of his shirt, then the zipper of his jeans, and then she was touching him, loving him, her hands and mouth and body enveloping him in magic.

He could hear someone groaning softly and realized it was his own voice as the silk of her tongue sent him swirling to the edge, and he reached up and found her again, naked now, the touch of her skin on his like the kiss of flame.

"I need you more than life itself," he murmured, the words catching as she eased herself down over him, silk on steel, wrapping him in herself. "My God, Linn, I don't know what you're doing to me...."

But there was only a breathing of laughter in the darkness as she started to move, loving him in ways he'd only dreamed of, touching him in ways and places he'd never known existed. She was witch fire and moonlight, surrounding him not just with satiny flesh but with the very essence of herself, sheathing him in an erotic fantasy of need and want and desire.

She took what she hungered for swiftly, deftly and he listened to her soft, tiny cries with pleasure and satisfaction. And then, with a breathless laugh, she started to give and give with a selfless joy, filling him with it, taking him further than he'd ever been before.

There was a moment or two when he instinctively fought it, struggling for control, fearing the consequences should he just let go and let himself be swept away. But then it suddenly didn't matter anymore.

He gave himself over to it with a reckless laugh, trusting in that moment more than he'd ever trusted before. He could hear her whispering his name and could have sworn the sound came from within his own skull, felt the beat of her heart, the rhythmic surge of her blood, the deep flex of muscle as she moved, all within himself. He called out to her and she answered, reached out for her and she was there, not separate, not simply female flesh and sweet laughter in the night but *there*, a part of him like the breath in his lungs, the blood in his veins, soul perfectly meshed with soul.

And then it broke, and breaking, broke again, and he was swept away on a riptide of physical sensation so crystalline it made him cry out. It was a primitive shout that was half conquest and half surrender and as he listened to his own voice, he found himself wondering dazedly if he could ever dare take all this woman had to offer, if he would ever survive the letting go it would demand. But if he didn't, would he ever be able to forgive himself?

"It's nice, isn't it, being one big happy family like this." Kathy helped herself to a slice of crisp bacon and neatly nipped the end off it, chewing thoughtfully. "We've been here four days now and so far Santos hasn't found us, you and I haven't argued even once, and Rod and Trey haven't killed each other yet. All in all, it's worked out better than I'd hoped."

Linn smiled as she started buttering the last slice of toast. Kathy was right: it *was* great having the family together again. Even Trey and Rod had settled down after the first couple of days, managing to be at least civil to one another if not actually friendly. "The problem," she said dryly, "is that they're both used to being in charge."

"That and raw pride. Rod sees himself as protector of the family, and feels his role is being threatened by Trey's relationship with you. And Trey figures that he, not Rod, should be protecting you."

"Nathan seems right at home, anyway." Linn nodded her head toward the far end of the kitchen where Nathan was sprawled on the floor beside Murphy. He was telling the big dog an involved story about a group of space-faring rabbits, and Murphy seemed to be listening intently to every word.

Kathy smiled as she watched her son, then she looked at Linn again. "I think Trey feels left out, if you want the truth."

"Left out?" Linn gave her a skeptical look. "He's pretty much running the show, in case you hadn't noticed."

"Yes, but you and I and Rod and Nathan are a fairly tight little group, and Trey's on the outside looking in."

"By choice," Linn said quietly. But she knew what Kathy meant. She'd sensed it herself at times, noticing how Trey would never join them after supper when she, Rod and Kathy would take their coffee into the living room. How he always managed to be elsewhere when they started playing one of the silly word games they'd invented just to keep boredom at bay. She'd seen him watching sometimes, off in the shadows, his expression carefully closed as he listened to their laughter and comfortable teasing. It was almost as though he was deliberately holding out on them, keeping temptation at bay.

"Are you going to stay up here with him when this is all over?" Kathy asked suddenly.

Linn gave her a startled look. "I don't know. I never really thought about it."

Kathy's gaze held hers. "You'd better *start* thinking about it, Linn. I see the way he looks at you. Especially when you don't know he's watching. Jack used to do the same thing— follow you around with his eyes, as though he just couldn't get enough of you."

Linn frowned slightly, wondering why Kathy's directness made her uncomfortable. Maybe because she didn't *want* to think about leaving. Maybe because, in spite of the ever-present threat of Santos and his people, she was finding it all too comfortable to simply let the days slide by one by one, enjoying Trey's undemanding companionship without having to face the unanswerable questions the relationship posed.

But they were going to have to be faced sooner or later, she reminded herself with an uncharacteristic sense of gloom. She couldn't stay in limbo forever, making no decisions about her life. She'd sold the business, the house, her very future before this nightmare with Santos started, and that was going to have to be dealt with. And that was going to mean dealing with her feelings about Trey and his about her. How they fitted into each other's life and future. More questions than she had answers for at the moment. More questions than she might *ever* have answers to.

Linn shook her head sharply, annoyed to discover she'd been staring out the kitchen window, lost in thought. Kathy was still watching her, her expression speculative, and Linn picked up the plate of cooling toast and shoved it into her sister's hand. "Don't get on my case, Kathy," she said with quiet warning. "I'll live my own life, thank you. You've got one of your own to worry about."

Kathy's mouth tightened and Linn regretted her sharp tone immediately. She had her own mouth open to apologize when Kathy tossed her head and wheeled away. "Well, excuse me! I didn't realize it was a crime to care about your own sister!"

"Kath..." Linn started after her, then subsided with a sigh. Stress was taking its toll on all of them. It wasn't like her to take Kath's head off over a bit of well-meaning meddling, and it wasn't like Kath to get onto her high horse like that, either. They were both reacting more to tension than to each other, the same way Rod and Trey were getting on each other's nerves.

"What was that all about?"

Trey's quiet voice made Linn glance around. He was leaning against the counter, eating a slice of bacon he'd taken off the plate beside the stove, watching her curiously. Just seeing him filled her with a sudden warm happiness and she smiled as she walked across to him. "Nothing much. Cabin fever, I guess."

He nodded and drew her gently against him so that she was standing in the cradle of his long, outstretched legs, slipping into his embrace as naturally as breathing. She rested one hand on his shoulder as she combed a tangle of dark hair off his forehead with the other. "Hungry?"

"Uh-huh." His dark eyes held hers, filled with mischief. "For more of you, mostly," he murmured, tugging her against him. "I just got my appetite whetted this morning when our guests started stirring and you felt obligated to jump up and make breakfast."

Linn gave him a slow smile and slipped her arms around his neck, toying with a tangle of hair at his nape. "We were well past the whetting stage when I heard Kath and Rod getting up," she reminded him softly.

Trey chuckled and lowered his mouth to hers, kissing her gently. "It was kind of good this morning, wasn't it?" He nuzzled her hair, rubbing his freshly shaven cheek against hers. "So good it begged for seconds. In fact," he added softly, running his hands down to caress the sleek contours of her denim-clad bottom, "I was thinking that we could—"

"No, we couldn't," she told him with a laugh, giving his hair a gentle tug to lift his head as he started kissing her throat.

"Inhibited all of a sudden?" He looked at her in amusement. "Rod and your sister know we're sleeping together. And I presume they're both bright enough to have figured out by now that's not *all* we're doing every night in that big bed."

Linn had to laugh, surprised to find herself blushing lightly. "I know. It's just that she's my *sister*."

"I've got news for you, sweetheart," he said with a chuckle. "I think your baby sister knows all about these things. I doubt they found Nathan under a cabbage leaf."

"That's different," she said with another laugh. "They're married."

"Is that a hint?"

Trey's tone was still amused and teasing, but there was something else in it that made Linn draw back to look up at him. "Of course not," she said in honest surprise. "I thought you knew me better than that by now, Hollister. If I figured you should be making an honest woman of me, I'd come out and say it, not drop oblique little hints here and there, hoping you'd fall over one."

One corner of his mouth tipped up in a wry half smile. "Rebuke accepted and duly noted," he assured her. "It's just that your brother-in-law seems to think I'm taking you for a ride. He advised me yesterday that you're still pretty vulnerable after losing Jack, and that if he finds out that I've wooed you into my bed with false promises, he'll use his service revolver on me. And I have a feeling he wasn't planning on shooting me in the *head*."

Linn had to smile. "I think Rod's having trouble dealing with seeing me with another man, if you want the truth. He really liked Jack. And even though Jack's dead, it's sort of like catching me in adultery. I know that sounds silly, but families are like that." Her smile widened. "Mine, anyway."

"So a man has to marry you to be considered honest, does he?" He was smiling as he said it, but his eyes were watchful.

"Not as far as I'm concerned," Linn told him easily, wondering even as she said it why his words left her feeling strangely empty. She'd entered this relationship with no illusions, no motives, no plans. How could she feel a sense of loss for something she'd never had?

"Good," Trey murmured, giving her a lazy, comfortable hug. "I had a bad feeling that things were suddenly going to get complicated or something."

"Not with me," Linn said lightly, easing herself out of his embrace. It was silly—the last thing on earth she'd ever contemplated was marrying again—but his easy dismissal of it sent a tiny jab of hurt through her. She shook it off impatiently and picked up the plate of bacon. "This is stone-cold by now, but it'll have to do. I just have to put Nathan's porridge in a bowl, and I'll be right in."

Did he really give her an oddly thoughtful look as he turned away? she wondered, or was she just imagining things? Linn watched him as he strode into the dining room, then shook her head again and turned back to the stove.

Without even planning to, she found herself suddenly thinking about their lovemaking that morning. He hadn't been worried about complications then. And neither, for that matter, had she. In fact, they'd come together in the pale light of dawn with nothing more complicated between them than blunt physical need.

They'd already been making love when Nathan's young voice filtered through the heavy bedroom door, and had been for what seemed like a long, sweet while, Trey's body so deeply joined with hers that Linn hadn't been able to tell her heartbeat from his. He'd been moving slowly and rhythmically, each unhurried thrust of his body like silken fire, and Linn had been responding in erotic counterpoint, legs drawn up over his hips, the covers thrown back to give them more freedom.

The only sounds had been the whisper of flesh on flesh, Trey's deep breathing and the tiny, muffled groans that Linn hadn't quite been able to bite back. She'd heard Nathan running up and down the corridor, had heard Kathy's quiet attempts to shush him, but absolutely nothing had been more important at that moment that the man locked in her arms and the spiraling tension centered within her, building with every passing moment.

She'd deliberately held herself back, so familiar now both with Trey and herself that she had no doubt of attaining that sought-after release, and concentrating instead on drawing out the last few minutes for each of them. And Trey, knowing exactly what she was doing, had laughed quietly and cupped her bottom in his hands, shifting his weight and his movements to correspond to hers, watching her through heavy-lidded eyes that smoldered with his own hunger.

But it had finally got away from her and she'd arched under him with a moan, straining and writhing against him as the tautness was pulled that last desperate distance, sending her senses and control and willpower spinning away. Then it had broken in a hurricane uprush of sensation so powerful it had made her cry out and she'd only dimly heard Trey whispering to her, urging her on and on and on.

She'd still been half-dazed with the power of it when Trey's movements had suddenly become rapid and erratic. Then he'd thrust himself against her with a breathless exclamation, his head thrown back so she could see the cords in his throat standing out. As skilled a lover as Trey was, he didn't always manage to bring them to satisfaction as one, and they'd relaxed in each other's arms, laughing and savoring the specialness of it. And then, regretfully, Linn had finally eased herself out of his arms and bed to dress and come downstairs.

A scant hour ago, she reminded herself. And she still tingled from the wonder of it, every nerve ending more sensitive than normal, the muscles in her inner thighs still tender enough to bring an evocative smile to her mouth. Damn that man! All it took was one look, one touch, one smile, and she turned to melted butter. If this wasn't love, it was a pretty good imitation. And maybe that was all she needed for now.

She was just turning away from the stove with Nathan's porridge when she heard the car and glanced out the window above the sink just as Murphy came hurtling into the kitchen. He started into a deep-chested baying that was nearly deafening in the confines of the room, and before she'd even finished drawing in a breath to call Trey, he and Rod were there.

They seemed to fill the room with a deadly competence, moving like cats, quickly, silently, guns out, eyes cold, in tandem like a well-matched team, neither getting in the other's way, seeming to know without words what the other was going to do, where he was going to step. Trey silenced Murphy with one sharp word and positioned himself at the door as Rod crouched low and eased himself toward the sink. He dared a swift glance out the window, then dropped like a stone, gun hand braced.

"One car," he said softly. "Gray four-door. Driver and a passenger, both male."

Trey frowned, searching his memory for a description of the car. He shook his head. "You get a good enough look at them to recognize them?"

Rod shook his head, wetting his lips.

Trey moved quietly away from the door. "I'm going to go out onto the deck and slip around behind them—I think I can make it without being seen. But if—"

"Rod? Hey, Rod, you in there, old buddy? It's Don!"

Trey saw Linn stiffen in disbelief and looked down at her. "It's Don Rasky," she said in astonishment. "Rod's partner."

"Rasky?" Rod sounded as surprised as Linn. He glided to the window and ventured another quick glance outside. "Well, I'll be damned. It *is* him!"

"Hold it!" Trey's hand shot out and grabbed Rod's arm as he started for the door. "It could be a trap."

Rod's eyes glinted. "He's my partner, for—"

"I don't like it," Trey said with quiet urgency. "How the hell did he find you?"

"Because I told him," Rod said with precision, wrenching his arm out of Trey's grasp. "I called him a couple of days ago."

"Damn it, Valencia, I told you not to—"

"You're not my keeper, Hollister." Rod shoved his revolver into his shoulder holster. "You might be hot stuff with security systems, but Don Rasky and I have been partners for five years. And we've been fighting garbage like

Santos for the same length of time. So don't tell me how to do my job!''

For a brief moment Trey was tempted to toss Valencia right through the damned door, just for the satisfaction it would give him. But he dragged in a deep breath and forced himself to relax, reminding himself that it *was* his fault the man was here in the first place. No two ways about it: he was getting too old for this kind of—

"Rod, you haven't stayed alive this long by being careless." Linn eased herself between them, her tone placating. "It can't hurt to be extracautious, can it? Let me go out and meet him, and—"

"No way!" Both men snapped it out at the same instant, trading hostile glares over the top of her head.

"I'll go," Trey growled, shoving Linn behind him. "Valencia, you—"

"Butt out," Rod snarled in return, roughly shouldering by Trey. "It's safe, I tell you! He's too damn good to let Santos put a tail on him."

"It's not a tail I'm worried about," Trey told him angrily, reaching across to unlock the door. He met Valencia's furious stare evenly. "It's your neck, *Detective*. But if something goes wrong, hit the deck and hit it hard—because I'm going to be right behind you, and I'm going to be firing at anything that moves. Got that?"

Rod's reply was an unintelligible mutter, but the pugnacious look he gave Trey needed no translation. And Trey, for his part, very nearly landed a knockout punch on the other man's chin there and then. He knew if he did there'd be hell to pay when Rod came to, but at least it would get him out of the way for long enough to confirm that everything was safe. And maybe save his damned life into the bargain. It wouldn't be the first time he'd had to use brute force to protect a man from his own stupidity.

As though knowing exactly what Trey was thinking, Rod eased his weight back, balancing himself on the balls of his feet, eyes narrowed as though waiting for Trey to make a move. They faced each other for a tense moment, then Trey whispered a savage oath under his breath and wrenched the door open.

"Just keep your eyes open, Valencia," he snapped. "I don't relish having to tell Nathan he has to face the rest of his life without a father because his old man was too damned thickheaded to listen to reason!"

Rod didn't answer. But he did, to Trey's approval, draw his revolver before stepping into the carport. "Don!" he called. "What's up?"

"We, uh ... we've got news. About the trial. New information." Rasky wet his lips and glanced around nervously. "You up here alone, buddy?"

Something was wrong. Trey eased himself through the door, gun hand braced, safety off. Rasky was scared—so scared Trey swore he could smell it. And why didn't he step away from the car? If these two were such good friends, there was no need for that much caution. Rasky's eyes kept darting this way and that and he was sweating heavily, even in the cool morning air. He looked like something trapped and afraid, backed so far into a corner that he knew there was no way out.

"Valencia ..." Trey kept his voice low, but he knew Rod heard him. Knew too he'd heard the warning in it, and the fact that he stopped abruptly told Trey that he'd also sensed something wasn't quite right. Trey glanced around swiftly, unable to see Joe but knowing the man was in position.

"What's going on?" Rod asked calmly. "Who's that in the car?"

"You ... okay?" Rasky seemed to be having trouble swallowing.

"I'm fine," Rod replied. "Are you coming in or what?"

Trey honestly didn't know if he actually saw the car door open, or if some gut-level instinct told him what was going to happen before it actually did. But he was moving before he'd even consciously made the decision to do so. His mind separated two distinct images as he dived toward Valencia: one of the car door swinging open and the figure of a man stepping out, the weapon in his hands turning toward Valencia, the other of Rasky wheeling around with his arms outstretched, his mouth wide as he screamed something.

A warning, maybe. No one would ever know. Even as Rasky flung himself at the man with the weapon, it swung up, fired a short burst and Rod's partner spilled back across the hood of the car, as limp as a rag doll. Trey only saw it happen from the corner of his eye; he tackled Valencia low and hard and they both went sprawling across the floor of the carport.

The assault rifle was firing as they dropped and Trey heard bullets stitch the air above their heads. The doors on the far side of the car opened and two men piled out, both holding small automatic weapons. Trey started firing even as he rolled free of Valencia, scoring at least one hit; he could hear Joe opening up from one of the upstairs windows on what sounded like an AK-47.

One of the gunmen sagged against the car door and for an instant there was a lull as Joe pinned down the remaining two. Trey was on his feet in a heartbeat, grabbing a stunned Valencia by the arm and dragging him toward the door. Trey gave Valencia a ferocious push that sent them both sprawling, a spray of gunfire coming so close behind that the edge of the door frame exploded into slivers of wood even as Linn was slamming the door shut.

Chapter 14

To Trey's relief, the metal lining in the door—untested until now—held firm against the barrage of bullets, and he breathed a prayer of thanks to whatever whim had made him install it in the first place. The glass in the window above the sink was bulletproof too, and although it had crazed badly it seemed to be holding. Long enough for them to get their wits collected, anyway.

Abruptly the shooting stopped. Trey cat-footed to the window and looked out, just in time to see the car backing rapidly up the narrow, tree-lined driveway. It vanished around a curve and a moment later he heard the engine stop. They, too, were clearly taking time to regroup.

Valencia was slowly getting to his feet, his face gray, looking so ravaged by disbelief and the shock of betrayal that Trey almost felt sorry for him. "You . . . you saved my life, man," he croaked, looking at Trey numbly.

"If anyone has the pleasure of killing you, Valencia, it's going to be me," Trey told him gruffly. "You hit?"

"No." Rod shook his head slowly. "You're bleeding pretty bad, though."

Trey blinked, then looked a trifle stupidly at his left arm, realizing that blood was dripping off his fingertips into a growing puddle by his feet. He flexed his fingers, relieved to discover nothing was broken, and peered gingerly at the deep gouge on the inside of his upper arm. There was no pain yet. Adrenaline, fear and shock were numbing everything but a peculiar heaviness in his arm, though he knew from experience that it would wear off all too fast.

Linn was there a moment later, looking grim-faced and pale; she ripped away the torn, blood-soaked shirt sleeve and wrapped a pressure bandage around the wound with the swift competence of someone used to medical emergencies. Suddenly he found himself thinking of Jack, wondering if she'd looked at him with the same fear in her eyes, and became aware—as she obviously already was—just what a close call he'd had. The bullet had passed between his arm and his body. A few inches to the right, and it would have been game over for one Trey Hollister, man of action.

"A little close for comfort, but I'm all right," he said quietly, holding her gaze. "How about you?"

"Scared," she said succinctly. "Joe called someone by the name of Ryerson, and apparently help is on its way. Thirty minutes at the outside."

Knowing he didn't have the time to waste, he slipped his right arm around Linn and held her against him, breathing in the wind-and-sea scent of her thick hair, letting her body warmth flow through him like a calming wave. He could feel her trembling slightly and tightened his embrace.

"We're barricaded in here pretty solidly. All we have to do is hold them off till the cavalry gets here."

She drew back after a moment, smiling humorlessly. "You're a damned liar, but I appreciate the thought." Then her smile faded and she looked up at him, eyes very calm. "I know what these guys are capable of, Trey. They've got the latest in sophisticated military weaponry—most of it bought from American suppliers, and all of it the best money can buy. Grenade launchers, rocket launchers...and every other kind of high tech killing toy available. And they're not going to wait around out there for the police to show up. Joe said another car came in a few minutes ago, so they've got reinforcements.'' She swallowed. "They're going to hit us with everything they've got. And I—''

"Linn…'' He stopped, not even knowing what he wanted to say. She was right. And they both knew it.

"I know this is incredibly corny,'' she said softly, "but if we don't get through this, Trey, I want you to know that you've made me unbelievably happy for these past couple of weeks.''

"Linn, we're—''

"Shh.'' She put her finger across his lips. Her eyes searched his, such a clear blue they were almost azure, and he felt something pull tight in his gut, a desperate kind of ache that was half wonder, half despair. "I do love you, Trey Hollister,'' she whispered. "No matter what happens, at least I've had that.''

The words hit him like a fist, knocking the wind—and whatever he'd been about to say—right out of him. He had to fight to catch his breath while his mind spun with a hundred possibilities, none of them making the slightest bit of sense. And it occurred to him that it was a little like getting shot again, every nerve ending as numb as stone.

Linn's mouth curved in a beguiling smile. "Don't look so scared, Hollister—I'm not putting you to the test. If we don't make it through this, it won't matter. And if we do, we can just put it down to the usual irrational things people say when they think they're going to die, and pretend it never happened, okay?''

He should be saying something, he knew. Something very wise and reassuring and preferably heroic. But the only words that kept spilling through his mind were the wrong ones, full of rash promises and hasty declarations he doubted he could ever live up to. The tangle of emotions within him seemed to wrap itself around his heart, a Gordian knot of wants and wishes and crazy, hopeless dreams, and for a split second he very nearly said the words he knew she wanted to hear, the words that kept filling his mouth with their sweetness.

"Damn it, Linn,'' he managed to growl, "this isn't—''

"They're starting to make their move." Joe's quiet voice brought Trey's head up, eyes narrowed, every sense alert. Joe was standing in the doorway, his arms full of weapons. "I counted six of them, but there may be more. Enough artillery to start a war. They've split up—two coming up from the beach, two from the north, two coming in through the trees at the front."

The icy knot in the pit of Linn's stomach tightened and she glanced around to find Kathy standing near the stove, her eyes wide and frightened, hands convulsively clenching and unclenching on Nathan's shoulders.

Trey nodded authoritatively. "Okay. I'll take the beach side. Joe, you take care of the ones coming from the north and—"

"I've got the front covered," Rod said grimly. He seemed to be over the worst of his shock now and although he was still pale, there was a glitter of healthy malevolence in his eyes that hadn't been there before. Joe tossed him a stubby, evil-looking weapon of some kind. Rod fielded it easily, then took the handful of magazines that Joe held out for him. "In case we don't make it out of this, Hollister, I want to thank you right now. For taking care of Linn and Nathan. For taking Kath and me in. Not many men would have done what you've done, knowing the odds."

"Forget it," Trey growled, slapping a full magazine into the weapon Joe handed him and checking it. "I didn't do it for you, I did it for me. And the kid." He flashed an unexpected smile at Nathan. "How are you holding up, sport?"

"Are those bad men going to kill us?" Nathan's voice was just a whisper.

"Not a chance," Trey said grimly. "Your dad's too good a cop to let that happen."

Rod cast Trey a startled look. Then he smiled faintly in appreciation. "I owe you, Hollister."

"Damn straight," Trey assured him with a reckless grin. "And I intend to collect, Valencia. So let's get it done. Linn..."

"Right here." She stepped forward and took the revolver he handed her, checking it expertly. "Where do you want me?"

Trey held out a plastic card. "Take this. It's a coded access card to a security room built in behind the sauna." Linn took the card, looking at him questioningly. "The linen cupboard swings out from the wall," he went on with quiet urgency. "The release catch is just inside the frame, about waist height. Swing the cupboard out of the way and you'll find a steel door—that card slips into a slot and unlocks it.

"Inside there's a couple of small rooms. It's built like a bomb shelter, sheathed in a special high-grade steel and stressed concrete, and can withstand even a direct rocket hit. Once the door is closed it's impregnable. The air is filtered and recycled, so it's completely self-sufficient. You can hole up in there for weeks if you need to—there are a couple of camp cots, a chemical toilet, food, water... everything you need."

"Trey..." she started warningly.

"I want you to take your sister and Nathan and lock yourselves in there," he said flatly. "No arguments, Linn. We don't have the time. Just do it. And take Murph with you," he added. "I don't want him hurt, either."

"I will not leave the three of you out here with—"

"Linn, do as the man says." Rod looked at her beseechingly. "If there's a chance to get Kath and Nathan through this..."

He didn't need to finish. Linn nodded once and wheeled away, smiling with false calm as she reached for Nathan's hand. Tears prickled behind her eyelids, hot and sharp, but she held them back through sheer force of will, refusing to look around. No goodbyes, she told herself fiercely. Goodbye means you don't expect to see them again. Goodbye means...

"Come on, Nathan," she said lightly. "We're going to find Trey's secret hideout."

He took her hand trustingly and Kathy stepped toward Rod, her eyes swimming. "Rod, please. I can't just—"

"Do it," Rod said roughly, scooping her into a fierce embrace, his own eyes squeezed shut. "Just do it, Kath. When this is over, I'm going to take you and Nathan for that tour of Ireland we've always been talking about. And Hawaii."

"I don't want to go to Ireland," Kathy whispered brokenly. "Or Hawaii. I just want to go home with you. So don't you do anything stupid and heroic, hear me?"

"We're running out of time," Joe urged tightly.

Kathy turned away from Rod and stumbled toward Linn, chin wobbling, trying not to let Nathan see her crying, and in that moment Linn's eyes met Trey's. They burned into hers, filled with all the things they'd never said to one another. Then he too turned away and walked from the room.

Linn, fighting to hold back her own tears, started for the back of the house where the sauna was. "Don't any of you do anything stupid and heroic," she told Joe sternly. "Murphy, heel!"

The linen cupboard built into the wall between the sauna and a luxuriously appointed bathroom ran from floor to ceiling, the shallow shelves filled with a rainbow of towels, scented candles and soaps, shampoos and other toiletries. Linn fumbled inside the door frame for the hidden lock, finding it easily.

It gave a muted click when she pressed it and the entire linen cupboard swung away from the wall on silent hinges, revealing the heavy, gray steel door that Trey had described. Her hand was shaking so badly that it took her two tries to slide the thin plastic code card into the slot, but it finally sank home and she could hear another quick click as it released some locking mechanism embedded deep inside the thick blast door. The door glided partly open, as silent as death, and Linn swung it the rest of the way back.

When the door opened, it activated a low-intensity, battery-operated lamp mounted high on one wall; the three of them peered mistrustfully into the dim interior. Cupboards lined one wall, presumably holding the supplies Trey had mentioned, and there were a couple of camp cots as well as two or three folded canvas chairs.

"Not exactly the Holiday Inn, but it's nicer than some of the places Rod and I have been staying," Kathy said with a forced smile. "Come on, Nathan."

"Take this." Linn held the revolver toward Kathy, who looked at it as she might regard a live viper. "Damn it, Kathy," she urged impatiently, "this isn't the time to be squeamish! You know how to handle one of these—Dad taught you, too, in spite of the fact you fought him tooth and nail over it. Now take it!''

Kathy took it distastefully. "Why? You're the Annie Oakley in this family.''

"Because I'm not staying with you," Linn said calmly. "Murphy, get in here. And guard, do you understand me? Guard Nathan!''

The shepherd gave a sharp bark and Linn nodded, looking at her sister. "Okay, you'll be fine in here. The door unlocks easily from the inside—see the catch? But don't open it unless you're absolutely sure you know who's out here.''

"But . . .''

"See this monitor screen?" Linn pointed to a small screen set in the wall beside the door. On it she could see the doorway where they were standing. "He's got a camera out there somewhere, focused right on this door so you can monitor who's outside at all times." She gave a soft, strained laugh. "Damn, he's good! He's thought of everything.''

"Linn, you heard what he said! You've *got* to—'' There was a sudden chatter of gunfire in the distance and Kathy flinched.

"You'll be as snug as a baby in bunting in here." Linn started to swing the door closed. "Now remember what I said—don't open it unless you're absolutely sure who's out here.''

"Linn, you're going too far this time!" Kathy caught the edge of the door before it closed, her face grim with determination. There was more gunfire, accompanied by the sound of breaking glass. "I am not letting you risk your—''

"Kathy, I'm not risking anything I haven't risked for the past month. Now the only thing that got me through it— that has gotten Rod through it—is knowing that Nathan is safe. That's all that matters! You get in this shelter and stay there!''

The door clicked shut, cutting off Kathy's protest in midword, and Linn watched it for a mistrustful moment, half expecting Kathy to fling it open again. But she didn't.

Linn stepped back and swung the linen closet into its niche. It fitted smoothly, with just a faint click, and all evidence of Trey's little bolt hole vanished as though it had never existed. Then, tucking the plastic access card into the pocket of her jeans, she turned and started making her way cautiously back to the kitchen.

There were more shots, coming from both inside and outside the house, and Linn ducked instinctively. She eased herself along the corridor, trying not to flinch every time a burst of gunfire shattered the stillness. It was coming almost continuously now and she could hear bullets raking the side of the house like hail, ricochets whining off the stonework of the foundation.

There was a resounding crash just outside the carport door, then a burst of gunfire; the bulletproof glass in the window above the sink, already badly crazed, seemed to crumble like old cheese. It sagged inward and spilled into the sink and Linn dropped like a stone as a spray of automatic weapon fire stitched across the far wall, filling the room with flying plaster, dust and noise.

It stopped after a moment and in the deathly silence that followed, Linn peeled herself off the floor and scrambled into the relative shelter of the island, pausing there to catch her breath and try to steady her shattered nerves.

Her knees were shaking so badly that she was afraid to even attempt standing up, so she just knelt there, wishing she hadn't been so damned impulsive. What in God's name had made her think she might be able to help? Sure, she knew how to handle a gun, but all her father's training and advice had in no way prepared her for facing a South American death squad! Even if she didn't get herself killed, she was liable to distract Trey or Rod at the wrong moment and get one of them killed.

She knelt there for another moment or two, trying to work up enough courage to make a dash for the living room. Trey would be there. And for some reason it seemed very important to be with him. Even now. Or maybe especially now.

She'd actually gotten her feet under her and was just about to bolt for the door when someone started firing through the window again and the row of brightly painted ceramic canisters right above her head exploded. She dropped back to her knees, arms around her head, as fragments of glazed earthenware poured around her. The filter coffee machine was the next to go and Linn sucked in her breath as she was showered with hot coffee and shards of glass.

She didn't even notice the man come through the window until she caught a movement out of the corner of her eye and glanced around the end of the island in time to see him jump lightly from the countertop to the floor. He crouched there for a heartbeat, glancing around swiftly to check his surroundings, and Linn flattened herself against the side of the island with an indrawn gasp.

He hadn't seen her! Linn's heart was pounding so hard that she was certain he must be able to hear it; she crouched there, absolutely frozen, not even daring to breath as every nerve ending screamed at her to head for cover.

But she ignored the impulse, knowing that if she ran the deadly looking weapon in his hand would swing around and he would bring her down with no more than a flex of his trigger finger. *Just please don't let him come around this end of the island,* she prayed silently. Why, oh, why hadn't she stayed with Kathy and Nathan, hidden and safe and . . . ?

The man moved, his feet crunching through the broken glass, and Linn stiffened. But he didn't move toward her. Instead, gliding as stealthily as a hunting cat, he started to make his way toward the door leading into the living room.

Paralyzed with relief and raw terror, Linn couldn't move. She was certain that if she so much as took a deep breath she'd shatter into a million pieces, so fragile was her control. Then she heard Trey's voice as he shouted something to Rod or Joe, and realized with sudden, brutal clarity that he had no idea their barricades had been breached.

Keeping the island between the intruder and herself, she peeked cautiously around the corner. He was in the dining room now, heading swiftly and silently for the living room. She could see someone beyond him, someone crouched by the ruins of what had once been the patio door, his broad back undefended.

Trey, Linn realized dimly. He had his weapon up and was firing through the shattered glass of the big door, spent shell casings raining onto the hardwood floor around him. The intruder paused at the door to the living room and stared at him, then, as though in slow motion, he raised his own weapon and aimed it right between Trey's shoulder blades.

Linn didn't even realize what she was doing until she was in motion. Without conscious thought she was on her feet and sprinting toward the crouched figure as though her very life depended on it, screaming *"Behind you!"* before she'd even cleared the kitchen door.

The intruder turned awkwardly and she was on him before he'd gotten the gun swung all the way around. If he hadn't been coming out of a crouch, it wouldn't have worked. But he was off balance and her flying tackle sent him staggering back against the wall with a grunt of pain, very nearly knocking the semiautomatic rifle out of his hands.

She caught a glimpse of Trey leaping to his feet, his face white with shock, heard him shout something... and then the intruder brought the butt of his weapon up and around so fast that it was just a deadly blur. In the next moment the very universe exploded and she was being sucked into a spinning vortex of bright-spangled darkness; she could hear her own cry hanging disembodied and distant in the air as she slid down and down and down....

"No...!" Trey's shout of anguish and rage echoed through the room, too late. He saw Linn's head snap back, watched her sag bonelessly to the floor and felt something within him tear loose, the pain more real than anything he'd ever experienced. He was still on one knee, knowing he was never going to get his own weapon up to snap off a shot before the intruder killed him. He watched the barrel of the semiautomatic arc smoothly toward him, thinking very calmly that it was all right, that there really wasn't a hell of a lot to live for without Linn, anyway....

"No! *No...!*"

It was a woman's scream this time, half terror and half fury, and for a split second Trey thought it was Linn's voice. But she was still sprawled limply at the intruder's feet. He blinked, realizing with some tiny, rational part of his mind that the shout had been real—real enough to make the gunman falter once more and glance around.

It was all the opening Trey needed. Bringing his gun the rest of the way around, he moved out of instinct and habit, but before his finger had even tightened on the trigger, a single shot cracked through the room.

It was followed almost instantly by another, the roar of Rod Valencia's service revolver this time, coming from so close behind him that Trey flinched, half-deafened. The intruder was slammed back against the wall so hard that the house shuddered, then he fell sprawling, the stubby weapon flying out of his hand and spinning across the polished hardwood floor.

There was a heartbeat of utter, stunned silence. Trey stared at the fallen gunman, then lifted his gaze to look at the woman standing in the kitchen doorway. It was Kathy, in perfect shooting stance, arms outstretched, left hand bracing her right, and she was holding the small revolver he'd given Linn. She was staring at the fallen man blankly, as though not really comprehending what had happened, and Trey heard someone behind him whisper a shocked oath.

Slowly Trey became aware of other sounds. Sirens, this time. And the thunder of a helicopter, the pulse beat of its rotors all but drowning the amplified, authoritative voice that was ordering everyone to lay their weapons down....

Trey closed his eyes for an instant, then lowered his own weapon and set it aside. It was over. Somehow, impossibly, they'd managed to hang on long enough.

Not wanting to startle Kathy, Trey gently eased himself to his feet. Rod stepped by him and walked cautiously toward his wife, holding out his hand. "Give me the gun, honey," he said quietly. "Come on, Kath—swing it down and put the safety on and hand it to me. You can do it, honey."

Kathy blinked, then looked at the gun in her hand as though seeing it for the first time. A look of revulsion crossed her face and she opened her fingers and let it drop, the sharp thud when it hit the floor making them all jump.

"I—I killed him," she whispered, starting to shake violently. "M-my God, I killed him...."

"No, you didn't," Rod said reassuringly. "It was my shot that hit him. You missed him by a country mile." He bent and retrieved the gun, then eased his arms around Kathy and drew her close. "I love you, honey, and I appreciate the gesture... but you're still one hell of a lousy shot."

Which was as fancy a bit of lying as he'd heard in a long while, Trey mused as he swiftly checked the gunman. The man was dead, all right, but it would take a forensic lab to tell which of the two bullets had actually killed him. Kathy might be a lousy shot—but when it counted, her aim had been as true and deadly as her husband's.

He touched Linn's cheek with the back of his hand, relieved at the warmth that rose from it, then placed his fingertips on the side of her throat. Her pulse was strong and regular and he let his breath out tightly, not even aware until then that he'd been holding it. There was a gash on her temple and her hair was sticky with blood, but it had obviously been a glancing blow, looking worse than it was.

"She isn't dead?"

It was Kathy's voice, tremulous with fear, and Trey shook his head. "No, but once she comes to and that headache sets in, she's going to wish she were." He brushed a strand of silken hair off Linn's cheek and gazed down at her, still aching with that deep, knifelike fear that had cut through him when he'd seen her fall. The realization, in that instant, that if he lost her, everything else just made no sense at all.

There were the sounds of running footsteps outside, someone bellowing orders through a loud hailer, someone else banging on the door and demanding to be let in by the authority of the Royal Canadian Mounted Police and half a dozen other enforcement agencies and official-sounding government departments.

Trey looked wearily at Rod. "How would you like to let those boys in before they bust my front door down?"

"With pleasure," Rod said just as wearily, walking across the room. "With pleasure."

* * *

The room was dark. Or almost so, illuminated only by the warm glow of naked flame. Someone had lighted the fire and Linn watched the flames weave intricate patterns on the ceiling. She could hear the murmur of voices nearby, blending with the murmur of the fire into a comfortable background noise that made her feel very safe and warm.

Her head had stopped aching. Or rather the potent little capsules that the doctor had ordered her to swallow had kicked in, and their narcotic haze simply made the ache bearable. She reached up very gingerly and touched her right temple, fingering the thick wad of gauze, and wondered if she dare try to sit up.

"Don't even think about it," a quiet baritone said from the shadows beside the fireplace. "You're supposed to be playing invalid."

"Trey?" Her voice sounded dry and raspy.

A lean shadow eased itself from the darkness just beyond the ring of firelight and Trey crouched beside the sofa, his dark eyes filled with concern. "How are you feeling?"

"Like I got run over by a herd of stampeding buffalo," she muttered.

"How many fingers am I holding up?"

Linn squinted at his hand. "What fingers?" The concern in his eyes turned to outright worry and she had to laugh, immediately regretting it. "Joke," she whispered hoarsely. "My God, it was just a joke!"

"Damn it, Linn," he protested tightly, "this is no—"

"Three fingers," she said consolingly. "But if you start asking me to count backward from fifty or repeat my name and address a dozen times, I'll strangle you."

He managed a fleeting grin. "Sorry. The doctor said your X ray came back clean—nothing cracked, concussed or bent out of shape. Except your sense of humor," he added as a dark afterthought. "And I still wish you'd stayed in the hospital overnight for observation like the doc wanted."

"No." Linn fought a sudden shiver. "I hate hospitals. I've spent too much of my life in hospitals, watching the people I love die."

He nodded, and she could see by his eyes that he understood. His face was pale and drawn, the lines bracketing his mouth deeper than she'd ever seen them, his hair matted with dried sweat. He looked worn-out and worn down, and she put out her hand and touched his cheek with her fingers. "Are you all right? No more bullet holes or anything?"

"Nope. Everyone's fine."

"And Kathy? They told me what happened...that she saved your life. And probably mine."

"She's okay. Pretty shaken up, but we all are."

Linn smiled. "She's something else, isn't she?"

Trey gave a snort of wry laughter. "You're both something else! What does it take to get either of you to do what you're told?"

"Whatever it is," someone growled from behind him, "I've never discovered it." Rod stepped into the firelight and grinned down at her. "How are you doing, Sis?"

Linn stared at him. "What happened to your eye?"

Rod grinned sheepishly, touching the puffy, bruised skin around his right eye. "Nothing much. Just stepped in front of an unfriendly fist, that's all."

"You and Trey weren't—!"

"Not Trey," Rod assured her. "Some government type in a shiny blue suit who kept getting in my way when we were trying to get you into the ambulance."

Trey's mouth canted to one side. "This brother-in-law of yours packs a pretty mean wallop. He just about caused an international incident, mind you, seeing as the guy he took a poke at was RCMP, and they're already a little ticked off at all the ruckus and paperwork we've caused."

"Are we all under arrest or anything I should know about?"

Rod snorted. "Trey seems to know everyone worth knowing in this part of the country. He spent the last couple of hours smoothing ruffled feathers." He gave Trey a speculative look. "One day, Hollister, I want to hear what you *really* do for a living. That guy was on the phone checking your credentials for about two minutes flat before he was standing at attention, calling you *sir* and doing everything but saluting every time you looked at him."

Trey just smiled lazily. "I write books, Valencia. I already told you."

"Sure," Rod said in a disbelieving drawl. "And my sister-in-law here is just another pretty face."

"Well, I won't argue with that." Trey gazed down at her, his eyes suddenly serious. "You saved my life, lady," he said very softly. "That guy had me cold. I'd have been dead before I hit the floor if you hadn't been there."

Linn shivered suddenly. "I don't even want to think about it. I've never been so scared in my life." Trey reached out and meshed his fingers with hers and she smiled, wondering what was going on behind those private, silver eyes. She still couldn't tell what he was thinking most of the time. Even now, even after what they'd been through, he had the barricades up, the action as automatic as breathing.

She stifled a sigh and turned her mind instead to other, more immediate things. "So what happens now? Can the police up here guarantee Rod some protection, or are we—?" She stopped dead, intercepting the look that Rod traded with Trey.

"I guess no one got around to telling her," he said with a faint, tired smile.

Linn looked at him sharply. "Telling me what?"

"It's over, Linn," Trey said quietly. "Santos is dead."

She heard the word, but her mind kept fumbling it like half-frozen fingers fumbling a ball. "Dead?" Even when she said it herself, it didn't sound entirely real. "You...don't mean that man who broke in here, the one I tried to stop, was—?"

Rod shook his head, managing a smile. He moved the big hassock across to the sofa and wearily sat down. "It would have made my day if it had been, but no such luck. That guy was just a hired gun." He blew his breath out and scrubbed his fingers through his hair, raking it back.

"One of Santos's competitors saw his chance to take over Santos's empire—just another two-bit hood with a billion or two to spend on weapons and hired assassins. He and his army took Santos down early yesterday morning. It happened in Santos's Caribbean stronghold, and not much news of it leaked out—which is why we hadn't heard anything."

"But if Santos was dead, why did these guys—?"

"They didn't know about it, either," Trey said. "Santos had dispatched this team three days ago, right after he'd found out that Rod was here. They were operating on their own, with no contact with Santos to minimize the chance of a leak."

"Dead," Linn whispered, feeling stunned. "I can't believe it."

"Believe it," Rod told her grimly. "From the pictures the RCMP showed me, it was a bloodbath. There aren't more than half a dozen of Santos's men still alive, and there are contracts out on all of them. The three that got picked up here are so scared, they're spilling everything they know, just for the promise of some protection."

"So...it's over." Linn drew in a careful breath, afraid of jarring her head. It didn't seem real, somehow. None of it seemed real.

"It's over," Trey repeated quietly, his fingers tightening on hers. His gaze seemed to burn into hers, seeking while giving away nothing, and she realized he was thinking the same thing she was. *Over. It's all over....*

Chapter 15

What are you two doing?" Kathy's voice was brisk with impatience, and Linn looked over Trey's head to see her sister bearing down on them like a wrathful spirit. "My God, I don't believe this! The doctor told you she had to have plenty of rest, and the minute I turn my back you're in here pestering her!"

"Filling me in," Linn protested with a smile. "How's Nathan?"

"He and Murphy are tearing around the beach like nothing has happened," Kathy said with a wondering shake of her head. "The first thing he asked when Rod told him Santos was dead was if that meant he could go outside and play now."

Linn smiled drowsily, the fire's warmth and the medication she'd been given making her so sleepy that she could scarcely keep her eyes open. "The kid's just got his priorities straight, that's all." She gazed up at Kathy for a long moment. "When I gave you that gun, you were supposed to use it to protect yourself and Nathan, not take Santos's men on single-handedly."

"I just got tired of you grabbing all the heroics for yourself," Kathy said lightly. "I thought it was about time Patrick Duffy O'Connor's younger daughter showed she was made of the right stuff. After all, a cop's daughter who's married to another cop shouldn't be hiding when trouble hits."

Kathy's smile was careless, but Linn could see the horror still lurking in her eyes, knew it was going to be a long while before either of them could get through a full night without meeting Santos in their dreams.

"You don't have to go proving anything to me," Rod grumbled, reaching out and taking Kathy's hand.

"I was proving it to myself," Kathy said quietly.

Rod smiled at her, then looked around at Trey. "That's quite a little bunker you've got built in there."

"In my line of work it's handy to have a secure place where you can stash someone and know he's safe. Politicians marked for assassination, court witnesses with a price on their heads—" he paused to give Rod a wry smile "—potential kidnap and ransom victims...." He shrugged. "Whatever."

"Whatever." Rod smiled and shook his head slowly. "Just a natural extension of the bulletproff glass in the windows and steel cladding in the doors and walls, right?"

"Right."

"Which is fine, providing the person you're hiding stays hidden." Linn gave Kathy a pointed look.

Kathy smiled faintly. Then the smile faded and she looked at Linn seriously. "I'd have lost my mind in there, not knowing what was happening. I just knew that if it was as bad as I suspected, Rod and Trey would need all the help they could get. I always swore I'd never have a gun in my hand, but when the people you love are in trouble..."

She shrugged, reaching down to run her fingers through Rod's thick hair. "I can't remember being as mad in my life as I was when I stepped through that door and saw that man hit you with his gun. And I knew Trey didn't have a chance—" She stopped again, shuddering lightly. "Anyway, it's over. I don't want to talk about it. Linn, are you hungry? I've made some soup."

Linn shook her head, wondering drowsily if Kathy really believed Rod's well-intentioned lie about having missed her target, or if she suspected the truth. Maybe she'd ask one day. Years down the road when the horror had finally faded.

Then she looked at Rod, knowing she had to ask, wishing she didn't. "And Rasky?" she asked softly. "He really was helping Santos, wasn't he?"

Rod's face went hard and cold. "Yeah," he said roughly, the disgust on his face almost palpable. "He was the key man—he knew every move we were making."

"But he was your partner," Linn whispered. "Partners don't sell each other out."

"Partner, friend," Rod said bitterly. "What's friendship and honor compared with a million in cold, hard cash?"

Linn closed her eyes, opening them a moment later to look at Trey. "You knew all along, didn't you? Both you and Joe. That's why you wouldn't let me call in anymore."

Trey's face was as hard, as cold, as Rod's. "I'd hoped I was wrong. But it was the only thing that made sense. I could see you letting Santos get the drop on you once, but not a second or third time—you're just too damned good for that. But from what you'd told me, every time you made a move, Santos's men would be there before you'd even unpacked. That information had to be coming from inside—and Rasky was the obvious choice."

"We could use you on the Miami force, Hollister." Rod gave Trey a humorless smile. "It was right in front of me—and all the others—and we couldn't see it."

"In my business you learn not to trust anyone," Trey said quietly. "I've seen brother sell out brother for a pocketful of cash."

"They'd planned to grab Nathan and use him to bring Rod out of hiding." Kathy stroked Rod's hair. "But catching you didn't turn out to be as easy as they'd thought." She laughed quietly and looked at Linn. "You outwitted Santos's hired muscle at every turn. You've been driving them crazy for three weeks, staying just out of reach."

"I wonder why Rasky didn't just take care of you himself," Trey said with a glance at Rod.

Rod managed a bitter smile. "I have a feeling that's why he was up here—that he hadn't delivered me as promised, and Santos sent him up here to finish the job in person." He stopped, a muscle along his jaw rippling.

"But he couldn't do it," Trey reminded him sofly. "At the end he tried to stop them. He died trying to save you, Valencia. It's not much, God knows, but you have to give the man that."

"He's been hooked on cocaine for the last year," Kathy put in. "His wife suspected that something was going on, but she couldn't pin it down. Even a couple of officers who have been working with Rasky while Rod's been handling the Santos investigation had a feeling he was into something heavy."

"One of them called a couple of hours ago to say that they found a note in Rasky's locker that suggested he was considering suicide," Rod added. "I guess the stress was getting to him, between being so strung out he'd hock his own grandmother for a few grams of coke, then selling me out to Santos."

Kathy looked at Linn, her expression cold. "I know I should feel sorry for him, but I can't. I can understand someone getting in too deep. I can even understand him being afraid to ask for help. I can't understand him selling out his own partner."

Rod shook his head wearily, shoulders sagging as though weighed down. "I don't know, man. Maybe if I hadn't been so obsessed with this Santos case I'd have seen something was wrong. Been there to help when he needed it. That's what partners are for...."

"It's over," Linn reminded them quietly. "We'll never know what demons were chasing Rasky, but I suspect he's more at peace now than he's been for months. And you can't start blaming yourself, Rod. Whatever turned Rasky bad came from the inside, not the outside. If he really wanted help, he knew all he had to do was ask and you'd be there for him."

Rod nodded, still staring at the carpet between his feet, and Kathy stroked his hair gently, looking pensive and sad.

"Why don't you catch some shut-eye?" Trey murmured, giving Linn's hand a gentle squeeze before unbraiding his fingers from hers and getting to his feet. "You've had one hell of a day."

Linn thought about arguing, wanting to hear more about what had happened to Santos, about what had gone on while she'd been unconscious. But her eyes kept sliding closed and finally it was just easier to leave them that way. She thought she felt the feather touch of Trey's lips against hers, but then they were gone and before she could catch herself, she felt herself slipping swiftly into the oblivion of sleep.

"We're really going home?" Nathan's small, dirty face was radiant with happiness as he gazed up at Kathy. "And Grandpa's coming home, too?"

"Yes, honey," Kathy assured him, "your grandpa's coming home. And your Aunt Linn's going to be staying with us for a while, too. So we're going to be a family again." Grinning broadly, Kathy looked up from her packing. "I honestly can't believe it's over, Linn. No more running and hiding. No more waking up in a cold sweat in the night, expecting to see Santos standing there with a gun."

She continued her packing, then looked at Linn. "Rod's quitting Vice."

"Quitting?" Linn stared at Rod in astonishment.

He nodded, his face grim. He still looked tired and haggard, and when his eyes met hers, they were the eyes of someone very old and very embittered. "It's a war zone out there," he said simply. "And it's no place for a thirty-five-year-old man with a wife and son. This last year working undercover on the Santos case made me look hard at my life. And one thing I realized is that a dead Rodrigo Valencia isn't a hell of an asset to anyone." He smiled at Kathy. "And my wife deserves more than I've been able to give her lately. A lot more."

"We want another child, for one thing," Kathy added. "We talked about it a lot during the last few weeks on the run from Santos. Neither of us is getting any younger, and

I think Nathan's at a good age to really enjoy a brother or sister.''

"A baby? And Rod quitting Vice. Good grief...." Linn looked from one to the other.

"The word 'quit' is purely relative," Rod told her with a smile. "We're putting together a new drug crime task force that will be working hand in hand with the feds, and I was asked if I'd like to head it up. I wasn't sure at the time—I was still too caught up in this Santos thing—but I've decided to take it."

"I'm glad," Linn admitted quietly. "My heart's in my throat every time the phone rings—I always expect it to be Kath, telling me something's happened to you."

"For a cop's daughter, you sure worry a lot."

"That's *why* we worry a lot!" Linn and Kathy chimed in unison.

"I got us seats on a three o'clock flight out of Vancouver, and a charter flight out of Tofino harbor at noon. That sound all right to everyone?"

"Yeah!" Nathan bounced around the room as though he were on springs, radiating boundless energy and excitement. "Wait'll Gandpa sees all the shells I found!"

"And I think one of the first things we have to do when we get home," Rod said with great seriousness, "is get you a dog."

"A dog?" Nathan stopped dead, his eyes widening. "For real? Do you mean it? A *dog*?"

"I think you're old enough to take care of one, don't you?"

"Yeah!"

Linn smiled to herself, watching the three of them. Kath and Rod had obviously used their time in exile to sort out their priorities and were bursting with renewed energy and ideas, anxious to get on with their lives. But she hadn't given the future a lot of thought at all. Content, she reminded herself, to simply take each day as it came. To savor this wonderful and completely unexpected magic she'd discovered....

Her heart gave a sudden thump. She swallowed, knowing she couldn't put it off any longer. "I'll...be back," she said quietly, looking at Kathy. "I have a couple of things to do before we leave."

Kathy's eyes held hers. "There's no rush, Linn."

Rod looked up. "We have to be in Tofino in an hour."

"Shut up, Rod," Kathy said calmly. "Like I said, Linn— there's no rush."

Rod opened his mouth to protest, then shut it firmly at a glare from Kathy, and Linn took a deep breath and started for the stairs.

Trey had opened the outside door of the kitchen and was standing in it, leaning against the frame and staring out toward the beach. The sky, a deep, sultry blue, promising late-day heat, was curdled here and there with clouds and the morning air was cool and smelled of sea salt, tidal beaches and forest. It was an earthy, primitive scent, one Linn had never entirely gotten used to, and she breathed it in deeply as she strolled across to stand beside him.

The tip of his cigarette glowed like a small jewel against the sky as he drew on it, eyes narrowed against the smoke. "So. I guess this is it." He didn't look at her as he spoke. He braced his forearm on the door frame, the cigarette in his hand, and stared at the rising smoke.

"Yes, I guess it is. Kathy's packing Nathan's things now."

He nodded, still not looking at her. "You're going, aren't you?"

Linn frowned, hearing something in his voice she couldn't quite pinpoint. Anger, perhaps. Wistfulness. "I have to. Kath could use a hand getting things back in order, and with Dad coming home and everything..."

He nodded again, taking another deep drag on the cigarette. He blew the smoke out slowly, watching it drift upward. "I guess neither of us really gave much thought to this part, did we?"

"No," Linn lied, her voice just a whisper. She'd thought of it a lot, wondering how—when the time came—she was ever going to leave. Wondering how much of herself she was going to leave behind. Wondering if...

"Trey, I..." She paused. "I don't even know where to begin thanking you," she finally whispered.

"I already told you I had my own reasons." He glanced aside at her, smiling very faintly. "Mind you, I'll admit I was hoping it was going to last longer."

"Me, too," she whispered.

"Damn it, Linn—" He stopped, swearing softly, then tossed the cigarette down and ground it out with his toe. "I don't want it to end like this," he said quietly, turning to look at her. "When I told you at the very beginning that I didn't want to be just a pair of arms in your night—damn it, I meant it. I thought you understood that."

"You've been a lot more than just a pair of arms in my night, Trey. And you know it."

"But you're leaving."

It was more accusation than observation and Linn frowned, not knowing what he expected her to say. What he wanted her to say. "I have to, Trey. My whole family's been torn apart, and we need time to get things back to normal."

He was looking at the sky again and she watched him for a silent moment, wishing he'd turn and look at *her*. There was anger in the set of his shoulders, in the way he held his head as he stared out at nothing, narrow-eyed and silent.

"And I... have things I have to sort out, too. Where I'm going to live, what I'm going to do. I just had to leave everything up in the air when this Santos mess happened, and I have a thousand decisions to make and..." She shrugged, willing him to turn around to look at her. To say something.

"You're not making this any easier," she said after a moment or two, her voice quiet. "We both knew this was going to happen, Trey. Sooner or later."

"Yeah." His voice was rough.

Linn ran her hand up his arm. "You...mmm...could always ask me to come back." She smiled, daring to touch his cheek with her fingertip.

"What's the point?" He turned his head from her touch and pushed himself away from the door, brushing by her as he walked back into the kitchen. A battered pack of cigarettes lay on the counter and he picked it up and shook it, swearing when it relinquished nothing but a few shreds of tobacco. He crumpled it angrily and tossed it away, pacing restlessly.

Linn felt a jolt of responding anger and tried to ignore it, knowing it was nothing more than a gut-level reaction to Trey's behavior and refusing to give in to it. "A lady sometimes likes being asked." In spite of her best efforts some of the anger got through, giving the words an edge she hadn't intended.

Trey gave her a sharp look. "I'm not into games, Linn."

"I'm not asking you to play games!" She caught the anger and swallowed it. "I'm just asking you to talk to me, Trey. I think I deserve some sort of... of explanation."

"For what?" He started rummaging through one of the kitchen drawers, not looking at her.

"For why you're acting like this!" She stared at him in frustration. "Why are you doing this to me, Trey? Why are you making it sound as though it's my fault we're arguing? As though I've broken some sort of promise I don't even remember making?"

Finally he found what he was looking for. Opening the pack of cigarettes impatiently, he took one out and lighted it, drawing on it deeply.

"Damn it, Trey, will you talk to me!"

"What the *hell* do you want me to say?" He wheeled toward her angrily, expelling the smoke in a thin stream. "You've already made up your mind, so what's the point in discussing it?"

Linn stared at him in exasperation. "So this is how it's going to end? Thanks for the memories, it's been nice... if you're ever in the neighborhood again, give me a call?"

His chin lifted fractionally and he held her gaze with faint defiance. "You're the one calling the shots, babe."

Linn turned away and walked to the open door, blinking back a prickling of tears. "You really know how to make a woman feel cheap, Hollister," she whispered, rubbing her bare arms against a sudden, deep chill. "I don't deserve this and you know it. I didn't just pick you up on some beach and take you to bed. It *meant* something. And you're turning it into something tawdry and... empty."

"You're the one who's leaving, not me," he said in a low, rough voice. "You're the one who's calling it quits."

"I'm not calling it quits!" Linn turned around to look at him, gesturing angrily. "My family *needs* me!"

"Damn it, *I* need you!"

His words rang through the kitchen, clipped with his own anger, and Linn glared at him. "Trey—don't *do* this to me! Don't make me decide between you and my family. It's not fair!"

"I'm not asking you to *decide* anything," Trey said tightly. "It's just that I thought we had something here. Something good. Something that was working. And then I wake up one morning and you're packing to leave."

His words were filled with such bitterness that Linn simply stared at him. Then slowly she started to understand.

This wasn't about her at all. It was about an eleven-year-old boy whose mother had died, abandoning him to strangers. It was about a young marine coming home from the horrors of Vietnam to discover his wife was suddenly someone he didn't know. And a few days later, that same woman walking out of his life forever, taking the son he'd never gotten to know but had never forgotten, whose picture he still kept by his bed.

And how many others? she found herself wondering. He'd built those barriers around his heart tall and strong to protect himself from further loss, yet their very existence made that loss all but inevitable. How many other women had simply walked out of his life, unable to break through the barricades and weary of trying, bruised and wounded like moths battering against a window, trying to reach the candle's flame?

It chilled her to the bone, thinking of all that loss. All that leaving....

"I just don't see why you're making it so damned difficult, that's all!" He stabbed the half-smoked cigarette into an ashtray. "We're good together, Linn. Hell, that's more than most men and women ever get. So why are you making it so hard?"

"Because I want it all, Trey," she replied wearily, wondering if he'd ever be able to understand.

"All? What the hell do you mean, all? All of what?"

"Of you." She looked at him calmly. "Trey, I'm not interested in a halfway love affair. I want something lasting. Something that's got the inner steel to withstand all the hard times."

"Damn it, do you want me to say I love you?" He sounded angry and confused, almost trapped. "If that's what you want, you've got it!"

"I don't need you to say it, Trey," she said softly, "I need you to *mean* it."

"Does anyone ever mean it?" he asked brutally. "You never know, Linn. It's like jumping into deep water blind, you told me that yourself. You take a deep breath and hope for the best."

Linn shook her head. "Not with love, Trey. You have to be ready to commit. Ready to *make* it work."

"Commit?" he barked. "Commit, hell, lady! *You're* the one who's running away."

"And you're not stopping me!"

"Didn't you hear what I just said? I said I love you! What in the hell else can I—?"

"Yes, I heard," Linn replied softly. "But they're just words, Trey. You say 'I love you' like it's some kind of magical incantation. But I don't think you really believe in it. And magic doesn't work unless you believe."

He was staring at her with such confusion and anger that her heart ached for him, yet there was no way she could make it easy for him. Or for herself. Because it would always be that halfway kind of love she swore she'd never settle for, requiring no more commitment from either of them but the assent of the moment.

"You said you loved me." His eyes held hers, almost daring her to deny it. "Didn't that mean a damned thing?"

"I do love you," she whispered. "Or at least as much as you'll let me. But that's the problem, Trey. You keep fighting me, holding me out."

"Fighting you?" He wheeled away with a bark of harsh laughter throwing his hands into the air. "God almighty, woman, what do you want from me?" It was a cry from the heart, a cry of anguish and anger and confusion, and Linn closed her eyes and turned away, her own heart aching.

"I want all of you," she whispered. "But you're fragmented and torn up inside, Trey. There's a vulnerable part—the part of yourself you never let me near. And a doubting, mistrustful part. It's as though there's another Trey Hollister inside you, detached and unaffected by everything that happens. I can sense him sometimes, even when we're making love, standing off to one side, watching and analyzing."

He stood there as though frozen, saying nothing, his face expressionless, and Linn felt a little part of her die as she realized he was doing it again: shutting her out, keeping her from getting too close to that vulnerable, private core.

Then he gave a snort and started pacing again. "If you think that's what love is like, you're dreaming," he said with a rough laugh. "No person can open up that much, Linn. You want something that isn't even possible!"

"It is possible, Trey," she whispered. "But this way it's just too...too one-sided. And I won't settle for that."

She'd thought she could. There had been a couple of times in his arms when she'd thought she might be able to do just that—to take the small bits of himself that he could bear to part with and make a life of it. To settle for *need* and *want* and *caring* instead of love.

But she knew now that it just wasn't enough. She'd had it all with Jack, and she wanted it all this time. Unless Trey could open up and accept her love, unless he could admit he loved her as much as she suspected he did, they simply had no future. It had to be real and it had to be forever.

"Will you be back?" His voice was ragged.

Linn looked at him evenly. "Do you want me to come back?"

There was a heartbeat's pause. "Do you *want* to come back?"

Linn simply stared at him, then she managed a sob of laughter. "My God, if you even have to ask, what's the point!" He was still staring at her, his eyes narrowed slightly now, and Linn sighed, suddenly so tired and dispirited she felt numb.

"Look," she said wearily, "if we keep this up, we're both going to say things we'll regret. We need time to work this out, and right now time is something we don't have. I'm going back to Florida to help put my family back together. And if you want me—*really* want me—you know where to find me."

She turned away and walked toward the door into the living room, willing him to call her back. Say it, damn you, she felt like screaming. Say it like you mean it, and I'll stay!

But he didn't.

And Linn somehow kept walking.

Chapter 16

Steele watched her walk to the door, feeling something tight and hot spill through his chest. He didn't want to lose her.

She paused at the car and looked back. He could see the tears on her cheeks, even through the rain. And the tightness, the heat in his chest, pulled even tighter. Then abruptly she turned, opened the door to the car and slipped behind the wheel.

"Wait!" He caught the door before she pulled it closed, and she looked up at him, startled. Steele braced one hand on top of the car and smiled down at her. "I don't even know your name. How will I find you?"

For one long moment he thought she wasn't going to tell him, that it had all been for nothing, after all. Then finally she gave him a small, wry smile. "I thought you'd never ask," she whispered. "And my name is . . .

What? Trey stared at the computer screen angrily. What *was* her name, this raven-haired beauty who had managed to send Steele into such a tailspin? Cleo, Damask, Rio... nothing seemed to fit. That was one of the reasons he'd left her nameless in the first place, because he couldn't come up with anything that felt right. There just didn't seem to be any name that captured the rarity and wonder of this very special woman.

Carolyn. Carol-Lynne. Linn....

Trey swore ferociously and shoved his chair away from the keyboard, reaching for the package of cigarettes. What the *hell* was the matter with him, anyway? Why was he having so much trouble getting this scene written? It wasn't even much of a scene—two pages maybe, three at the most. Yet he'd been grinding away at it for over two weeks now, ever since his household had gotten back to what passed for normal. He'd written the damned thing every way he could think of, and it *still* didn't work.

He toyed with the cigarette, then tossed it back onto the desk. It wasn't working this time, either. Another day wasted, and all he'd managed to do was get Steele out that damned door and into the rain, putting his heart and guts on the line.

There had been a time or two during the past few days when he'd been ready to throw the whole thing out. The problem was, he'd already made the mistake of letting his publisher see the first hundred or so pages. They were back there now talking about breakthrough books and fifty weeks on the *New York Times* bestseller list and publicity tours and God knew what else.

And here he was, sweating his way through three pages that just would not take shape.

He rubbed the back of his neck wearily, tempted to call it a day. Except that would leave him with nothing to do for the rest of the afternoon and evening. As long as he kept busy, he was fine. But when he had too much time on his hands, he started to think about Linn, about the hurt in her eyes when she'd turned away from him that last time. And that led to a whole lot of brooding and sleepless nights.

He wrenched his mind back from the course it was following and pulled his chair over to the desk, eyes narrowing.

No. Steele gritted his teeth, strode down the stairs and out into the rain. No, damn it, he wasn't going to let her get away that easily. They had something, he and this raven-haired beauty, and he wasn't going to let her just slip through his fingers....

"I cannot believe you just did that."

Linn glanced at her sister. "Did what?"

Hands planted on hips, Kathy gazed at her in exasperation and Linn looked at the wall she was papering. And realized, after a moment or two, that she'd put the last strip on upside down.

"Oh, brother," she sighed. "Sorry. It's still wet—I can pull it off and turn it around."

"I'll pull it off and turn it around," Kathy said none too patiently. "Honestly, Linn, what is the *matter* with you? It's been a month since we got back, yet you're still wandering around in a fog."

Linn brushed her hair off her forehead with her wrist, eyeing the upside-down tulips with annoyance. "Look, you go on back to your painting—I'll fix this. You wanted this paper on all four walls, didn't you?"

"No," Kathy said succinctly, taking the ladder and moving it. "The tulips go on these two walls, the coordinating stripe on the other two." She looked around. "Linn, don't take this the wrong way or anything, but I wish you'd go on a long vacation or get a hobby or just go read a book—because you're driving me crazy!" She gave her stomach a gentle pat. "I've only got eight months before the kid is born—and with the kind of help I've been getting from you lately, I'll still be papering this room when the contractions start."

"Sorry," Linn muttered. "I guess I was just thinking about something else...."

"No kidding," Kathy said dryly. "I'd never have guessed."

Linn looked at her sharply, then gave a rueful laugh. "You and Rod have been wonderful, letting me stay here while I figure out what I want to do. But I'm beginning to think it's time I got a place of my own." She sighed and tossed the wallpaper smoother into the bucket at her feet. "That editorial job they've offered me at *Florida Straits* magazine is a good one, and I've pretty much decided to take it. It'll mean moving down to the Keys, but I've always loved it there. I was thinking about heading there next week to look for a place to stay."

"Linn, I was *not* hinting that I want you to move out. I love having you here, you know that. It's just that you seem to be in some never-never land half the time." She smiled. "I'm worried about you, that's all."

Linn smiled thinly. "I'm just tired. And it's been odd, coming back to nothing—no house, no job, not even a family crisis that needs handling." She managed another wan smile. "Once I get back to work, things will settle down to normal."

"I don't think it's that at all," Kathy said with a shrewd look. "I think it's Trey Hollister. I think you're in love with him."

"Kathy..." But she sighed and turned away, not even having the energy to lie. She walked to the window and stared out at nothing. "It's the first time since Jack died that I found a man I could honestly care about. And I guess it's not written anywhere that just because I fell in love with him he has to love me back." She laughed ruefully and glanced around at Kathy. "If love ran that smoothly, all the country and western singers would be out of work."

"Are you really all right?" Kathy's voice was soft.

Linn swallowed, nodding. "I will be. It hurts like hell, that's all."

"Oh, Linn." Kathy came over and slipped her arm around Linn's shoulders. "I wish there was something I could do. I remember all those boyfriends and broken hearts I went through before I finally met Rod, and you were there for me every time. Now it's you who needs someone to hold your hand and pass you tissues and tell you what a bastard he is ... but I don't think I'm doing a very good job of it."

Linn had to laugh. "You're doing fine. And I'll live. I went through this a time or two myself, remember, before

Jack and I got married." Although not like this, she reminded herself. She'd been a girl back then, brooding over lost boys. But this was a woman's loss, a woman's hurt.

"Linn . . ." Kathy paused, biting her lip. Then she swore with uncharacteristic fervor and took a deep breath. "I wasn't going to bring this up, but . . . why are you still here?"

Linn blinked. "Here? Because you—"

"Not *here*," Kathy interrupted impatiently, her gesture taking in the entire house. "I mean here in Florida. Why aren't you up there with Trey where you belong? You've already admitted you're in love with the guy. So—"

"He's not in love with me," Linn said quietly. "And I'm not so desperate for a man that I'll go chasing after some poor guy who doesn't want me."

"Oh, for—" Kathy bit it off. Took a deep breath. "I was up there with the two of you, remember? I saw the way he looked at you. And you can't tell me he doesn't love you, Linn."

Linn smiled wearily. "Oh, I think in his own way he probably does—as much as he can let himself love anyone. But it's not enough, Kath." She got up and wandered toward the window again. "Maybe I am being unrealistic, I don't know. But I want the kind of love I had with Jack. The kind that Mom and Dad had. The kind that you and Rod have. Open and sharing and—"

"Do you really think that Rod and I got to where we were today without a lot of hard work?" Kathy moved to stand beside Linn. "Rod's got a lot of Latino machismo in him, Linn, don't let him fool you. It took two years for him to really relax and open up with me. But I knew I had to give him time to get used to being loved. It takes a while sometimes for a man to really trust something like that."

She looked at Linn. "You were lucky with Jack—he was open and loving right from the start. But a man like Trey needs patience, Linn. That's part of what loving him means. You stayed by Jack's side because you loved him—and because you never gave up hope. Yet you're giving up on Trey after only a few weeks. It just doesn't seem fair, if you ask me. If he's worth loving, it seems to me he's worth a bit of extra effort."

Linn looked at Kathy quizzically. "So you're saying I should go back."

"I think you should give the guy a chance."

"And if he can't do it? Even if I go back and he keeps me shut out?"

"I can't answer that, Linn. You'll have to decide for yourself how much you can live with. But it seems to me you've written him off without even giving him a chance to show you he can change."

Linn opened her mouth to protest, then closed it again thoughtfully. Maybe there was a kernel of truth in what Kathy was saying. Love was something she'd always been comfortable with, but it was an alien emotion to Trey, something never given freely, always suspect. A man—even one as strong and single-minded as Trey Hollister—would have trouble turning that around in a mere three weeks. *If he's worth loving, he's worth a bit of extra effort....*

She looked at Kathy. "Are my suitcases in the basement?"

A slow smile lifted Kathy's mouth. "I'll bring them up while you have a bath and wash the wallpaper paste out of your hair. And I'll call my travel agent and see what kind of connecting flights you can get to Vancouver tonight."

Linn slipped off the old plaid shirt of Jack's she was wearing as a smock and draped it over her shoulder, smiling as she headed for the bathroom. No doubt about it, pregnancy had brought Kathy's nesting instinct up to a full boil.

If he's worth loving, he's worth a bit of extra effort....

If he let her, she reminded herself. But who knew what had happened in the month since she'd left? All those barricades might have gone back up again, twice as high, twice as thick. And this time, abandoned once too often, he might not be inclined to let her anywhere near his heart again.

She ran the water deep and hot and sank into it with a sigh, deciding it was pointless trying to second-guess how he'd react to seeing her again. But Kathy was right about one thing—she owed it to him to at least give him a chance. And if it didn't work...well, there was always that job with

Florida Straits to come home to. And broken hearts, after all, did eventually heal.

The hot water made her drowsy and she relaxed against the bath pillow and closed her eyes. Nathan was playing just outside the window and she could hear him and the kids from next door chattering happily, their laughter punctuated with excited yips from the pup Rod had brought home three days ago.

She must have dozed, because she didn't hear what had started the commotion. She'd been vaguely aware of hearing the doorbell ring, had heard the sound of running footsteps as Kathy had sprinted down to answer it, but then she'd let her mind drift again.

"But you can't go in there!" It was Kathy's voice, right outside the bathroom door, and it snapped Linn wide-awake. There was an indistinct reply, then Kathy's voice again, edged with laughter. "I'm serious—she'll kill me if I let you in there!" She was reaching for the towel when the bathroom door burst open. She uttered a gasp of shock and instinctively submerged to the shoulders as Kathy backed into the room, obviously trying to block the intruder's path.

"Daddy's going to be here any minute," she was saying, "and if he catches you in here with—"

"Lady," grunted a husky, familiar baritone, "you're in my way." Two tanned hands gripped Kathy's slender shoulders and moved her gently but firmly to one side. Trey stepped fully into the bathroom, his lean, handsome face set with what bordered on defiance as he gazed down at Linn. "I have to talk to you."

Linn stared up at him in utter astonishment. "What in heaven's name are you doing here?"

"Getting himself arrested if he doesn't get out of here," Kathy said, still laughing. "My God, Linn—Dad and Rod are due back any second! If Dad finds Trey in here, and you as naked as the day you were born—"

Trey turned and gently pushed Kathy from the room, then pulled the door closed and pushed the knob to lock it. He took a deep breath, as though bracing himself, and turned back to look at her. "I finished the book."

Linn blinked. *"Steele on Ice?"*

"*Steele and Flame.* I changed the title."

"Oh." Linn blinked again. "And you came all the way down here to tell me that?"

"No. I came all the way down here to tell you that you were right." Trey squatted on his heels beside her, seemingly unperturbed by the fact he'd caught her in midbath. He set a large manila envelope on the side of the tub and drew out a sheaf of paper. "Page 234."

"Katherine!" It was her father's voice, coming from the front door, and Linn winced. "Who owns that car in the driveway?" Linn could hear Kathy's voice, too faint for her to make out the words, then a querulous reply.

But she ignored it and reached around Trey for the towel, drying her hands before taking the page Trey was holding for her. "Kind of a long way to come for editing services, isn't it?" she teased gently. "What if I don't like it?"

"You'll like it," he said softly, his eyes locked with hers. "After all, you helped me write it."

"He's *where*?" It was her father's voice again, in the corridor now. "She's *what*?"

Steele watched her walk to the door, feeling something tight and hot spill through his chest. He didn't want to lose her.

She paused at the car and looked back. He could see the tears on her cheeks, even through the rain. And the tightness, the heat in his chest, pulled even tighter. Then abruptly she turned and opened the door of the car and slipped behind the wheel.

"Wait!" He caught the door before she pulled it closed. "It can't end this way," he said roughly. "I don't want to lose you, Rebecca. It's...hell, it's just too easy this way."

"I can't stay," she whispered. "You know I can't...."

"I love you." The words came easier than he'd ever dreamed possible. They sounded natural and right on his tongue, as though weighted with honey. "Damn it,

Becky, I love you. And you can't just leave. Not without giving it a chance.''

Linn looked up and met Trey's eyes across the manuscript page. "So. He actually did it."

"Yeah." Trey slipped the sheet of paper from her hand and put the manuscript aside, catching her hand and braiding his fingers in hers. "It took me nearly three weeks to write that scene. I finished it two days ago. And caught the first flight down here I could get."

"Aislinn O'Connor Stevens, just what in the good Lord's name is going on in there?" Her father's bellow made the door rattle. "Talk to me, girl!"

"It's probably going to be a bestseller."

"Marry me."

Linn looked closely at him. "I . . . pardon?"

"I asked you to marry me," he repeated quietly.

"I . . . well, yes, that's what I thought I heard," Linn allowed.

"Linn! Linn, darlin', it's your father! Just hang on, girl, and I'll be getting that madman out of there. Katherine, will you stop your bleatin' and get out of the way!"

"Daddy, for heaven's sake," Kathy was saying, "don't you dare try kicking that door in! I tell you, it's perfectly all right!"

"All right?" her father roared. "My daughter's in there naked and drippin' wet with a strange man, and you're telling me it's all right?"

"I love you, Linn." Trey cupped her chin in his hand and turned her face so that she was looking straight at him. "I have never said that to a single person in my entire life. Not even to Diane. But damn it, I do love you. I never knew what it felt like to love someone—or what it felt like to have someone love me. It spooked the hell out of me, Linn. I felt wide open and more vulnerable than I've ever been in my life. When you were standing in my kitchen looking at me that last morning, it was as though you could see right through into my soul. There were things in there I'd never shown to anyone. Things I never even looked at too closely myself. And it scared me to death."

Linn simply stared at him, scarcely daring to breath.

"It wasn't until you walked out that I realized how deep you'd touched. I don't want to lose you, Linn Stevens. You've changed me in ways I still only half understand, and if I lose you, I'm losing part of myself. And I don't want to live like that anymore. I don't want to be just half-alive anymore."

"Linn!" Her father was pounding on the door now. "Linn, damn it, if you don't talk to me I'm going to—"

Linn's heart did a slow cartwheel and she slipped her arms around his neck, heedless of dripping water, heedless of the pounding at the door, heedless of everything but the unconditional love glowing in Trey Hollister's eyes. "We should discuss this, you know. There are hundreds of things we've never talked about. Kids, for instance."

"As many as you want, as soon as you want." He kissed her gently. "I've wasted my life running from myself. From feelings I didn't understand and didn't want to understand. But I don't want to waste any more time, Linn. I love you. I want to have children with you and grow old with you and hell, even fight with you now and again. I want to wake up in the morning and find you there beside me, and I want to look across the room and see you there. I want kids underfoot, and an Irish flatfoot and a Miami vice undercover cop as in-laws.... Say you'll marry me."

There was a ferocious banging on the door. "I've got a gun and at the count of three I'm kicking this door in. *One....*"

"Speaking of Irish flatfoots," she murmured, "that'll be one now. I think you're about to meet your future father-in-law."

"Two!"

"Can he shoot straight?"

"I'm afraid so." Laughing, she lifted her mouth from his. "Dad, I'm perfectly all right! And for heaven's sake, don't try kicking that door in or you'll sprain your bad knee again."

"Kathy says some madman's gone charging in and—"

"His name's Trey Hollister, Daddy." Linn smiled, eyes locked with Trey's. "And you can't shoot him because I'm going to marry him."

The silence outside the bathroom door was deafening and Trey smiled. "Was that a yes?"

"A definite and absolute yes, Mr. Hollister. And if you'll hand me that big towel over there, I'll get out of this bath and introduce you to your new family."

"Sainted Mary and Joseph," came a bemused voice from outside the door. "Kathy, would you mind tellin' your old man what's goin' on here? Does she know him, do you suppose?"

"Of course she knows him Daddy! She loves him."

"Does she?" whispered Trey as he wrapped the towel around Linn, brushing her lips with his.

"She does," Linn murmured back. "Yes, I think she does...."

Epilogue

It came in the morning mail, and Trey smiled as he read it. Picking up his cup of coffee, he carried it and the letter across to the sliding door leading to the big sun deck, standing there for a moment to look out at Linn.

She was sitting cross-legged in the sun, nursing the baby, and as it did every time he saw her, his heart took a leap. The sun surrounded her like a mantle of gold, making the loose torrent of dark hair spilling around her shoulders gleam, and she was smiling down at the child cradled in her arms. The small, dark head at her breast moved and he saw a tiny fist clench, heard the music of Linn's soft laughter, and found himself having to swallow at a sudden thickness in his throat.

It caught him unawares like that sometimes. All it took was a sidelong glance from Linn, filled with unspoken love so deep that it never needed words. Or the unexpected sound of his new son's laughter. Or just waking in the night and seeing her lying there beside him, smiling in her sleep, and knowing that smile was for him.

You're a hell of a lucky man, Hollister, he told himself silently. To finally be in the right place at the right time....

Smiling, he pulled the door open and stepped into the sunshine. He held up the clipping. "It came."

Linn's eyes widened. "And?" she urged gently.

Trey's smile widened. "It's . . . good."

"Read it to me!" She bent to kiss the baby's head, smiling down at him. "Listen up, kid—the *New York Times* has reviewed your daddy's new book."

"In *Steele and Flame*, author T.C. Hollister has given us one of the best reads of the entire year. And certainly one of the best books of his career. That Hollister has reached a new plateau of excellence is an understatement—this book isn't just a rousing good action story, it's a story of life, of change, of growth and, yes, even of love."

Trey skipped a few lines. "He runs through the plot, tells what's going on. . . ."

"Get back to the good stuff."

"There are segments in this book that makes this reviewer wish he could read it all over again for the first time. Hollister has reached down so deep inside himself—inside all of us—that it is not merely a story but a reflection of life itself. The reflection of a man finding himself through love. There is a sensitivity never seen in his writing before, passion and compassion, a sense of wonder and joy that have always been missing in previous Steele novels. It is, quite simply, the story of how love can transform a man's life. Steele will never be the same. And, based on the dedication Hollister has made to 'the woman who loves me, and made it all possible,' neither will his creator. Thank you, T. C. Hollister."

Trey smiled and leaned across to kiss her. "All he needed to add," he murmured, "was that they lived happily ever after. . . ."

He drew back after a moment and gazed down at his son, smiling. The baby was still nursing, making soft sucking noises as he tugged gently at Linn's breast. "I got a letter from Craig today," he said quietly, stroking the baby's cheek.

He sensed more than heard Linn's breath catch slightly. "I wrote to Diane a few months ago," he admitted softly. "I didn't tell you because I didn't want you worrying about it. Worrying about me." The baby gripped Trey's finger fiercely and, as always, he was astonished at the strength in that tiny hand. "She wrote back telling me she was glad things were working out so well. And she said that she thought it was time she had a long talk with Craig. She said that he knew about me, that she'd told him years ago. But he'd never seemed very curious about what happened, and she'd never pressured him."

"And now?" Linn asked softly.

"He...uh...wants to come up. Next month, maybe." He looked at Linn, grinning. "He's getting married, can you believe it? He wants to bring his fiancée up and get to know us. Get to know...me." He gave his head a wondering shake, laughing. "I've barely got used to having one son, and suddenly I've got two."

Linn smiled, reaching out to run her fingers through his hair. "It's called a family," she teased gently. "And they're pretty nice to have around...."

"I know," Trey whispered, leaning down to kiss her again. Knowing, too, that the peace he felt was real. And forever.

*   *   *   *   *

Diamond Jubilee Collection

It's our 10th Anniversary...
and *you* get a present!

This collection of early Silhouette Romances features novels written by three of your favorite authors:

ANN MAJOR—*Wild Lady*
ANNETTE BROADRICK—*Circumstantial Evidence*
DIXIE BROWNING—*Island on the Hill*

* These Silhouette Romance titles were first published in the early 1980s and have not been available since!

* Beautiful Collector's Edition bound in antique green simulated leather to last a lifetime!

* Embossed in gold on the cover and spine!

This special collection will not be sold in retail stores and is only available through this exclusive offer.
Look for details in all Silhouette series published in June, July and August.

DJC-1

Silhouette Romance®

LONG, TALL TEXANS

Diana Palmer's fortieth story for Silhouette . . . chosen
as an Award of Excellence title!

CONNAL
Diana Palmer

Next month, Diana Palmer's bestselling LONG, TALL
TEXANS series continues with CONNAL. The skies
get cloudy on C. C. Tremayne's home on the range
when Penelope Mathews decides to protect him—by
marrying him!

One specially selected title receives the Award of
Excellence every month. Look for CONNAL in August
at your favorite retail outlet . . . only from Silhouette
Romance.

CON-1

A TRILOGY BY PEPPER ADAMS

Pepper Adams is back and spicier than ever with three tender, heartwarming tales, set on the plains of Oklahoma.

CIMARRON KNIGHT ... available in June

Rugged rancher and dyed-in-the-wool bachelor Brody Sawyer meets his match in determined Noelle Chandler and her adorable twin boys!

CIMARRON GLORY ... available in August

With a stubborn streak as strong as her foster brother Brody's, Glory Roberts has her heart set on lassoing handsome loner Ross Forbes ... and uncovering his mysterious past....

CIMARRON REBEL ... available in October

Brody's brother Riley is a handsome rebel with a cause! And he doesn't mind getting roped into marrying Darcy Durant—in name only—to gain custody of two heartbroken kids.

Don't miss CIMARRON KNIGHT, CIMARRON GLORY and CIMARRON REBEL—three special stories that'll win your heart ... available only from Silhouette Romance!

Back by popular demand, some of Diana Palmer's earliest published books are available again!

Several years ago, Diana Palmer began her writing career. Sweet, compelling and totally unforgettable, these are the love stories that enchanted readers everywhere.

Next month, six more of these wonderful stories will be available in DIANA PALMER DUETS—Books 4, 5 and 6. Each DUET contains two powerful stories plus an introduction by Diana Palmer. Don't miss:

Book Four	**AFTER THE MUSIC** **DREAM'S END**
Book Five	**BOUND BY A PROMISE** **PASSION FLOWER**
Book Six	**TO HAVE AND TO HOLD** **THE COWBOY AND THE LADY**

Be sure to look for these titles next month at your favorite retail outlet. If you missed DIANA PALMER DUETS, Books 1, 2 or 3, order them by sending your name, address, zip or postal code, along with a check or money order for $3.25 for each book ordered, plus 75¢ postage and handling, payable to Silhouette Reader Service to:

In the U.S.	In Canada
901 Fuhrmann Blvd.	P.O. Box 609
Box 1396	Fort Erie, Ontario
Buffalo, NY 14269-1396	L2A 5X3

Please specify book title(s) with your order.

DPD-1